ALSO BY KRISTINA ADAMS

What Happens in...
The Real World (free prequel about Liam)
What Happens in New York
What Happens in London
Return to New York
What Happens in Texas (free blog series about Astin)
What Happens in Barcelona
What Happens in Paphos

Hollywood Gossip (*What Happens in...* prequel spin-off about Tate and Jack)
Hollywood Gossip
Hollywood Parents
Hollywood Destiny (coming 2021)
Hollywood Heartbreak (coming soon)
Hollywood Romance (coming soon)
Hollywood Nightmare (free ebook about Trinity)

Spotlight (*What Happens in...* spin-off about Cameron and Luke)
Behind the Spotlight (runs alongside *What Happens in London* and *Return to New York*)

Nonfiction for Writers

Writing Myths

Productivity for Writers

How to Write Believable Characters

Writing as K.C.Adams

Afterlife Calls

Ghost Call (coming 2021)

Empath

Empath (coming 2021)

Seeker (coming 2021)

Hero (coming 2021)

WHAT HAPPENS IN BARCELONA

KRISTINA ADAMS

To Nan. Thank you for everything you did for me.
I wouldn't be the person that I am without you.

DECEMBER

ONE

'Hey Bea, I think that guy's checking you out,' said Fayth.

Hollie froze. 'What guy?' She stopped drying herself off and placed the towel over her body like a blanket. Nobody ever checked her out. Usually the main reason she attracted attention was her blood-red hair and bold fashion choices. But her hair wasn't red anymore, it was a muted brown. Even her outfits weren't so bold lately. The less she stood out, the more comfortable she felt. A blue and pink polka dot bikini wasn't that interesting, was it? Why would someone check her out at a spa, anyway? Her old feelings of self-consciousness rose within her like magma inside a volcano.

Cameron shifted up in his lounger. Not to be obvious or anything. 'Oooh, he's cute. You should go say hi.'

'Shut up,' said Hollie. She slumped farther into her lounger between Fayth and Cameron, pulling her towel up to her neck. A part of her was curious to see who was supposedly checking her out, but the other, stronger part of her wanted to become invisible.

'Do you have any idea how many diets I'd have to go on to get your body?' said Cameron, snatching the towel from her.

'And you'd still have bigger boobs than me,' said Hollie.

'You're just jealous you can't fill a C-Cup,' said Cameron, jiggling his manboobs.

'Well duh. Now give me back my towel!' she said, snatching it from him and covering herself back up.

'What are you *doing*?' said Cameron. 'He's hot!'

'Shut up. You're taken.'

Cameron shrugged. 'Taken. Not blind.'

Fayth snorted. 'Why not go say hi?'

'Because I'm in a bikini?'

'That's *exactly* why you should go say hi,' said Cameron.

'I swear if you make another generalised comment about men,' said Hollie, resisting the urge to roll her eyes.

'What? I'm a man. I know men.'

'You know male stereotypes,' Hollie corrected.

'He's moving!' said Fayth.

That's when Hollie noticed him. He stood up from a lounger opposite them and climbed into the heated pool. His crimson swimming trunks complimented his dark skin, and his graded haircut framed his cheekbones. Oh shit. He *was* hot. And he was staring right at her. He smiled.

She looked away. There was every chance her cheeks were as red as his trunks.

'*So* hot,' said Cameron.

'Shut up,' repeated Hollie.

'If you don't go say hi I'm going to do it for you,' said Cameron.

'Seriously? You know I'm not interested in anyone right now,' said Hollie.

'It's just a conversation,' said Cameron.

Hollie chanced a look at Fayth – she was unusually quiet.

Fayth shrugged. 'I'm staying out of it this time.'

This time. As in, the last time she forced Hollie to talk to a guy look what happened. It had all gone so right…until it had all gone so wrong.

Hollie checked the clock above the pool. 'I have a massage in half an hour.'

'Then that gives you 25 minutes to talk to him before you need to leave,' said Fayth. 'If you want to, that is.'

She really had changed her tune since the start of the year.

'You never know – talking to him might cheer you up. I know a conversation with anyone I find attractive always puts me in a better mood,' said Cameron.

'I thought there was only one thing that put you in a better mood?' said Hollie with a smirk.

'What can I say? I like the exercise,' said Cameron.

'What a shame you didn't bring Luke with you,' said Hollie, referring to Cameron's boyfriend, member of boy band HATT.

'There are other things I can do,' said Cameron with a grin.

'And on that note,' said Hollie, pulling the towel from herself, 'I'm going for a swim to get that image out of my head.'

'You love it,' said Cameron as she climbed into the pool.

She loved Cameron, but she did *not* need an image of him wanking in her head. She shuddered, partially at the image and partially at the heat of the pool as it hit her. She swam a few laps, then found her way to the jacuzzi in the centre. It was currently empty, making it the perfect time for her to sit under the jets and have her tense shoulders massaged by them. She pressed the button on the edge of the jacuzzi. The jets sprang to life. She settled underneath one of them, her eyes closed. Water massaged her aching shoulders, tense from hunching over a sewing machine. Damn, that felt good.

When she opened them, Mr Red Swimming Trunks was sat opposite her, grinning.

Hollie jumped, almost hitting her head on the top of the water jet. Thankfully she was too short to actually hit it. Now that would've been embarrassing.

'Sorry, I didn't mean to scare you,' he said in a smooth Spanish accent.

'It's OK,' she said. She must've looked like a right moron.

'Is that an accent I detect?'

'Yeah. I'm from England.'

'Which part?'

'The Midlands,' she said. 'Are you local?'

'Yes. I live a couple of blocks away. This is my local gym, although I don't usually swim. I'm glad I did now.'

'Oh? Why's that?'

'Well, I got to meet you, of course.'

Hollie blushed, looking away. He was cute, and he was flirting with her. It was weird being flirted with, but kind of nice.

'I'm Hollie,' she said with a smile.

'Like the Christmas berries,' he said.

'Exactly.' As if she hadn't heard that one before.

'It's nice to meet you, Hollie. I'm Santiago. How long are you in Barcelona for?' The way he said Barcelona was sexy. Super sexy. He almost purred it.

'A few months. I'm working out here. Although my friends insist that I take a break over New Year.'

'Breaks are important,' he said. 'What work are you doing out here?'

'I've got a fashion show coming up in a couple of months. I'm out here putting the finishing touches to it while running my fashion line.'

'That sounds amazing,' he said. 'What's your line called?'

'Hollie Baxter,' she said. Not the most original name…

'Simple but memorable. I like it,' he said.

Hollie checked the clock. It was almost time for her massage. 'I have to go. It was nice talking to you.'

'Perhaps we could go out somewhere while you're here?' he suggested.

Ah, there it was. The request she'd been dreading. But would going on a date with a cute guy really be that bad?

'Sure,' said Hollie.

'How's tomorrow lunchtime?'

'That works,' she said. 'We're staying just down the road from the Sagrada Família. I'll meet you there at one?'

'See you then.'

Two

Hollie hated dates. Just thinking about them made her nervous. She tried not to think of it as a date, but really, that's what it was. There was so much pressure on dates. They were worse than job interviews. You had to look a certain way, act a certain way, not mention your ex or what had gone wrong with them, not talk about politics or religion or anything remotely controversial. There was so much to worry about it was painful.

Not to mention she had no idea where he was taking her. Why did people insist on surprises? Surprises were annoying. She liked to know what was going to happen. Or did she? It had never bothered her with Astin. She'd liked it when he'd surprised her. They were always good surprises. Well, when he was in control of them they were. The accident hadn't been so good. It had been fucking awful, in fact.

Oh for the love of clothes.

Would she ever get over her comparisonitis? Would Santiago help her to get over it? Cameron always said rebounds were the way to go, but then, when he and Luke had broken up – both times – he'd gone in the opposite direction. Funny how he said one thing and did another…

Why were relationships so complicated?

'Come on, Bea!' said Fayth. 'You've been in that bathroom forever!'

'Sorry!' said Hollie. 'My stomach is killing me.' It felt like her insides were trying to come out through her arse. She was afraid that if she moved, she'd end up getting internal organs all over the bathroom floor. Ugh. Stupid digestive system. 'Why can't you use the other bathroom?'

'Cameron's showering. Am I going to need a gas mask to go in there when you're done?' called Fayth from the other side of the door.

'Er…it's possible,' said Hollie.

'Lovely,' grumbled Fayth.

Hollie knew that Fayth understood, but she also knew how annoying it was waiting for someone to finish doing bad things in the bathroom. It wasn't like she could control it, though. Her stomach had been behaving questionably for the last few months. As soon as she thought it had calmed down, it would start doing a jig and make it almost impossible for her to leave the toilet again. Her body seemed to really hate food lately. It was behaving like she was stressed. But she wasn't. Nope. Not at all.

The cramping subsided – for the most part – so she cleaned up, opened the bathroom window, and walked out into the living room.

'Finally!' cried Fayth, running towards the door. She put her hand on the handle and hesitated. 'How bad is it?'

'You might grow an arm or two. No big deal,' said Hollie with a shrug.

'You can't be that nervous about seeing whatshisface again,' said Fayth, tightening her ponytail. Curly dark hair tickled her shoulders. Fayth's hair was getting super long, and it suited her. The high maintenance of it would just make her tie it up more, though. Fayth didn't have the patience to faff about with her unruly hair.

'It's not nerves about that. I don't know what it is. Or maybe it is nerves about that. I don't know. Ugh.' She sunk into the red leather sofa. 'My body just hates me right now.'

'Join the club,' said Fayth with a sigh. 'But we're here to have some fun and a couple of nights off.'

'But back to work tomorrow,' Hollie reminded her.

'No, tomorrow is New Year's Eve,' said Fayth. 'Back to work in the new year.'

'Yes boss,' said Hollie, but she fully intended to get some sewing done the following morning. She couldn't afford to take any more time off. Being forced not to work for four days by Fayth and Cameron was bad enough. She had orders to fulfil! People were depending on her! They also weren't expecting anything to be shipped until after the new year, but still. It was always better to keep on top of things.

Fayth disappeared into the bathroom.

Hollie went into her room and raided her wardrobe. She narrowed it down to two outfits.

'Decided what you're wearing yet?' asked Cameron, walking in.

'I didn't say you could enter,' she said, mock glaring at him.

He shrugged. 'I've already seen you in a bikini. Not much left to see. Plus you're like a sister to me anyway.' He sat on the edge of the bed. 'So, what are our options?'

'"*Our* options"? You remember the part about me being a fashion designer, right?'

'Yeah. I also remember how indecisive you are.' He leaned forwards, a wry grin across his face. 'So. What are our options?'

Hollie rolled her eyes. She wasn't indecisive, she just liked to take her time making decisions. 'Black sheath dress with gold zip or jeans and fluffy jumper.'

'Jeans and fluffy jumper. This in a *lunch date*, not an evening date. You don't want to look too dressed up,' said Cameron. 'Shoes?'

'Vans. I don't have any daytime heels.'

'And with it being a *lunch date* on a nice day, you might go for a nice walk,' said Cameron.

Hollie sat beside him. 'Why do you keep saying lunch date like that?'

'Like what?'

'Like it's in italics.'

Cameron chuckled. 'Come on, Hollie. It's a *lunch date*. You don't take someone you're serious about on a *lunch date*.'

'Not everyone uses the same play book, you know.'

Cameron grumbled. 'I suppose. But a *lunch date* in Barcelona when there are so many great bars? Come on.'

'Maybe he's busy in the evenings.'

'Doing what? Nobody's busy between Christmas and New Year.'

'He might have plans with family. Isn't that what most people do this time of year? Not everyone avoids their relatives like you do.'

'I don't avoid them,' he said. 'I just go out of my way to not see them.'

*

Hollie stared up at the Sagrada Família. It was huge. And unfinished. They'd been building it for almost a century, and the behemoth still wasn't complete. Given how quickly apartment buildings and housing complexes seemed to be assembled, it surprised her how long it was taking to build the cathedral. But then, it was so intricate. She couldn't help but admire the beauty of its design. It was regal. Modern. Retro. Everything she wanted to create with her clothes but didn't know how to embody. Could she get some inspiration from exploring inside it? Would she even have time to explore it while she was there?

'Hollie,' a voice called.

She turned around. Santiago walked towards her wearing a black shirt under a red jumper with black jeans and black brogues. Ew, brogues. What was he, a middle-aged man? He wasn't, was he? He looked in his twenties…

He put his hands on her shoulders and kissed her cheeks. Cheek kisses always made her uncomfortable, but she reciprocated the gesture so as not to be rude. She didn't like new people in her space.

'It's beautiful, isn't it?' said Santiago, gesturing to the cathedral.

'Yeah,' said Hollie. 'Have you been inside?'

'A long time ago, yes. You?'

'No, but hopefully I'll get a chance to while I'm here,' she said, craning her neck to look all the way up. The thing was never ending.

'You can see it from all over the city,' Santiago informed her. 'It's so huge compared to everything else around it. You don't get a true feel of its size so close up.'

'Where's the best place to see the view?'

'The cable cars that take you to Montjuïc Castle. We could go there now if you like?'

'Sure.'

*

Fayth and Cameron were lying on the sofa watching *Clueless* and drinking cider when Hollie got back a few hours later. As soon as the door was closed behind her, Cameron swung around and grinned at her eagerly. 'Well, how'd it go? Where'd he take you?'

'Dude, let me get through the door before giving me the Spanish Inquisition,' said Hollie. She dumped her bag by the door and unfastened her Vans.

'No. I want the gossip. So…?'

Fayth paused the film and swirled around too.

Hollie sat on the sofa perpendicular to them and tucked her legs underneath her. 'We went in the cable cars up to Montjuïc.'

'That's the castle, right?' said Cameron.

'That's the one,' said Hollie.

'It was gorgeous. You need to go up there and take some photos, Fayth. My phone doesn't do it nearly enough justice.' She took her phone from her bag to show them the photos and saw a text from Santiago: *Thanks for a great afternoon. We should do it again some time. Santi x*

She smiled, making a mental note to reply once she'd shown Fayth and Cameron the photos.

Hollie handed her phone to Fayth.

'They're blurry,' said Fayth, pinching the screen to try to see more detail.

'I said my camera didn't do it justice! It's an old phone. And I had no idea we were going up there. It's a good job I wore sensible shoes. We walked back down the hill. That was murder. My legs are going to kill me tomorrow,' she said, massaging her calves.

'Is it steep?' said Fayth.

'Very, but you can get the cable car back down if you want.'

'I think I'll go for that option,' said Cameron. 'I prefer to preserve my energy.'

'You mean be lazy?' said Hollie.

'The preservation of energy is important,' said Cameron. 'So anyway, what's Santiago like?'

'He's nice,' said Hollie. 'He's 27, has no pets, and works in HR.'

Cameron's eyes widened. 'Sounds…riveting.'

'You work in a music shop,' Hollie reminded him.

'And I see all sorts.'

'So does he by the sounds of it, but he didn't give much away. Confidentiality, and all that. He's really into history and old buildings. He's the perfect person to explore the city with.'

'Maybe we could double date when Liam gets here?' said Fayth. 'I know he's eager to see the sights.'

'Sure,' said Hollie.

'Did he walk you back to the apartment?' said Cameron.

'No, just the Sagrada Familia. I don't know him well enough to want him to know where we're staying just yet,' said Hollie.

'Did you get a goodbye kiss?' continued Cameron.

'Give her a break,' said Fayth.

'I want details! She asked me for them when she found out about Luke!'

'That's because you hadn't told me that you lost your virginity to a member of the world's biggest boy band,' said Hollie.

'They break up when the clock strikes midnight tomorrow, so he'll no longer be a member of the world's biggest boy band. Anyway. Back to you.'

'No, no kiss. It was too crowded. People kept pushing into us. And you know how I feel about PDAs...I said a quick bye then scurried off down the park.'

Cameron rolled his eyes. 'Amateur.'

Fayth nudged him. 'It's not that big of a deal.'

'Yes it is. That first kiss means *everything*,' said Cameron.

'Which is precisely why it's better to wait,' said Fayth.

Hollie sighed. 'While you two compare my first date to your relationships, I'm going to go—'

'You'd better not finish that sentence with "work",' interrupted Cameron.

'In the bath,' she said. 'I'm going to go *in the bath*. Is that all right, Mum?'

'Yes. Good girl. You go have a nice, hot, steamy bath and dream of what it will be like to—'

'Stop. I beseech you, stop.'

'Does he have an off switch?' said Fayth. 'We really need to find one.'

Cameron glared at her. 'I'll remember that.'

JANUARY

ONE

Hollie stared at the white ceiling. It was her favourite hobby wherever she was, it seemed. She'd hoped a change of scenery would help her to sleep, but it wasn't meant to be. How many nights had she spent staring at ceilings lately? Some were artexed (ew), some had mirrors on them (creepy), most were white (yawn). She'd started to hallucinate pictures in the artex. Faces that were secretly judging her. In the mirrors she'd studied her reflection in the darkness, imagining fine lines that weren't there and willing the purple bags under her eyes to disappear. In the white ceilings she'd stared at the shadows; the figures cast by lights from vehicles as they drove past in the night. She'd heard the sound of car engines humming as they waited to pick someone up or dropped them off. If she did drift off to sleep, all it took was the sound of one of those engines or a shadow moving in the room to wake her up. Then she'd be back to staring at the ceiling.

They'd only been in their new apartment for just over a week, but she was already familiar with every mark on the ceiling. Where they'd painted over the damp patch in the far corner. Where the wardrobe cast a shadow across the room. Where parts of the cheap roller had broken off and left permanent lumps on the ceiling.

She rolled on to her side. The red cotton pillows were soft against her dry skin. They smelled of lavender. The smell didn't relax her like it was supposed to.

On the wall opposite the window was a black-and-white picture of a chicly dressed woman carrying a red umbrella. The woman was judging her with that smug look on her face. It was a look that said, 'I'm classier than you. And you know it.' Stupid picture.

Hollie lay on her back again. She couldn't maintain the pace she'd been running at the last few months for much longer, but she had no idea how to stop. Not to mention she couldn't. The fashion show was two months away. There was too much to do. She'd outsourced some things, but she liked being in control. That's why she'd chosen to be self-employed in the first place. As her friend and investor, Tate had suggested outsourcing the making of the clothes for the show too, but she couldn't. Sewing was her favourite part of the process. If she didn't do that, why was she even bothering? She'd sooner outsource the boring business stuff than the creative side.

She threw the covers away and sat up. She wasn't getting back to sleep any time soon. May as well get some work done.

*

'How'd you sleep?' Fayth asked as she and Hollie sat eating their breakfast of egg muffins at the glass dining table. Even with make-up on, Hollie looked tired. When would she give herself a day to rest? She knew Hollie had sneaked some work in when she'd thought nobody was paying attention. Would she give herself a proper day to rest, or would she burn out first?

'Meh,' said Hollie with a shrug. 'Same as ever. You?'

'OK. Ish. I never sleep that well in new places,' said Fayth. 'It always takes me a few days to adjust.' She shoved another bite of egg muffin into her mouth.

'Same. Not that I really sleep anywhere anyway.'

'Is it today you pick up the keys to the studio?'

'Yeah,' said Hollie. 'It looked pretty good online, so fingers crossed it's as good in real life and not just some clever camera work.'

'It was rated pretty highly, wasn't it? Hopefully that's a good sign. Do you want me to come with you, check it out, since Tate isn't here yet?'

'Don't mind. I figured you'd want to go and do touristy stuff.'

'I'm saving that for when you give yourself a day off or Liam gets here. Whichever comes first,' said Fayth with a small laugh. She knew which was likely to come first, but she hoped planting the idea of exploring a beautiful city like Barcelona in Hollie's head would mean that at some point she'd want to do it.

'Probably Liam, then,' said Hollie.

Or not. But maybe in a few days' time when she was fed up of thinking about clothes…

'I pick up the keys in an hour if you want to come with,' said Hollie.

*

Hollie and Fayth stepped into the studio, otherwise known as Hollie's new home for the next couple of months. It was bigger than it'd looked in the photos, which was good. More floor space for cutting out patterns. Four mannequins lined the wall by the door, with a table in front of them and a couple of beanbags underneath the window. A desk was on the other side of the window, and the far wall was taken up by a kitchenette and a bathroom. Everything she needed in one place.

'I can work with this,' said Hollie, nodding.

'Yeah, it's nice,' said Fayth. She went over and jumped onto a beanbag. 'Yep. I think I've found my spot.'

Hollie giggled. She dumped a bag of patterns and fabric onto the table. She sighed. Where was she supposed to begin?

'Do you need help with anything?'

'Not really,' said Hollie. 'Just need to get on with stuff.'

'There must be *something* I can do.'

'I don't have anything for you to photograph if that's what you mean.'

'I do have other skills you know.'

'I'm fine, really. You go play tourist. Or maybe you could get some experience in a photography studio or gallery while you're here? That might be good for you.'

'I never thought of that. I did put together a portfolio as part of the course I did in New York.'

'Perfect!'

'Are you trying to get rid of me?'

'Maybe a little.'

Fayth stood up. 'All right. I can take a hint. I'll see you later.'

*

Job hunting without a CV was hard. Fayth had tried to put one together, but the only job she'd ever done was for the family pub. That wouldn't help her to stand out. So, camera in one hand and portfolio in the other, she hoped that her decent camera skills would help her get an internship at a gallery or studio. It wasn't about the money (although she wouldn't mind some form of income), it was about getting some photography experience that wasn't her friend's fashion line or related to her celebrity boyfriend.

Hugging her portfolio to her chest, she stepped inside the third studio of the day. The first one had practically shoved her out the door, while the second had kept her talking for half an hour before deciding they weren't interested. She was getting desperate. But she refused to return to the apartment until she had something. *Anything.*

The inside of studio number three – called Regina K Photography – was a bright white, with black-and-white photos adorning the walls. A bored guy around her age stood at the counter, flicking through his iPhone.

'Hi!' said Fayth in her chirpiest voice.

'*Hola*,' he replied, completely uninterested.

'Is the manager about?'

'Uh…'

Shit. Did he understand English? She hadn't come across someone that didn't speak English yet. She should've learned some Catalan, or at least some Spanish. Her accent didn't help. Maybe if she enunciated?

The receptionist held his index finger up, then walked out of the room, leaving her alone. What was she supposed to do? Wait? Was he brushing her off?

She turned to look at the photos behind her. The contrast was high. Every detail of the subject's faces were defined down to the very last wrinkle. It made them look so much more human than the airbrushed stuff from magazines.

The back door opened and out stepped a middle-aged woman in a sharp suit. 'Hi. You were looking for the manager?'

'Hi, yes. I'm Fayth,' she said, stepping forwards to shake the woman's hand. She held out her portfolio. 'I'm in Barcelona for a few months and looking to get some experience at a photography studio. I came across this place and really like your style.'

The woman took Fayth's portfolio but didn't look through it. She scanned Fayth up and down. 'Why do I recognise you?'

Oh no.

'I don't know,' lied Fayth. She wasn't getting into the Liam discussion.

'You look familiar.' She put her weight on one foot and placed her hand under her chin. 'I don't know. Hmm.'

'I must just have one of those faces,' said Fayth, desperately hoping that would be enough for her.

Regina studied Fayth for a moment. Fayth held her breath. Had she seen photos of Fayth in the gossip blogs or magazines? Was she the kind of person to read them? God, she hoped not. She didn't want to work somewhere that was more interested in her personal life than the quality of her work. She'd had enough of that at the pub. Don't let her figure it out. *Please* don't let her figure it out.

Regina opened the portfolio and scanned through it. Fayth exhaled, taking that as a sign she didn't know or care where she recognised Fayth from.

But then, Regina spent so little time on each page Fayth doubted she'd paid any attention to the photos. Another waste of time. Until Regina asked: 'Can I keep this?'

*

When Fayth opened the apartment door, she was exhausted. Her legs were protesting from all the walking and her shoulders were tight from all the stress. She'd have to wait to find out whether or not her job hunt was successful. Regina keeping her portfolio was a good sign though, right?

All she wanted was to collapse onto the sofa and watch something tedious that she could fall asleep to.

Wait. Why did the apartment smell of French toast?

Fayth followed the smell into the kitchen area. Liam stood over the cooker, his hair flopping into his espresso-coloured eyes. He flicked it out of his face and turned to her, a big grin on his face. Fayth ran to him, embracing him tightly. Had it really only been a few weeks since she'd last seen him?

'What are you doing here? I thought you weren't due to arrive for a couple more days. Not that I'm complaining,' she said.

He kissed the top of her head. 'Recording my voice over for *Sea of Dogs* didn't take as long as they thought it would, so here I am. I brought Wade and Ola with me too.'

Fayth squeezed him tighter. If he'd brought his bodyguard and assistant, that meant he planned to stick around for a while...

'It's only been a couple weeks. You can't have missed me that much.'

'Long day,' she mumbled, squishing her face into his shirt.

'Why?'

'Job hunting.'

'Did you find something?'

She pulled away from him so that she could look at him as she spoke. 'Maybe. Not sure yet. I left my portfolio with someone so fingers crossed.'

Liam crossed his fingers. 'In the meantime, French toast?'

'Yes please.'

Liam kept one arm around her and used the other to flip the French toast over. It was becoming his signature dish. Considering when they met a year ago he couldn't even make toast in a toaster, it was a substantial improvement.

'Hang on, isn't it HighCon today?' said Fayth. HighCon was the annual event celebrating all things *Highwater* – the fantasy film Liam and his ex-girlfriend Trinity Gold had starred in together. At the previous year's HighCon, Trinity had very publicly announced that she and Liam had broken up…because of Fayth.

He faked a cough. 'I have the flu.'

Fayth shoved him. 'Liam! I thought you loved spending time with your fans?'

'Yeah, but after the stunt Trinity pulled last year…don't you think it's better if we stay away from each other?'

'I guess, if that's what you want to do.' She didn't agree with cancelling on people last-minute – especially not when people had paid good money to see him – but it was his choice. He wasn't sure on his future in Hollywood already. Was pulling back from doing events his way of slowly starting to separate himself from Liam York, Actor?

'Is Hollie in?' said Fayth, deciding it was better to change the subject than dwell on a something that wasn't up to her and was too late to change.

'Nope. I texted her when I got here so that she could let me in, but after saying a quick hello she went back to the studio.'

Two

The apartment door swung open. Tate burst in looking like a millennial Elle Woods. Her latest hair colour was rose gold. She complimented it with a fuchsia wrap dress and matching lipstick. Moxie, her morkie, wriggled in her arms. 'Good morning ladies!' she chimed.

It was far too early to be *that* chipper. Then again, Tate was *always* chipper.

Hollie and Fayth walked over and hugged her. They'd only been awake for half an hour, so they weren't ready for Tate to be so bright-eyed. How was she so awake after such a long flight?

'How was your flight?' Hollie asked.

'I wouldn't know – I slept through most of it!' she said with a giggle. Of course she did. Oh, to be able to fall asleep so easily.

Maddy – Tate's assistant – and the tallest woman Hollie had ever seen followed her through the door, piled up with bags. Hollie assumed she was Tate's latest bodyguard. Tate got through them like Emily Gilmore got through maids.

'Hey,' said Maddy.

The bodyguard raised her head in greeting. 'Sup.' They didn't usually speak; this was new.

'What have we missed?' Tate asked, narrowing her eyes at Hollie. Hollie instantly felt self-conscious in her knitted tartan shift dress and thermal tights, even though she knew there was nothing wrong with either of them.

'Nothing much,' said Hollie.

'Bea has a boy,' said Fayth with a smirk.

Hollie elbowed her. Tate did *not* need to know that. Not when she insisted on bringing up Astin at least once a week. They'd been broken up for over six months. Everyone else around her had moved on. Why couldn't Tate?

'Oh?' said Tate, cocking her head.

'I'll tell you later,' lied Hollie, secretly hoping she wouldn't have to. 'We have work to do.' She grabbed Tate's arm, glaring at Fayth as she dragged Tate out of the door. They didn't have time for small talk. They had go-sees to deal with.

*

Fayth tidied up the kitchen after Hollie had left. She loved Hollie and Liam, but they could be such slobs. Why couldn't they just put stuff in the dishwasher? She reached under the sink to get a dishwasher tablet out, but the box was empty. Typical. She'd have to get some more when she went out. As she scribbled it on the notepad attached to the fridge/freezer, her phone started ringing.

Could it be…?

She dove into her bag for her phone. The call was from an unknown Spanish number. Could it really be…?

'Hello?' said Fayth, forcing her voice to stay even.

'Hello, is this Fayth?' said a voice with a Catalan accent. It sounded a lot like Regina. Was she about to get her first real job?

'Yes.' Her blood pressure rising, she began to pace around the open-plan living and kitchen area.

'This is Regina from Regina K Photography. I had a look through your portfolio, and I'm impressed. I'd like you to intern for us.'

'That's great! Thank you! I'm so glad you liked my shots!' Stop sounding so obsequious. Ask something useful.

Regina cut her off. 'Can you start on Thursday?'

'Yes, of course!' said Fayth. Did she have anything planned? Probably not. Hollie and Tate would be so busy with fashion show stuff they'd barely be around, and Liam preferred to make things up as he went along. 'What time?'

'9am.'

'Got it. See you at 9am.'

Regina cut off without saying goodbye.

*

Hollie rubbed her face. So far they'd seen five models and picked one. They needed ten for the show. But almost all of the ones that they'd seen so far were totally lacking in personality. Sure, it was their job to model the clothes, but they had to be somewhat interesting too. She wanted to hire people, not zombies.

'When's the next one arriving?' Hollie asked.

Maddy scanned her iPad. 'Tomorrow.'

'*Tomorrow?*' echoed Tate.

'Yep,' said Maddy.

'Marvellous,' said Hollie. It was turning into one of those days. Perhaps it would be better to do something else and return to finding models in the morning.

'You two can go if you want,' said Hollie. 'I'm going to stay and work on a couple of things.'

'All right,' said Tate. 'I need to go to the gym, anyway.'

'Damn right you do,' said a husky voice as its owner walked through the door.

The hairs on the back of Hollie's neck pricked up. No. It couldn't be. What would *she* be doing in Barcelona? She lived in New York. Which was good, because the farther away she was, the better.

But when Hollie looked up…there she was.

Trinity Gold stood in the door of the studio, her hands on her hips and her head high. She wore a white shirt underneath a green trench coat with cigarette jeans and black stilettos. Her dark hair was plaited down to her waist.

Hollie, Tate, and Maddy stared at her, agape.

'I heard you were looking for models,' said Trinity, unperturbed. She wrinkled her nose. Her make-up crinkled, revealing the shapes of scabs around her nose which she'd cleverly disguised by heavy foundation and concealer. No amount of make-up could cover up how red and bloodshot her eyes were, though. Was she high?

Trinity had done modelling before, that was true, but why would she want to model for Hollie? Every other time they'd met Trinity had either ignored her or planted some sort of seed to create an argument. It seemed to be Trinity's lifelong mission to cause hell, and she was bloody good at it. What hell did she plan to raise this time?

'You're not serious?' said Hollie.

'Why wouldn't I be?' said Trinity, strutting towards them. She was good, Hollie had to give her that. But she couldn't work with her. She *wouldn't*.

'Trinity, I feel it's best that you go,' said Maddy. She was the only one who'd remained calm. Tate's face was turning increasingly red at the sight of her ex-best friend.

Trinity fixed her gaze on Tate's assistant. 'I don't feel that decision is up to you.' She turned to look at Hollie. It was the first time she'd really looked at Hollie – her gazes at Hollie were usually fleeting or snide. If she even acknowledged Hollie's existence at all. This time, it was determined. 'It's up to the business owner.'

'Please leave,' said Hollie. She kept her tone even. Lashing out wouldn't fix anything, only encourage Trinity, and who knew what she'd end up doing then? She'd retaliate in some way for being kicked out of the go-see, anyway. That was inevitable. But they'd be prepared for that. Her turning up to model for Hollie Baxter they had not anticipated.

'Fine,' said Trinity. She spun on her heels and left, leaving the door open behind her.

Maddy got up and closed the door. The anger in the room hung around like a thick, dense fog. Tate's hands were curled into fists, her eyes unmoving from the door.

Hollie got up and looked out of the window. She saw Trinity leave the building and hop on a moped just outside. Trinity could ride mopeds?

'She's gone,' Hollie confirmed as Trinity rode away.

Tate remained still. Her lips were pursed into a straight line, her eyes fixed on the door.

In what world did Trinity think they'd choose her to model? After everything she'd done? After causing her and Astin to break-up in New York? After accusing Fayth of ruining her relationship with Liam? After causing the horrible argument that had happened at Tate's charity gala? Hollie shuddered. That was the last time she'd seen Astin. The distraught look in his eyes when she'd told him to fuck off still haunted her. She saw it regularly in her nightmares. Like a wounded puppy, those blue eyes bored into her even when he was thousands of miles away.

'I'm going home,' said Hollie. 'I need to lie down.'

Tate still hadn't moved.

'Tate?' said Maddy.

'Bitch,' mumbled Tate.

'She's gone,' said Maddy.

'Not for good,' mumbled Tate.

*

When Hollie and Tate returned to the apartment, Fayth was out and Liam was experimenting in the kitchen.

Tate went into her room and slammed the door without speaking to anyone.

'It doesn't smell that bad, does it?' said Liam, frowning. 'I wanted to surprise everyone with cake.'

'Are you sure you put sugar in that?' said Hollie. It didn't smell like cake. It smelled…salty. She didn't cook much, but she loved to bake. Her nan had taught her when she was younger, and she'd inherited her nan's affinity for it.

'What else would I have put in it?'

'It smells salty,' said Hollie.

'Shit, is that what that smell is?' His shoulders slumped. He went over to the oven and opened the door. 'You're right. It does smell salty.' He kicked the oven.

'That'll do more damage to your foot than to the oven,' said Hollie.

'What's up with Tate, anyway?'

Should she tell him about Trinity? He was a hot head at the best of times. Telling him that his ex-girlfriend was lurking in Barcelona and wanted to be back in their lives was far worse than using the wrong ingredients in a cake.

He turned the oven off and shoved the cake onto the countertop. It was half-cooked and had barely risen. 'Fuck.' He scraped the cake out of the tin and into the bin, then tossed the empty tin into the sink. His arms folded, he turned back to Hollie. 'Did you and Tate get into an argument?'

'No.' Hollie swallowed. She couldn't lie to him. 'You might want to sit down.'

'I don't want to.'

Hollie closed her eyes. 'Someone unexpected turned up for a go-see.'

Liam looked at her as if to say, *And…?*

'Trinity.'

'*WHAT?*' His face turned so red Hollie was worried he might explode.

How could she calm him down? Fayth was good at that. What did Fayth do? Was her just being Fayth enough? Dammit, where was she?

Liam stormed past her and out of the apartment.

Shit.

THREE

Liam knew exactly where she'd stay. She stayed in the same hotel every time she visited Barcelona. There was no reason she'd stay anywhere else.

It was a long walk from where they were staying to her favourite hotel on Passeig de Gràcia, but it was a sunny day and the walk helped him to clear his head. He called Wade, knowing that he'd get an earful if he didn't let *someone* know where he was going. Wade tried to talk him out of it, but Liam hung up on him and put his earphones in. People did double-takes as he walked past, but he marched on, unable to face any fans while in such a bad mood.

As he walked through the crowded streets, he noticed a moped shop. Fayth had always wanted to ride a motorbike. A moped would be the perfect starting point. *And* it was their first Valentine's Day soon. *And* it was easier to get around Barcelona on a moped. He could get them to customise it, too. He went inside with a broad grin on his face, ready to spend a whole lot of money.

Buying the moped took longer than he'd expected because of all the customisations he wanted. He clutched the handle of the gift bag with all the information inside, pleased that he'd found her the perfect present. He couldn't wait to see her face on Valentine's Day!

He'd almost forgot about the reason he went out in the first place until he walked past a shop that was blaring Trinity's song about them, *The Joke's on You*. Fayth had been upset at the time, but she'd learned to accept that Trinity would never change. But she shouldn't have had to. Trinity should've stayed away from them. Why couldn't she stay away from them?

The rage building back inside him, he marched towards where she was staying.

The doorman stepped aside to let him in.

Out of the corner of his eye, he saw a woman toss a long, dark plait and get into an elevator. Could it be her? Would it really be that easy? He ran to the elevator, putting his hand out to stop the doors from closing. The door reopened, and there she stood. Her smile was as fake as ever.

'Liam!' she cooed, her face brightening. She was the only one in the elevator. He got in and stood beside her.

'What are you doing here?' growled Liam as they went up to her usual suite.

'I got invited to a *Highwater* event and thought it would be a good chance to practise my Spanish.'

'What *Highwater* event? I'm here and I didn't get an invitation,' said Liam, offended. How dare they invite Trinity and not him? He was the star!

'Maybe they thought you still had "the flu",' she said, narrowing her eyes accusingly.

Liam ground his teeth together.

'Anyway, I thought I'd offer Hollie my help while I was here but she didn't want me.' Trinity faked a pout.

The elevator doors opened and Trinity stepped out. Liam followed her to her suite. She wobbled as she walked, unstable in the black stilettos she wore.

They reached a door and she put her keycard to it. She held it open for Liam, then closed the door behind him.

Once they were inside, Trinity cocked an eyebrow as if to say, *Well?*

'You knew Hollie wouldn't want you to be a part of her fashion show. Why are you *really* here?'

Trinity crouched down, probably intentionally sticking out her ass, and took a bottle of gin from a shelf that didn't require her to bend down at all. She offered it to Liam. He shook his head. 'This heat makes me so thirsty,' she said, tugging on the neckline of her blouse and unfastening a couple of buttons. He rolled his eyes. It wasn't warm. In fact, it was freezing out. Unless of course you were high…

She unscrewed the lid and gulped several mouthfuls without stopping.

'What are you doing?' said Liam.

'Drinking, silly!' said Trinity, raising the bottle in the air. 'Learn to have some fun, would you?' She took a few more chugs.

'*Fun*? Do you have any idea how much trouble you've caused? Fayth and I were nearly killed because our stalker blamed us for *your* meltdown on live TV! Hollie and Astin might've been back together by now if you'd kept your mouth shut!'

Trinity sat on a grey corner sofa and patted the spot beside her. He ignored her, preferring to stand. If he sat, she'd think he was staying. He placed the bag holding the details of Fayth's present on the glass coffee table, his hand hurting from holding it so tightly.

'You can't blame me for the actions of a total stranger. I had no idea I had a fan that was so *cray*.' She took more gulps of the gin. 'And as for Hollie and Astin, I was trying to help!'

Liam scoffed. As if.

'I *was*!' she insisted. 'I heard that they'd broken up, and I thought changing the seating arrangement might help. I'd put them beside each other, actually, but someone must've noticed and changed it. The HATT kids that were sat with you originally are so *boring*. You didn't miss anything.'

He actually liked the HATT 'kids' but let that one slide because there were bigger things to worry about. 'Why did you have to be there if you were so bothered about them reconciling?'

'I wanted to help them talk through their issues!'

Liam furrowed his brow. 'And you thought they'd do that with an audience?'

She shrugged, then took a few more sips of her gin.

'Trinity, you need to stop,' said Liam. He reached out and tried to take the bottle from her.

She pulled it towards her and hugged it, her expression like that of a hurt child. 'No. You don't get to tell me what to do any more. You lost that right when you broke up with me.'

'Why won't you let me help you, like you helped me when I came out of rehab?'

'You don't want to help me, you just want the badge of honour that comes with helping someone like me! You want the world to know how good you are; how noble you are; what a fucking Prince Charming you are. But if you wanted to help me so badly, why'd you dump me, huh? Why didn't you give me a break? Why didn't you give me a chance?'

'You broke your promise to me! I was upset!'

'So, what, you threw yourself into the arms of someone else?'

'No! You know nothing happened between Fayth and I for months.'

'Not physically it didn't, but I lost you the moment you saw her. She was everything you wanted and everything I'd never be.' Trinity shook her head. 'You know what? It doesn't matter. I'm so done with you.' She pointed to the door.

'Trinity, don't be like that. Please. Let's talk.'

Trinity flashed him a down-turned smile. He'd never seen that look on her before. It was odd. Like she'd given up. 'I'm done being angry. At you; at Tate; at the world. It's exhausting. I don't want anything more to do with you or your little clique. I've got the hotel for another few days, then I'm going to hide out somewhere quiet for a while. Maybe I'll get clean, maybe I won't, but for once, I'm going to do things on my own terms. Not for any boy, any manager, any fan. Not for anyone but me.' She opened the terrace door. Cold air filled the room. Trinity grinned, tugging at the neckline of her blouse as sweat dripped down her decolletage.

'I think a break will do you good,' he said.

'Stop that! Stop telling me what to do, or agreeing with me, or acting like your opinion matters to me at all! God, why do you always do that? Why do I even want to tell you all this stuff? Ugh.' She scrunched her face up. 'How many more times do I have to ask you to leave?'

'OK, if that's what you want.' He left her alone, guilt swirling him like piranha around blood. Should he have given Trinity the chance to explain herself after the breakup? But then, if that had happened, he may not have started dating Fayth. And he loved Fayth more than anything. She made him happy. Happier than Trinity ever had. She may have helped him after he came out of rehab, but she was just as broken. Being around her was dangerous; she could too easily have led him back down the path of addiction, and that wasn't a path he was comfortable with. It wasn't a path he was comfortable Trinity going down, either, but he had to respect her decision. He'd interfered enough. Was that why she resented him so much? Did she see his trying to help her as him trying to control her? Is that what had driven such a wedge between them in the weeks before the breakup? He almost turned back to ask her, but thought better of it. No, she'd asked for space. It was about time he respected her wishes.

*

'Where've you been?' Fayth asked as Liam walked back in. She lay on the sofa, reading a photography magazine. When she'd gone out to pick one up, Liam had been baking. When she'd returned, he'd gone out.

'Doesn't matter,' said Liam.

Fayth closed her magazine. 'That sounds very ominous.'

His shoulders were slumped and his head bowed. What on earth had happened while she was out? 'Have you spoken to Hollie?'

'No; I didn't realise she was in.'

'She came back while you were out. She said…Trinity turned up for a go-see.'

Fayth sat upright. *'What?'*

'I went to ask her why she's here.'

'Why would you do that? You know that's exactly what she wanted!' Fayth stood up and started pacing the living area.

'Because she shouldn't be here!' He crossed his arms.

'That's not your problem!'

'Yes it is! She's always causing problems for us! I wanted to stop her before she had the chance this time!'

Fayth stopped pacing and turned to face him. 'Was that really all it was?'

He put his hand on her arm. 'Of course it was. Fayth, it's you that I love and want a future with.'

'Then why do you look so sad?'

'She just…said some things that upset me, that's all.'

Fayth kissed his cheek. 'You're a good person, Liam York, but you've got to stop trying to save everyone. It'll be the death of you if you don't.'

He rested his head against hers. 'If only it were that easy to stop.'

Four

Her bag was packed. Her lunch was in the fridge. Her outfit was laid out. Everything was ready for Fayth's first day at Regina K Photography. Except for Fayth.

Even with Hollie and Liam's reassurances, she was terrified. She'd slept for a couple of hours the night before and that was it. She hadn't slept that badly since she'd started therapy. What, exactly, her mind thought the folks at Regina K Photography would do to her she didn't know. Maybe that was part of the problem.

She stared at herself in the bathroom's full-length mirror and sighed. Would Hollie have some concealer she could borrow to hide the bags under her eyes? She didn't want to turn up to her first day of work looking like a zombie.

'What time do you need to be there for?' asked Liam, appearing in the doorway. He leaned against the bathroom doorframe and sipped his tea. In nothing more than a pair of jogging bottoms, he was a wee bit distracting. They hung loosely around his waist, a narrow strip of hair leading from his belly button into the waistband. And that strip of hair lead to...

Nope. No time for that.

She snapped her head away from his treasure trail and focused on his face. 'Nine.'

'Do you want me to come with you?'

'Thanks, but I'll be OK. I don't want to attract any attention.'

'All right,' he said, kissing her cheek then leaving her alone in the bathroom again.

Fayth still had half an hour before she had to leave, so she went in search of Hollie and her concealer. She knocked on Hollie's bedroom door but there was no answer. Dammit.

Tate poked her head out of her room. 'She's already at the studio,' said Tate.

'Oh,' said Fayth. Her shoulders fell.

'What's up?' Tate rubbed her eyes.

'Nothing,' said Fayth.

'Mm-hmm,' said Tate.

'I just wanted to borrow some make-up so that I look less dead.'

'Oh. Well that I can help with.'

*

Fayth stared up at the metallic sign above the entrance. Its crisp, clean font and silver lettering were sleek and modern. It was also terrifying. What if the rest of the team didn't like her? What if they still thought she looked dead when she walked in, even after Tate had worked her magic? What if they judged her because of her relationship with Liam? Sigh.

Deep breath. Head high.

She walked under the metallic sign and through the doors into the studio. The same snooty guy that had been on reception when she'd applied was there. He greeted her with the same snooty reaction then told her to wait for a moment and disappeared. So he did speak English, he was just ignorant. Why couldn't people just be polite?

She waited for what felt like forever, but eventually a smartly dressed woman not much older than Fayth came out alongside the snooty receptionist. Where was Regina? '*Bon dia*,' she said. 'I'm Elissa. Regina has asked me to show you around.'

Oh. She'd hoped Regina would be the one to show her around. But then, she had a business to run, so getting someone to show her around made sense. Elissa didn't wait for Fayth to respond before continuing to speak. 'This is our reception area, and to the left are the changing rooms. Through this door is where we store everything we need.' She pushed through the door. It led into a room filled with backdrops, lighting kits, props – everything a photographer would need to take the perfect photograph of their subjects.

Fayth gazed around, not even noticing that Elissa had walked off until she heard giggling. She looked over to see Elissa talking to a couple of others. They were talking, laughing, and looking at her. There was no denying that they were talking *about* her. Ugh. She was pretty sure she heard them say 'Liam', too, but she couldn't be certain as she was too far away and they were talking in Spanish. Or Catalan. Or some other language she didn't understand. Why hadn't she learned some of the language before heading to Barcelona?

Was she being paranoid? Of course she was. She was being silly. Not everyone knew she was going out with Liam. And what did it matter if they did? She hadn't included any of her photos of him in her portfolio because she'd wanted to stand out on her own. But what if they noticed anyway? All it took were a few flicks through the gossip blogs to see unflattering photos of her.

'Fayth,' called Elissa, gesturing for her to join them.

Fayth did so, although the hairs on the back of her neck pricked up. Something was off.

'Is it true you're dating Liam York?' said Elissa.

Five minutes. She'd lasted five bloody minutes before someone had asked about her boyfriend. Ugh.

Five

Hollie leaned over her sewing machine, her earphones in and Taylor Swift drowning out everything around her. For the first time in ages, she was focused on nothing but her sewing. She was completely wrapped up in her own world.

Until *Shake it Off* was abruptly interrupted by her phone ringing. Dammit, why had she plugged her earphones into her phone? Oh. It was Santiago. Shit! They were due to go for lunch. How had she forgotten? Did that make her a bad girlfriend? It still felt odd calling herself his girlfriend. She hadn't had any relationships for the first 22 years of her life, then she'd ended up having two in a year. Life was weird.

'Hey,' said Hollie, answering the call. She peered out of the window. It was pretty gloomy out. With that weather, she might as well have been back in England.

'I'm outside your studio,' he said. 'I knocked but nobody answered.'

'Shit. Sorry,' she stood up and opened the door. He stood before her and smiled. She pulled out her earphones so that she could hear him properly, then pecked him on the lips.

'Ready to go?' said Santiago.

'Should I get changed?' she asked, not knowing where they were going.

'No, but you might want to put a jumper on; it's cold out.'

'OK.' She pulled on the turtleneck jumper that was sat on the back of her chair and grabbed a hooded bomber jacket from the coat stand.

'Is this one of your outfits for the show?' Santiago asked, gesturing to a drawing of a black jumpsuit that was sitting beside her sewing machine.

'Yeah,' she said.

'What's with the bit on the shoulder? It looks…weird.'

'It's recycled carrier bags,' she said. Did it look weird? It was intended as a statement about waste and consumerism, but was it a step too far? Did it just take it from a classic piece to something really over the top?

'But plastic clothes? Who's going to wear that?'

*

Hollie couldn't stop thinking about what Santiago had said about her outfit. Was plastic really that weird on an outfit? Katy Perry and Lady Gaga had worn it before. Hell, Lady Gaga had worn a meat dress. Plastic shoulders weren't *that* weird.

They pulled up outside a posh-looking restaurant, gave the car to a valet, then headed inside. Hollie had nothing against posh restaurants, but she wasn't used to them. Even though Astin had celebrity friends, he'd always preferred to go to more low-key places, like burger joints.

But she wasn't with Astin. She really had to stop thinking about him.

Their table was by the window – her favourite place to sit as it meant that she could people watch. And distract herself from the people who were silently judging her outfit. Surrounded by people in fancy dresses and smart suits, she was completely underdressed. Santi's default outfit of trousers and a jumper blended in fine just about everywhere. Maybe there was something to wearing the same outfit all the time. No. No there wasn't. What would he do in the summer? There was no way he'd be able to wear a jumper in the Barcelona heat. Would he?!

'Are you OK?' said Santiago, pouring some water that had been left on the table into her glass.

'I'm fine,' she said. 'Just been a long morning.'

'Well at least you get to relax now,' said Santiago.

'Yeah,' said Hollie, forcing a smile. Truth be told, she wanted to get back to work. She didn't feel like she had time for a lunch date. Which was exactly why she hadn't been interested in a relationship. But Santiago was sweet. He texted her every day to say good morning and good night, and in between they talked about nothing in particular. Everything was so easy and relaxed around him, and she liked that. He didn't force or nag her to do anything; for the most part, he just let her be.

They ordered their food then sat talking about nothing in particular. It was like he was consciously trying to keep her mind from work. Which was practically impossible, but it was cute that he tried.

'We should go to a flamenco show while you're here,' said Santiago. 'I think you'd like them.'

'Yeah, that would be cool,' agreed Hollie. She opened her mouth to continue her thought but was cut off by a waiter tripping over right next to them…and spilling red wine all over Santiago's red jumper.

His jaw tensed. Why was he so upset? With how often he wore red jumpers he had to have a wardrobe full of them.

'I'm so, *so* sorry,' said the waiter. 'Let me go get some white wine to clean that up.'

'No!' said Hollie. 'The white wine thing is a myth! It's fine. We'll sort it. Just get our food to us ASAP please.'

The waiter scurried off.

'Are you sure it's salvageable?'

'Yes.'

'My apartment is nearby if you'd like to come back with me and show me how to get the stain out?'

Going back to his apartment. She hadn't been there yet. What would that lead to? Would it lead to anything? Was she overthinking it? Of course she was. She didn't know how not to.

*

Santiago's apartment was neat and tidy. Everything had its place. There was only one other place she'd ever been to that was so tidy, and that had belonged to Astin. So much for dating someone completely different. How did she always end up with the neat freaks?

Hollie filled the sink up with water and poured some bicarb into the sink.

Santiago took off his coat then pulled his jumper over his head. The t-shirt he wore underneath rose up with it, revealing the sleek muscle underneath. Mmm. He wasn't as ripped as Astin, but he was definitely buff.

'Enjoying the view?' he said, raising an eyebrow.

'What if I am?' she said.

He stepped closer, his jumper still in his hand. He pulled her into him with his spare arm. Damn, he was nice to look at. She wrapped her arms around his neck, going on to her tiptoes. He leaned forwards and kissed her. His lips were soft and comforting. Being around him made her forget all the stresses of life. All she saw, all she thought about, was him.

He tossed the jumper into the sink. Water splashed everywhere, but they didn't care. He used his spare arm to pull her even closer, then carried her onto the sofa. She straddled him, desperate to feel closer to him. He was a good kisser. If he was that good at kissing, what else could he do with those lips…?

She pulled his t-shirt over his head then kissed him some more, running her hands over the smooth skin of his body. He unzipped her coat and threw it to the side, then began to peel off her layers until she was straddling him in nothing but a bra.

'Perhaps we should relocate to somewhere more intimate,' he suggested.

'Oh? And what do you intend to do when we relocate to somewhere more intimate?'

He leaned forwards, his breath tickling her ear as he spoke. 'Come with me and find out.'

*

Whoa. Hollie had not expected that. But damn. Like, *damn*. She hadn't orgasmed like that since – well, that didn't matter. For the first time in ages, she felt relaxed. She lay back on the soft sheets, listening to the sound of the shower running in the background.

The jumper. She should really check on it. It hadn't exactly been put into the sink strategically. For all they knew, the part that was stained wasn't even in soak. Sighing, she went into the living room, pulled Santi's white t-shirt over herself then peered into the sink. The bicarb had worked its magic, but the jumper needed to soak a little longer. She topped up the water, stirred it, then left the bicarb to keep doing its thing.

What else did he have in his wardrobe? She'd only seen him in red jumpers so far. If his wardrobe was full of them, surely he wouldn't miss one being damaged? She went into his bedroom and opened his wardrobe. It was a sea of red jumpers. Different fabrics and cuts, but all red jumpers. And black chinos. The odd pair of black jeans. Then white t-shirts. That was it. Did he have a separate summer wardrobe? There was no way he was wearing red jumpers in the Barcelona heat. He'd fry faster than a churro.

Why were they all the same colour, though? And why were they all the same thing? Where were the patterned shirts or the blue jeans or the graphic tees? Who didn't own a pair of blue jeans? She'd have to change that. She couldn't let him go on wearing the same thing every day. Who even did that? *Why* would someone do that? It was so boring! Clothes were about more than just comfort.

They were about expression. They were a form of art. She'd have to teach him that.

'Admiring my wardrobe?' he said, emerging from the bathroom wrapped in a towel that wasn't red. It was purple. An improvement. There was some hope.

'It's very…red.'

'I like red,' he said, taking another jumper from his stash. 'It looks good on me.'

'Yes it does,' she agreed, but so would a lot of other colours.

Six

Fayth fell back onto the plush red sofa. Ah, comfort.

'Hello,' said Tate from downward dog. Fayth jumped. Why was Tate doing yoga in the living room?! There was a gym downstairs! Was Tate trying to give her a heart attack?

Tate turned her head to face Fayth. 'How did your first day go?' She jumped her legs to her hands, then slowly stood up.

'Don't ask,' said Fayth.

'It can't have been that bad,' said Tate, raising her hands above her head.

'It was,' Fayth reassured her. She couldn't explain why to Tate, though. Tate wouldn't understand.

She placed her hands at her heart centre, bowed, then said: 'Why?'

'Doesn't matter.'

'You do that a lot, don't you?'

'Do what?'

Tate sat beside Fayth on the sofa. 'Dismiss your pain.'

'I'm not in pain.'

Tate nodded. 'Uh-huh. That's what you said last time.'

'What last time?'

'When we were in New York. You said you were fine even though you'd just had a panic attack.'

Fayth lowered her gaze. What was Tate getting at? She wasn't one for talking about her problems, that was all. She still talked to her therapist on Skype once a week and was feeling loads better because of it, but this wasn't the kind of thing to bother a therapist about.

'Where's Hollie?'

'Where'd you think?'

Fayth sighed. Of course Hollie was working. What else would she be doing? Talking to Hollie when she was so stressed out would just make her stress out even more, though. Maybe it was a good thing she wasn't there. Fayth rested her elbows on her lap and her head in her hands. 'I don't fit in there.'

'Says whom?' Tate crossed her legs.

'I felt like I was three inches tall. They don't like me there.'

'They don't know you there.'

'Has that ever stopped people from judging you?'

Tate gave a small laugh. 'People will find a reason to judge you no matter who you are. What matters is how you respond.'

'What do you mean?'

'Well, when people say that they don't like me, I remind myself that I've sold several million records and their biggest fan is likely to be their cat.' As if on cue, Moxie hopped onto the sofa and curled up in Tate's lap. Tate scratched behind her ears. 'People being mean doesn't always come from a place of jealousy – some people are just vile – but you have to remind yourself what you have to be proud of.'

Fayth raised an eyebrow.

'I'm serious. You're a great photographer, Fayth. Don't let them tell you otherwise.'

'But how do I know when to take the criticism and when to dismiss it?'

Tate moved her lips from side to side. 'You learn who knows what they're talking about, and who's full of hot air. Of course, knowing the difference comes with experience.'

Fayth glowered.

'I know, I know, it's easier said than done.' She took Moxie off her lap and stood up. The small dog glared at her from the sofa, circled a few times, then curled back up into a ball. Tate held out her hand to get Fayth to stand up.

'What are we doing?' said Fayth, standing up too.

'I'm teaching you a quick fix.' Tate raised her head and squared her shoulders. 'Now, feet hip-width apart. Hands on hips. Head high.'

Fayth raised an eyebrow.

Tate tapped her arm. 'Come on. What have you got to lose?'

She was right, of course. Fayth adopted the Wonder Woman pose. Tate stood beside her in the same position, a grin on her face.

'Now what?' said Fayth.

'Just hold it.'

'That's it?'

'It's called a power pose. If you hold it for a couple minutes, it gives you an instant confidence boost.'

Fayth snorted. 'Right.'

'It's not a panacea, but our body language is just like our outfits or our hair and makeup – it's a reflection of who we are and how we feel about ourselves. If we walk around with our shoulders slumped and our heads bowed, we're showing the world that we're afraid. It makes us *feel* afraid. And that makes us a target.'

'How do I usually stand?' Fayth asked, but she already knew the answer.

'In a way that we can change,' said Tate. 'How do you feel?'

'A little better, actually.'

'See? I told you: it's no panacea, but it can make you feel almost as good as a sneaky chocolate bar. You'll always have to face horrible people, but if you carry yourself in the right way, they're less likely to see you as a target.'

'But what if they've already established you as a target?'

*

Reception duty. That's what Fayth had spent most of her time at Regina K Photography doing. Didn't they already have someone to do that?

It wasn't that she thought that reception duty was beneath her, it was the fact that she'd hoped to be more involved in the photography side of things. But you had to work your way up, right?

She answered the phones and greeted customers as best she could, but most of them couldn't understand her thick Scottish accent. She was pretty sure most of her coworkers couldn't, either. Since there was no one around most of the time, she couldn't even get up to go for a pee or make a brew. Hollie wouldn't have lasted five minutes. But it was Fayth's first Proper Job and she was determined to make it work.

She was only there a few of days a week. It was money in her pocket. More money to buy equipment and chip in to the rent (not that Tate would let her). It was all experience, and that's what really mattered, wasn't it?

Elissa and a couple of the other photographers went off on lunch and walked past her without saying a thing. When Elissa returned half an hour later, the other two had been replaced by a cardboard coffee carrier. Fayth eyed it, desperate for a drink. Her mouth was like sandpaper from talking so much without so much as a sip of water. 'Sorry, didn't have enough hands to carry any more,' said Elissa as she went past. Bitch.

*

Fayth leaned back in the chair. The day was almost over. And then the phone rang. Of course it would ring at the end of the day. She picked it up and spoke broken Catalan in the brightest voice she could. She had no idea what the person on the other end was saying. Why they'd put someone with a rural Scottish accent on phone duty was beyond her. Where was the sense in that? She asked the person to hold for a moment – that line she'd become more than familiar with in her short time there – and went off to find someone. Unfortunately the only person free was Elissa.

She was in the staff area, leaning back and typing away on her phone.

'Elissa, have you got a minute? There's someone on the phone and I've no idea what they're saying,' said Fayth.

Elissa didn't even hide her eye roll. She stood up and went with Fayth back to reception. She picked up the phone, spoke in Catalan for a few moments, then hung up. That was it.

As she went to go back to the staff room, she turned back to Fayth. 'You know, you really shouldn't be on phone duty.'

'Then why'd you put me on it?' grumbled Fayth.

Elissa shot her a challenging glare then disappeared through the back doors. What *was* her problem?

*

Fayth grabbed Hollie as she walked through the front door and pulled her into a hug.

'Is it that bad?' said Hollie, wrapping her arms around her friend.

'It feels like I haven't seen you in forever. And yes, yes it is.'

Hollie rubbed Fayth's back. 'Why?'

'It's super bitchy there. It's like being back at school. Do some people just never grow up?'

'Pretty much,' confirmed Hollie.

Fayth's shoulders slumped. She and Hollie walked over to the sofa and sat down.

'So what's up with you anyway? Tell me something happy. How are things with Santiago?'

Hollie shifted in her seat, smiling sheepishly.

Fayth beamed. 'That looks promising.'

'I mean, yeah,' said Hollie, tucking her feet underneath her. Fayth forced herself to ignore the shoes on the sofa thing. 'It was…whoa. But…'

'But what?'

'I had a nosey at his wardrobe while he was in the shower, as you do—'

'As *you* do,' corrected Fayth.

'As *I* do, and it's not that he has no fashion sense, it's just that…'

'It doesn't change?' offered Fayth.

'You've noticed, then?'

'It's hard not to, even for me,' said Fayth.

'Does that seem weird to you?'

'Not everyone has the wardrobes of you and Tate,' said Fayth with a small laugh.

'I wish I had Tate's wardrobe,' said Hollie. 'I'm serious, though. Is it weird?'

'Nah,' said Fayth. 'Isn't it one of those productivity hacks? You wear the same thing everyday so that you don't have to waste time and energy deciding what to wear? It's why Steve Jobs always wore turtlenecks. Sounds like a pretty good plan to me.'

Hollie glared at her.

'But I'd never do it because I have a very talented best friend who's also a fashion designer and I wouldn't want to miss out on any of her designs,' added Fayth.

'Nice save,' said Hollie.

'I thought so,' said Fayth with a grin. 'I wouldn't worry too much about the whole Santiago and his wardrobe thing, though. Opposites attract, right?'

'So you don't think I should try to encourage him to wear something different?'

'Trying to change people in a relationship never works. It's like forcing yourself into a size eight when you're really a twelve. You're just kidding yourself.'

'Did you just make a clothing analogy?'

'Oh yeah. I did. Looks like your fashion advice is finally paying off.'

SEVEN

Liam's phone buzzed. He rolled over in bed and picked it up. It was a photo from Trinity. Of the bag filled with the paperwork for Fayth's present sitting on her coffee table.

'Shit,' he said, darting out of bed. Thank god Fayth was at work.

If it had been anything else, he could've just bought her a new one. But the proof of purchase for Fayth's moped? That he needed for when he went to pick it up. He'd had custom features put on it just for her. There was no way he was going through all that again. He'd have to deal with Trinity. One last time.

*

As Liam and Wade walked into the hotel, Trinity's jet black hair caught his eye. She was sat in the window of the buzzing restaurant, alone, eating a salad and flicking through her phone. Her head was propped up by her hand; she looked bored. He approached her, Wade a few feet behind. She didn't stir. He cleared his throat. She looked up. Her eyes widened; her back stiffened like a threatened cat.

'Can you get Fayth's present for me please?'

'*Pfffft.*' She practically spat at him as she said it. Gross. Liam wiped spit from his Tommy Hilfiger shirt. When had things become so awkward between them? No, that one was obvious. It was when Trinity had started to get jealous of Fayth. Anyway.

Trinity pushed her salad away from her, stood up, and walked out of the restaurant. Were they supposed to follow her? Liam glanced at Wade, who shrugged. He decided to chance it, and the two of them followed her into the lift. She didn't say anything, which he took at least as a sign that she didn't object to them following her.

When they arrived at the suite, she continued to ignore them. She sat on one of the sofas, picked up a bottle of gin that was lying on it, and spun it around.

Wade hovered awkwardly by the door, his gaze flitting from Liam to Trinity and back again.

Liam found the bag on the coffee table where he'd left it. He turned towards the door. Trinity opened the bottle and began to chug. What was she doing to herself? Was that really the life she wanted to live? Did she really want to end up like her mother?

'Wade, could you give us a minute please?' he said.

Wade glanced at Trinity, his eyes conveying concern.

'I'll be fine,' said Liam.

'I'll be in the corridor if you need me.' His jaw was set. It was obvious he didn't agree with Liam's decision, but, as Liam's employee, he had to obey. His arms folded, Wade left them alone in the suite.

Liam needed to talk to her. He needed to try. At least then, his conscience would be clear.

He approached his ex-girlfriend, his hands behind his back. Keeping his body language open would show that he was open to talking. Whether or not she was open to talking, on the other hand, was yet to be decided.

'Did you find what you were looking for?' said Trinity. She slammed the gin bottle onto the coffee table and wiped her mouth with the back of her hand. When she pulled it away, it was speckled with blood. Her nose was bleeding.

'Did you?' She cocked an eyebrow.

He held up the bag in his hand. 'Yeah.' He passed her a tissue from the box on the table. She snatched it from him and dabbed at her nose.

'Then why are you still here?' she asked, taking her phone from a concealed pocket in her orange lace dress, checking it, then returning it to her pocket.

'Trinity please, let me help you,' he said, lowering his head.

'What happened to staying out of it!' she said, standing up. 'You really don't know how to back off, do you? It's my life, my decision. You don't get to dictate that.'

'I'm not trying to. I just want you to know that you're not alone. Why is that so hard?'

Trinity scoffed. 'I've been alone my whole fucking life.'

'No you haven't! Why would you say that?'

'My mom left me when I was two.'

'She died, that doesn't count.'

'She killed herself! She couldn't handle living with my fuckwit of a father, so she overdosed instead. Then there's my father, whom we both know wasn't exactly a role model. Tate stabbed me in the back. You gave up on me. Tell me, Liam, who do I have? Who's ever really been on my side?'

Liam forced back tears. She was right. Everyone she'd ever trusted had betrayed her. 'I'm…I'm sorry.'

'No you're not. If you hadn't broken up with me, you wouldn't have started dating Fayth. You got what you wanted.'

'I wanted to help you!'

'There! There it is!' said Trinity, jabbing her finger at him. 'You never loved me. You just wanted to *help* me. Who are you, Florence fucking Nightingale?'

Was she right? Was that why he'd fallen for her? Not out of love, but out of an attraction to broken people and broken things?

'See? You know I'm right. It's written all over your face. You may be a great actor, Liam, but you're a shit liar.' She shook her head. 'We could've been great together, you and me. The next great Hollywood power couple.'

'We were toxic and you know it. If we'd stayed together you would've dragged me back down the path of addiction.'

'I was snorting coke the whole time we were together and you didn't even notice! How much attention were you paying to me, huh? You never would've found out if it hadn't been for your bitch of a girlfriend!'

'Don't you dare talk about Fayth like that!'

'Why? Is she the only good thing in your life? Does she make you really, *really* happy?' Trinity said mockingly.

'Save me the jealous speech, would you?'

Trinity almost choked on the gin she was drinking. 'Jealous? Don't flatter yourself.'

'Then why are you really here? Why did you come all the way to Barcelona?'

'I told you – I was at an event! It's not my fault they didn't invite you because you're a fucking flake.'

'*I'm* the flake? That's rich!'

'Right, because I'm the one that used to turn up late to set,' said Trinity, rolling her eyes.

'I was grieving!'

'And getting high.'

'You don't get to judge me,' said Liam, crossing his arms.

'What, but you get to judge me? You get to tell me the best way to deal with this shit life that I've been given? You get to control me, like everyone else?'

'I'm not trying to control you! Why can't you see that!'

Trinity took the gin bottle, opened the terrace doors, and stepped outside. Cold air swept through the suite. It was a clear but windy day. It wasn't the kind of day to hang out on the terrace. She turned back to Liam. 'You can leave now.'

He followed her on to the terrace. 'I want to help you. What's so wrong with that?'

'You gave up your chance to help me when you dumped me. You don't get to judge me *and* help me. That's not how you help people. Not unless you want to push them farther into their black hole.' Is that what he'd done by trying to help her?

'If you don't want my help, why do you keep showing up? Why were you at Tate's charity gala? Why did you reach out to Fayth in New York? Why are you *here*?'

'This is *Hollywood*, Liam! It's a small world. It's difficult *not* to run into each other. Not every decision I make is about you.' She climbed on to the edge of the terrace and looked over it. The stone wall was just wide enough to hold her feet.

'Come down from there Trinity, it's dangerous.'

'Oh, stop it, would you? Do you ever take risks? Do you ever do anything outside of your comfort zone?'

'You're standing on the edge of a terrace several stories up. That's not taking a risk. That's playing with fire.'

'Then let the fire rage on.' She took a swig of gin and stumbled. Liam reached out to help her. She regained her balance on her own. 'If I'm the fire, you're the water that's trying to put me out. You're right. We never would've worked together.'

No. That's not right. He wasn't trying to kill her fire. He'd never do that to her. To anyone. Would he? *Had he*?

'I didn't do that. I wouldn't do that,' he said, half trying to convince himself.

'Whatever,' said Trinity. 'You can go back to your apple-pie life now.'

'It's not an apple-pie life! Does she make me happy? Yes. Are we perfect? No. But no couple is.'

Trinity laughed. It was shrill, high-pitched; almost like a cackle. He'd never heard her make that noise before, not even when playing the villain in *Highwater*. 'So, what? You can accept her faults but not mine? You can give her a second chance when she makes a mistake, but you couldn't even listen to me when I tried to explain to you why I was back on the coke? Let's face it, Liam: you never really cared. You wanted to care, but really, you liked the attention that I gave you. I was something stable for you to cling to after rehab. I wouldn't suffocate you like your parents would've if you'd stayed with them, or like your staff wanted to. I let you be you, but you could never let me be me.'

'That's not true! Stop saying that!'

'Oh, Liam. You really have never been any good at seeing what's right in front of you.'

'What's that supposed to mean?'

Trinity stared at the gin bottle. There were only a few drops left in it. She tilted her head back, pouring the liquid down her throat. Then she fell.

Eight

He'd thought the streets of Barcelona were busy before. They were nothing compared to the crowd that had gathered to see Trinity Gold lying on the ground.

A middle-aged man crouched down and checked Trinity's pulse. He noticed Liam. Recognition passed over his face. Please. Please please please. She was horrible at times, it was true, but she didn't deserve to die like that. Liam turned back as the man stood up. He shook his head. 'I'm sorry.'

Liam turned into Wade, suppressing tears. Wade put his arm around Liam. Trinity was dead. He hated her – that he couldn't deny – but he didn't want her *dead*. He wanted her to get better. She could've done great things if her fucking addiction hadn't got in the way. But none of that would ever happen now. She was dead. Dead dead dead.

The man took off his coat and placed it over Trinity's body.

Bile rose in Liam's throat. His body was ready to purge whether he wanted it to or not. He found a gutter a few feet away and threw up into it. What if they thought it was his fault? He was the last person to see her. He was there when it had happened. It was common knowledge they didn't get along like they used to. It wouldn't take much for the police to label him as guilty. He threw up again. And again. And again, until there was nothing left in his body.

A hand touched his back. He flinched.

'It's me,' said Ola. How had she arrived so quickly? She guided him back inside the hotel and into a conference room. The walls of the narrow room were dark grey, and Liam couldn't help but feel like they were closing in on him.

'The hotel have cleared this room for the police,' said Ola.

'Oh god,' said Liam. He sunk onto a metal chair and began to sob.

'Wade's talking to them now. Fayth's on her way.'

'Fayth? No! She needs to stay out of this.'

'Too late,' said Fayth. How long had he been throwing up for if Fayth had arrived from the other side of the city?

Fayth stood in the doorway, her face sombre. He ran to her and hugged her like he hadn't seen her in years. She didn't speak, just hugged him back.

'How did you get out of work?'

She shrugged. 'Said it was a family emergency. They don't need to know the real reason.'

He kissed the top of her head. She was so good to him. Would he lose her if they thought that he did it and they sent him to prison? No, they wouldn't think that. Would they?

'*Hola*,' said a police officer.

Ola replied in Spanish, then, after a brief conversation, the officer began to speak in English. 'I'd like to speak to you, please.' While he said 'please', his tone informed them that wasn't a request – it was an order. Liam pulled away from Fayth but didn't let go of her hand. He knew how it looked. Bad was an understatement.

The police officer pulled up a chair opposite them. 'Tell me what happened,' he said, licking his fingers to flick to a new page in a reporter's notebook.

Liam told him what he remembered. It was starting to blur. The sooner he got it out of his system, the sooner he could relax. If they hadn't already decided that he was guilty.

The officer – who hadn't introduced himself – interjected Liam's story with questions, wanting clarification on this and that. He was very interested in Liam and Trinity's relationship, and that worried him. Them arguing right before she'd fallen didn't look good. It couldn't have looked worse. He could lie, but then, what if someone had heard them arguing? That would look even worse than them arguing right before she fell. Oh fuck.

'Thank you,' said the officer, standing up. 'Please wait here.'

The three of them alone again, Liam curled into his girlfriend. She was the only one who made him feel safe.

'It won't be long before the press pick up on this,' said Liam.

'No,' agreed Ola. 'I'll speak to your PR team ASAP and get them to do some damage control.'

Fayth rubbed Liam's back. 'We don't need to think about that right now. There are more important things to worry about.'

'You mean like how they think I did it?' said Liam.

'Don't be silly,' said Fayth.

'Didn't you see his face?' said Liam. 'You know they think I did it.'

'No, I don't,' said Fayth.

The officer returned, another one in tow. 'We'd like you to come to the station to answer a few more questions.'

Liam kissed Fayth, slow and hard. Would he ever get to kiss her again? To fall asleep with her in his arms? Would he ever see her again? He had no idea what was about to happen. He needed to feel her close to him just in case that was the last time. It was the only thing that gave him any real sense of comfort. She was everything to him, and he was terrified that after what had just happened, he was about to lose her.

The police officer cleared his throat. Liam sighed, gave Fayth's hand one last squeeze, then let go.

Nine

Wade wasn't allowed into the interrogation room with Liam. He was alone, in a foreign country, where his ex had just fallen off a terrace. Right after he'd had a massive argument with her. It looked bad and he knew it. It *was* bad. He'd grabbed her and she'd slipped through his fingers. His fingerprints would be on her body. Oh god. Her *body*. That's all she was now.

He ran over to a bin in the corner and threw up into it. He'd been talking to her a few hours ago. How had everything changed so fast?

The door to the interrogation room opened as he finished throwing up. 'You must be Liam,' said a man with an embarrassing comb over. 'I'm Ashleigh. Your lawyers sent me over to assist you.'

So they'd come through for him. That was something.

'Thank you,' said Liam.

'How are you feeling?'

Liam glanced at the bin. 'Not great,' he said as he sat back down.

'You didn't do anything wrong. Remember that.'

Ashleigh sat down beside Liam and flicked through a folder. He asked Liam a few questions about the situation. A few minutes later, a female police officer walked in with a cup of water. She placed it on the table then sat down. 'Good afternoon, both. I'd like to ask you some questions about what happened earlier, if you don't mind.' Liam and Ashleigh remained silent. They waited for the officer to sit down. She pressed record on a recording device, stated the day and time, then addressed him: 'You were present when your ex-girlfriend fell off a balcony. That had to have been difficult.'

Understatement, much? 'Yeah,' said Liam.

'Witnesses heard you arguing. Can you tell me more about that? What were you arguing about?'

'I don't really remember,' he said. 'She just seems to show up wherever I am. I'm trying to move on, and she won't let me.'

'I see,' she said, making some notes. 'That must have been annoying.'

'It was. I kept offering to help her, but then she'd shut me down. I didn't get what she wanted.'

'What would you say it was, if you had to guess?' The officer took a hair tie from around her wrist and tied her blonde bob into a short ponytail. It made her long nose look even more pronounced.

'Me? For us to have some great Hollywood romance, probably. She always did love old movies.'

'And what about you? What did you want from your relationship?'

He ran his hand through his hair. 'To move on.'

'Her not letting you must've made you angry.'

He sighed. It was pretty obvious where things were going. 'That didn't mean that I wanted to kill her.'

'You have a history of shooting people. It doesn't take much to move that up to anger.'

'My client shot *one person* in self-defence, in the leg,' said his lawyer. 'That's not the same.'

'Isn't it?'

'I didn't kill her! You have to know that. *Please.*' Was he pleading? Did he sound desperate? Then again, he was desperate. He'd never survive in prison! He'd watched enough documentaries to know what they did to pretty boys in prison.

Ashleigh put his hand on Liam's arm. What was that supposed to mean? Was it to try to stop him from getting hysterical? Wasn't he allowed to be, all things considered?

'My colleagues are talking to people who were in and around the hotel at the time and scouring the CCTV. We'll get to the bottom of what happened.'

'I'm *telling* you what happened!'

'We need someone else to corroborate what you're saying.'

'My bodyguard was outside! He can vouch for me!'

'He already has,' she informed him. Phew. 'But he wasn't inside when it happened. He can only tell us what he heard, and what he thinks of you as a person. That's not enough. Anyone can commit murder if the wrong buttons are pushed.'

'Do you really believe that?' If she did, he was in serious trouble.

'Yes. Now, tell me what happened from the start.'

Goosebumps formed on his skin. He was being interviewed like some sort of criminal. There'd be a permanent record of his involvement in her death. He had to remain calm. Looking nervous would just make him look guilty.

He recounted everything that had happened – or as far as he could remember it, anyway. Everything was already starting to blur. He wanted to block out seeing her fall, seeing her motionless body lying on the ground. The sooner he erased those images, the calmer he'd feel.

The police officer let him speak, only asking questions when he paused or she felt that something needed more detail. She was nice; a calming presence. Was she meant to be good cop?

Every so often, Ashleigh would chime in and say that Liam didn't have to answer that question and ask if he was being charged. For the most part, though, he was useless.

When he'd finished, she leaned back in her chair. 'See it from our perspective: you get into a huge argument, she falls. You're her sole heir—'

'Wait what?'

'You're Trinity's sole heir. Everything she owns goes to you. That's motive, Liam.'

'What? Since when? She never told me any of that!'

'With all due respect, it's clear that my client had no prior knowledge of this arrangement,' said Ashleigh.

'Are you sure about that? The documents have your signature on them.'

Liam widened his eyes. 'Pardon?'

'The documents have your signature on them to confirm that you've seen them.'

Liam shook his head. That bitch. 'She can – *could* – fake my signature. It's something we used to do when giving out *Highwater* merch. I didn't even know she had a will. She was always the irresponsible one.'

'Not this time,' she said.

Liam rested his head against the table. What had Trinity done?

*

'What if they charge him?' said Fayth, pacing the apartment.

'They won't,' said Hollie. She sat on the sofa, hand sewing something. How was she so calm? Liam was being questioned by the police!

'You don't know that. You don't know what's going to happen. None of us do!'

'We have to trust the police to do their jobs,' said Hollie.

'You don't know what the police are like over here. They'll want a quick resolution because of the press,' said Fayth, rubbing her hands together.

'Don't paint all police officers with the same brush,' said Hollie. 'You don't know what they're like over here either.'

'They took him down to the station!' said Fayth.

'To ask him questions. Let's not get ahead of ourselves,' said Hollie. 'They're just taking his statement.'

'Since when are you the calm one?' said Fayth.

'I'm not calm, I'm keeping myself busy.' She gestured to her sewing. 'And I trust the justice system. There's bound to be a witness in a busy street like that.'

'What if there isn't?' said Fayth.

'Then there'll be a CCTV camera that caught something. The more we worry about what could happen to him, the worse we'll feel.'

'That doesn't make me worry less!'

'What will?' said Hollie.

Fayth sunk onto the sofa beside her. 'Liam walking through the door.'

*

A jail cell. They were keeping him in a jail cell overnight.

They'd stripped him of his clothes and of his dignity. It wasn't the first time he'd been arrested, but it was the first time it had happened in a foreign country. And for *murder*. He wasn't that kind of person. Why didn't they believe him?

He sunk onto the solid mattress and curled up into the foetal position. How much longer were they going to keep him? What the hell were his lawyers even doing? What did he pay them for if they couldn't keep him out of a jail cell for the night?

He swatted at his face as he began to cry. No. He wouldn't do that. That was exactly what they wanted – to make him sweat. Doing that would make him easier to coerce into a confession. And he wouldn't confess to something he hadn't done.

He rolled over and closed his eyes. He saw Trinity's face as she fell. She'd looked serene. Almost happy. How was that even possible? Had he made that up, or had she really looked like that as she'd fallen? Had he even looked, or had he darted for the stairs as soon as her fingers had slipped through his, knowing that there was nothing he could do and hoping that, by some miracle, she'd be fine by the time he got there?

How much longer would he have to spend in that jail cell before they let him go? They knew he was claustrophobic, right? It was on his IMDb profile. His stunt doubles had had to do any *Highwater* scenes involving small spaces so that he didn't have a panic attack. It had been written into his contract.

What if four small walls were all he'd ever see for the rest of his life? What if they found him guilty without any proof? Surely him arguing with Trinity – no matter how bad that argument was – wouldn't be enough for them to charge him with murder? Would it?

Would it?

He started to cry uncontrollably. Of all the futures he'd envisioned for himself, prison wasn't one of them. Not since he'd been clean. Fear of ending up dead or in a jail cell was one of the reasons he'd got sober in the first place. What if all that effort had been for nothing?

What about Fayth? What would she do? He couldn't ask her to wait for him, but he couldn't stand the idea of her with someone else. She meant everything to him. So long as he had her, he could get through anything. Couldn't he?

Keys clattered. Liam sat up, scrubbing at his face to hide that he'd been crying. But nobody came. The sound of footsteps echoed down the corridor, then there was silence.

His hair fell into his face. He brushed it away with his hands. It stood up on its own because it was so greasy. Was there anywhere he could wash it? Would he be made to shave it if he went to prison? His hair drove him mad sometimes, but it was part of who he was. He didn't want to lose that. But prison changed you. He wouldn't be the same person when he got out. *If* he got out. He sobbed harder. What if they gave him a life sentence? The world would keep moving without him. His fans would move on and swoon over a new Hollywood face. His friends would move on and meet new, better people that weren't falsely accused of murder. They'd slowly visit him less and less, leaving him even more isolated from the outside world. Eventually he'd be a friendless nobody that used to be in the movies.

Then what?

He'd get beaten and raped for being a pretty boy pacifist film star. He'd have *TARGET* written on him in blood. His life, as he knew it, would be over.

Ten

'Liam?' called a voice.

Liam opened his eyes. He'd cried himself to sleep dreading what would happen next. He didn't want to speak to anyone; he wanted to be left alone. No, that wasn't true. He wanted Fayth. He needed to feel her close to him. She'd make him feel better, she always did.

The door to his cell opened. The officer that had interviewed him the day before walked in. She'd been the one to take him to the jail cell, too. Even though she'd been nice to him, he couldn't forgive her for that. Him being stuck there was her fault. Even if she was just following orders.

He didn't respond to her, just stared up at the ceiling.

'We found a witness. You're free to go.'

He sat up.

'What?'

'A gentleman in the hotel opposite Trinity's was on the balcony having a cigarette when she fell. He saw her topple over as she took a drink and you reach out to try to help her. It took a few hours to go through all the witness reports. I apologise for that.'

She apologised, did she? Well that was just great. An apology fixed how shitty he felt and how stiff he joints were from the crappy bed.

Did they have any idea what staying in a jail cell could do to his career? There was a reason his fans didn't know about his previous arrest! Hiding that had *not* been easy.

The officer guided him into an area where he could get changed, returned his things to him, then took him to the reception area where Fayth was waiting. He ran to her and wrapped his arms around her.

'It's OK,' she cooed. 'It's OK.'

'Take me home,' he begged.

She took his hand and led him out of that place, hopefully never to return.

*

'Are you sure you don't mind me going to work? I don't want to leave you,' said Fayth. She'd called in late to work so that she could pick him up. He loved her for that, but would it get her into trouble? She hadn't been there long. Calling in late because of personal problems wouldn't look good. Especially not when she'd left early because of Trinity's death. She needed to go in and not stay home to look after him. Even if a part of him wanted her to.

'Don't worry about me. I could use the alone time,' he said. It had been an overwhelming 24 hours and he needed the time to recover and process everything. It wouldn't happen in a few hours, but it would hopefully help him relax at least a little. If not, he could at least get in some game time…

'All right, if you're sure.' She kissed him, then left him lying on the sofa and went off to work.

Ah, peace.

He took out his phone and flicked through Twitter. He'd always had a bittersweet relationship with Twitter. He loved the idea of it, but he got so much shit on it that he couldn't enjoy it as much as he wanted to.

One of the tailored trends suggested to him was #TeamLiam. Oh no. He clicked on it. It wasn't pretty.

Liam is so full of it. He totes killed her. #TeamTrinity

Don't blame Liam! She was a psycho. She was bound to die young. #TeamLiam

Stop defending him! #TeamTrinity

Stop defending her! She was always dragging him down. And oh look – she's still doing it even now that she's dead. #TeamLiam

The fans' words were harsh. Really harsh. They'd started to split into #TeamLiam and #TeamTrinity. And, to his dismay, #TeamTrinity had way more tweets than #TeamLiam. And, if those numbers and his timeline were anything to go by, the fans were mostly on her side. What was he supposed to do? What could he say to convince them that he was innocent? He couldn't stay silent or avoid the spotlight forever. Maybe doing an interview would convince them that he wasn't the murderer they thought he was?

Then again, there was every chance it would go the opposite way and just reinforce the fans' opinion of him instead. People read what they wanted to into things. If they thought he was guilty, they'd take whatever he said as confirmation of his guilt.

He slumped onto the sofa and tossed his phone across the floor.

Hollie walked through the front door, put some churros in front of him, and walked out again. Bless her for thinking of him without pushing him to talk. No wonder Fayth said she was good at being there for people. But when it came to letting people be there for her, she was just as bad as Trinity. He just hoped Hollie wouldn't end up pushing people away like Trinity had.

*

Fayth walked into Regina K Photography desperately hoping that they hadn't heard of Trinity's death. Or even better, that they didn't care.

They knew she was in a relationship with Liam. If they knew about her death, there was every chance they'd want details. But she couldn't handle any questions about Trinity. It had been bad enough before, but now that she was dead? How could she possibly answer questions about someone she was glad to be rid of? What a horrible thing to think. She hadn't wished Trinity dead. She'd never wish that on anyone. But she *had* wanted Trinity out of their lives. After her death, Trinity was more of a presence than ever.

Everyone was gossiping loudly when Fayth walked into the staff room. When they saw her, they stopped. The room fell silent. Shit.

'Fayth, could I speak to you for a moment please?' said Regina. Regina was *never* in the staff room – she was always hiding in her office. It had to be bad.

Fayth gulped. 'Sure.' She followed Regina into her office. Regina closed the door and gestured to the chair opposite her desk. Fayth sat down; Regina chose to stand behind the desk. It made her already imposing air even more intimidating.

'There have been…rumours. I'd like to hear the truth from you.'

'What have you heard?' Fayth asked. Anything but that Liam killed Trinity. Anything but that Liam killed Trinity.

'Is it true that you're Liam York's girlfriend?'

Shit.

'Yes,' said Fayth, keeping her voice as even as possible.

'Why did you not mention this sooner?'

'I didn't think it was relevant,' said Fayth.

'I see,' said Regina, placing her hands on her hips. The queen of intimidation. 'And are the rumours about Liam true?'

'What rumours have you heard?' There was no way she was going to play into Regina's hands. If Regina wanted Fayth to confirm or deny a rumour, she'd have to spell it out.

'That Liam York killed Trinity Gold.'

There went Fayth's hope that Regina would mince her words or feel uncomfortable saying the accusation out loud.

'No.'

'Are you sure?'

Rage built inside Fayth. How dare she usher her into a private room to accuse Liam of murder?

Fayth stood, her hands clenched into fists. 'Yes, I am bloody sure. He's in pieces because he actually thought he could help her, and now the world is accusing him of murder. The police have found no evidence *because there isn't any*.'

Fayth turned on her heels and began to walk out.

'Fayth—' started Regina.

'Stuff your internship. The atmosphere here sucks anyway.' Her head held high, Fayth left Regina's office and made her way to the exit. Everyone's eyes burned into her, but she kept going. She had to. She needed to be around people who really knew her, who didn't judge her, and who didn't care for celebrity gossip (or at least knew it was bullshit). A couple of people tried to speak to her, but she had no idea who they were or what they were trying to say. None of them had been on her side. They'd all been gossiping. They'd all played into Elissa's bitchy behaviour. As far as she was concerned, there was no redemption for any of them. She was *glad* to be leaving. She didn't need them, anyway.

*

Hollie's studio was closer than the apartment. Since Fayth grew angrier with every step – and she didn't know if any press were lurking – she made her way inside. The door was unlocked. Hollie was sat at the desk by the window, typing away on her laptop. She jumped at the sound of the door.

'Fayth! Not that I'm not pleased to see you, but what are you doing here?'

Fayth slammed the door shut, leaned against it, and began to cry. Hollie ran over. 'What did they do to you?'

'Regina…Liam…m…m….'

'Regina accused Liam of murder?'

Fayth nodded, then sobbed even harder. She loved Hollie for figuring out what had happened from her ramblings, but hearing it put so bluntly was like reliving it all over again.

'Oh, Fayth,' said Hollie, pulling her friend into a hug. 'You cry as much as you need to. I have a cookie stash in the drawer if you want it.'

'Tea. And cookies. And more tea. And more cookies,' pleaded Fayth.

'Whatever you need,' said Hollie.

Eleven

Brrrrr. Brr brr. Brrrrr.

Fayth kicked Liam. 'That's your phone.'

Liam reached for his phone on the bedside table. It was four o'clock in the morning. Who'd ring him so early? His eyes flitted to the caller ID. It was Jim, his agent. 'Mmm,' Liam said as he answered. He climbed out of bed so as not to disturb Fayth any further and went into the living room.

'Sorry for calling at such a stupid time. I have…news. I didn't want to wait and have you hear it from someone else.'

He sat on the sofa. It had to be bad news or Jim would've waited until the sun was up in Spain.

'Liam? Are you still there?'

'Mmm.' He was too tired to speak. He just needed him to get to the point.

'They dropped you from the Baz Luhrmann film.'

Liam's grip on his phone tightened. He'd left Fayth on her own in New York at the height of her PTSD to film those scenes. He'd been a horrible boyfriend, and for what? 'Is it because of Trinity?'

'They didn't say that, but…'

'But you're pretty sure that's why?'

'It's possible. I tried, Liam. I really tried. I'm sorry.'

'What about *Sea of Dogs*?' He'd loved recording the voice over for that before arriving in Barcelona. He didn't need to worry about looking good for the camera because it was animated, *and* he got to play the villain. *And* it was about dogs.

'I haven't heard anything from them, but…'

'But what?'

How much worse could it get?

'*Little Empire*'s distributor pulled out.'

'But it's such a great film!' *Little Empire* had struggled to find a distributor for months – he'd filmed it almost two years earlier – but he'd had faith that it would find one eventually. It was a biopic about a businessman who'd built an empire in a small town in Tennessee. For a guy who'd only lived to 40, he'd lived a hell of a life. And now most of the world would never know his story. And it was all his fault.

'The producers won't give up, obviously, but it's not looking good.'

'This is ridiculous. I didn't kill her!'

'I believe you.' Jim sighed. 'Hollywood is fickle, you know that. Give it time to calm down. I'm sure everything will be fine.'

'Sure it will,' said Liam.

FEBRUARY

ONE

Fayth stood in the bedroom doorway as Liam packed for his trip to New York for Trinity's funeral. 'Could she really have faked your signature on her will?'

'How else could my name have ended up on it? I sure as hell didn't sign it,' he said, shoving a couple of pairs of jeans into his suitcase. How was he such a messy packer with all the travelling he'd done?

'Then what happened?'

'I don't know!' snapped Liam. 'Sorry,' he said, shoving his hands into his pockets and rocking on his heels. 'I wish I knew.' He sighed. 'Are you sure you don't want to come?'

'Do you need me there?' said Fayth. What would the press say if they saw her there? That it was out of guilt? Would they say that about Liam when they saw him there? Then again, they'd already said far worse about him.

'I'll have Tate and Wade there,' he said. 'It's not right to drag you to a funeral for someone you hated.'

Fayth sat on the edge of the bed beside his suitcase. 'I didn't hate her, I just didn't understand her. Not that she ever tried to understand me.'

'She never tried to understand anyone,' he said, throwing a handful of boxers into his suitcase. 'I'll only be gone a couple days. You sure you'll be all right?'

The last time Liam had left her in an apartment alone, she'd had a panic attack. But a lot had changed since then. 'I'll be fine. Dr Kaur's magic therapy has helped a lot. Plus, Hollie will be here. I can't leave her. You've seen the state she's worked herself into.'

'Yeah,' said Liam with a sigh. 'You stay and look after her. Ola will be here if you need anything.' He kissed the top of her head.

'Thanks.'

*

While in New York, Liam decided to meet with his PR team and lawyer to discuss what they'd dubbed 'The Trinity Situation'. They may have given it a catchy name, but beyond that, they were useless. They'd suggested he conduct interviews to help save his image. He doubted interviews would do much with the way everyone was talking about him lately, though. The interviewer would just twist his answers to fulfil their own agenda. No thanks.

After wasting his time with the PR team, he went to speak to his lawyer, David, about Trinity having faked his signature on her will.

'Is there anything we can do? Any way we can prove that she faked the signature?' said Liam. He was sat across from David, a cup of bad coffee balancing on his knee. 'I mean, it's not an easy thing to do. There must be *someone* who witnessed it. Don't these things need to be countersigned?'

David leaned forwards, rested his hands on the desk, and frowned. 'Not unless the people involved admit to it, but we both know that won't happen.'

'But we have proof!' said Liam, spilling coffee on his jeans as he waved his arms in protest.

'It's your word against theirs, Liam. You're outnumbered. They'll just say it happened when you were under the influence.'

'They'd *what?*' he said. He glared at a portrait of a regal-looking man on the wall to his left. It had beady eyes that followed him around the room. He shuddered, then turned back to his lawyer.

'It's not pretty, but that's how it works,' said David.

'Surely, if I was too high to remember doing something, I shouldn't have been allowed to sign it?'

David shrugged. 'I believe you, I do, but everyone is remaining silent. I'm just giving you the other side of the story so that you don't get blindsided. I'm doing what I can to look into this, but is receiving the money really such a bad thing?'

'I was accused of murder because of that money! If there hadn't been a witness to what happened I might be in prison! Doesn't that seem a little too *Gone Girl* to you?'

'Are you suggesting she did this intentionally?'

Liam ran his hand through his hair. 'I don't know. It didn't look intentional, but who knows with Trinity? I wouldn't put anything past her.'

'You don't have to spend the money,' said David. 'You could put it towards a good cause.'

'What do you mean?'

'Like a charity or something. Something she would've liked.'

Liam scoffed. 'Trinity didn't believe in giving to charity. She thought she *was* charity.'

'But Trinity can't make that decision any more. What happens to that money is either up to you, or up to the state. And frankly, I think you'd find a much better use for it.'

*

The next stop was his club, Inferno. He'd set it up at the height of his *Highwater* fame, but he'd never bothered managing it himself. It was an investment; a way to ensure he still had money even if his film career didn't survive. And it was looking increasingly like it wouldn't.

He met up with Drake, the manager, a couple of hours before he was due to go to the funeral.

'Hey man, I'm sorry about Trinity,' said Drake, pouring them both a pint of Guinness from behind the bar.

Why did people keep saying sorry to him? They hadn't been together for over a year. Was he really all that she'd had left?

'Thanks,' said Liam, perching on a barstool.

Turned out, Inferno was more popular than ever because it had been one of Trinity's favourite hangouts. Visitors were also hoping to catch sight of Liam (and no doubt check his mental state after everything that had happened). The fans still couldn't decide if he was guilty or innocent. He'd stopped checking his emails and social media because he couldn't handle the constant notifications. If it wasn't fans arguing about him, it was journalists asking him for an official statement. Which he hadn't given. Why should he? He wasn't her boyfriend and hadn't been for a long time. Why did his opinion matter so much to people? Fame was exhausting.

'You still there?' said Drake, waving his hand in front of Liam's face.

'Sorry, zoned out. It's been a long few days.'

'Yeah, I'll bet. How you holding up?'

Liam shrugged. He didn't know. One minute he was fine, the next he was angry, then sad, then confused. He couldn't keep up with his emotions. How could he expect anyone else to?

'Well, listen, you don't need to worry about this place. We've got this. You stay away for as long as you need to,' said Drake.

'Thanks.'

Knowing his club was in safe hands reassured him a little. He'd expected the fact that half his fanbase hated him to have killed custom. He'd never expected it to increase it. But at least if his acting career did nosedive – or he quit before it could plummet any further – he'd still have his investments. If he got really desperate, he could sell Inferno. But he didn't want to. He liked the place. It felt more like home than any apartment he'd ever lived in. It was his. He'd sell his other investments off before he had to sell Inferno. But it wouldn't get to that point. Would it?

Two

Astin didn't know why he'd decided to go to Trinity's funeral. He hadn't even been that close to her. But he knew that Liam had been, and that Liam could use as much moral support as he could get. Even with the police ruling Trinity's death an accidental suicide, there were plenty of fans that still blamed him. Trinity's death was on the verge of becoming one of the great Hollywood conspiracies. Nobody wanted someone so talented or popular to die in such a sudden and tragic way. But life didn't work that way…

Slipping during a stunt and ending up bed bound for months had taught him that all too well. If it hadn't been for the crash mat below, his friends would've attended his funeral less than a year ago. Hollie never would've had the chance to dump him because he wouldn't have survived long enough to treat her like crap.

Was Hollie going?

No. She had fashion show prep to do in Barcelona. It wasn't like she and Fayth got on with Trinity, either. Not that he had. He'd avoided her as much as possible. It wasn't his place to tell Liam who to date, but he wasn't going to hang around people he found draining or toxic, either. At least, he didn't until he became that person.

Some days he still wished the fall had killed him. He wished he could've stopped the pain that he'd caused Hollie, his little brother, his grandparents, and his friends.

After hearing about what had happened to Trinity, he'd realised he didn't want to leave the world without having really left a mark on it. Sure, he'd been in a few movies, but only as a stunt person. What could he do that would *really* leave a mark? Not the physical kind – like what the camera crane had done to the back of his neck – but the psychological kind. The emotional kind. The kind that left people awestruck.

He'd always dreamed of achieving something like that. If only he could work out what kind of achievements fell into that box.

Stunt work wasn't enough. And anyway, he'd been told he could never go back to it by his original doctor. Doctors didn't get everything right, though. Could he prove them wrong?

The church where Trinity's funeral was being held appeared through the trees. Astin and his flatmate Jack walked down the road in silence. Trinity wasn't even religious. Why were they having it in a church? Whose decision had that been? Who'd even organised the whole thing? It wasn't like she had any friends or family. Was it her assistant? Another staff member? Who else had any loyalty to her?

He recognised some of the faces in the crowds. People who'd worked with or for Trinity over the years; people from her circles (some of whom he'd met, too, mostly because of Liam); other Hollywood faces. It was a who's who of Hollywood. Helicopters buzzed above them. Of course they did. They loved her just as much dead as they did alive – they'd continue to draw blood from her for as long as they could.

Not that Trinity would've wanted it any other way.

A group of people from the *Knight of Shadows* set – the film where he'd had his near-fatal accident – came into view. He was finally rid of his head brace, wheelchair, and even crutches, but he still couldn't walk far. He'd insisted on getting out of the taxi at the end of the road to get some exercise, but every so often he'd have to lean on Jack for support. Jack had helped him in London after Hollie had left so he didn't mind, but it bothered Astin that he still wasn't back to his full health. Did the *Knight of Shadows* crew care? What had they done about that scene after he was injured? Had they rewritten it? CGIed it? Worse still, used the clip of him falling?

His legs grew wobbly at the thought. He grabbed on to Jack.

'You all right, man?'

'Yeah,' said Astin, tightening his jaw. His body would do as it was goddamn told.

He spotted Tate – dressed in a black shift dress and wearing a huge black sunhat – talking to her bodyguard. He and Jack made their way over. 'Hey,' he said.

'Hey,' she said. She gave Jack a quick kiss, then hugged Astin.

'Sorry I haven't spoken to you much lately,' said Astin.

All things considered, he was starting to realise just how important it was to stay in touch with the people he cared about. The truth was, though, Tate was working closely with Hollie to help her get her line off the ground. There was no way Tate couldn't talk about her. There was also no way he could handle hearing about her. Just the sound of her name tugged at his heart.

'He's not that interesting anyway,' said Jack.

Tate nudged him, half playfully, half scoldingly. 'It's OK,' she said. 'I get it.' She patted his shoulder. Out of everyone, she was the one most likely to understand. Every time she and Jack broke up, she couldn't stand to hear his name or anything about him. It seemed like things were going well between them lately, but their relationship was unpredictable at the best of times. He'd never been able to keep up.

'Hey,' said Liam, joining them. His hands were stuffed into his pockets, his head bowed. His face was red.

Astin patted his friend's shoulder. 'I'm sorry, man.' It sounded pathetic, but what else could he say?

Liam gave a small nod.

A gigantic man with a comb over began to walk up the church steps. He struggled with each step, taking a moment to pause and take a few breaths. Astin hadn't met him, only heard of him, but he was fairly sure he was Trinity's biological father. They hadn't spoken since Trinity was a teenager. She hated him. It was an open secret in Hollywood how horrible Peter Baum was not just to his children, but to anyone that worked with him. New people didn't believe the rumours, though – they fell for his charming exterior. They fell for his talent. And when you can put out great movies, studios will keep hiring you.

Tate narrowed her eyes at the sight of Peter. Even when Tate had been friends with Trinity, she'd never liked Trinity's dad. Hardly surprising given that he abandoned her for long periods of time and forced her to work in the movies when she didn't even want to. What a horrible, tragic existence.

Liam took a deep breath, his eyes glued to the crowds going inside.

However they felt about her, it was time to say goodbye to Trinity Gold.

*

There was no wake. Everyone had work to get back to. Well, most people did. Jack returned to the studio to help Camilla Persia with her latest album, while Astin, Liam, Tate, Wade, Liam's driver Thalia, and Tate's latest bodyguard went back to Liam's apartment. They didn't speak much. What was there to say?

Thalia made them all a hot drink, then the staff disappeared into the games room and left the three of them to talk.

Tate sipped her almond milk hot chocolate. 'It reminds you of how short life is, doesn't it?'

'Yeah,' said Astin with a sigh.

Liam got up and walked out.

Tate sighed. She placed her mug on the table, reached across the sofa, and held Astin's hands. Oh god. What else had gone wrong? Was someone terminally ill? Was it her? Was it Hollie? 'We need you in Barcelona.'

Astin blinked at her. 'What?'

'Look at him,' said Tate. 'He's a mess. He blames himself for Trinity's death. And so do a lot of his fans.'

'Why does that mean he needs me?'

'He's surrounded by women. Wouldn't you want a guy friend to play *Call of Duty* with?'

'Liam doesn't play *Call of Duty*.'

Tate slapped his leg. 'And women can play games just as well as men. You know what I mean!'

Astin leaned back against the leather sofa. Was Tate right? Did he need a friend? Hollie had dropped everything when her nan had needed her. He'd never done that for anyone before. Was it a good way to show everyone he'd changed, or would going back to Barcelona when Hollie was there – when she'd said she never wanted to see him again – look selfish? Or worse, creepy and stalker-like?

'I can't,' said Astin. 'I'm sorry.' He stood up and walked over to the window. Cars zoomed past 20 storeys below. Carrying on with life like nothing was wrong. If only he could do the same.

Tate walked over to him and placed a hand on his shoulder. 'Do you really want to die having never apologised to her?'

He swotted her hand away. 'I did apologise! She ignored me!'

'And how do you know she doesn't regret that?'

'I don't, but I doubt that you do either. There's only one person she'd admit that to, and it isn't you or me.'

'True,' said Tate, 'but every time your name comes up, she flinches, just like you do when I say her name.'

'That doesn't mean that it's meant to be, Tate. That's not how life works. You should know that better than anyone.' He crossed his arms, his jaw tight.

'That's how I know what's worth fighting for,' said Tate.

'She has a boyfriend,' he reminded her. Liam had *not* wanted to tell him about that, but it had slipped out. They'd double dated. How fucking nauseating.

'Him? He's wonderful to look at but just so *safe*! He wears the same outfit every day. Every. Day.'

He wore the same outfit every day and was dating a fashion designer? How did that not drive Hollie mad? 'That's very... practical of him.'

'It's very *boring* of him!' said Tate. 'She needs someone who brings out the spark in her, and that someone is *you*.' She jabbed his chest.

'Did you miss the part where she told me to—'

'Do you have any idea how many times I've told Jack to fuck off? That doesn't mean that I don't love him. It means that I do.'

'Slow down a minute, Freud.'

'She lashed out because she was angry at you. Only people who strike a nerve are capable of doing that. And that only happens when it involves someone or something that we love.'

'Even so, it's been months. She's moved on.'

Tate shrugged. 'He's a rebound. And that doesn't change the fact that Liam needs you. Or that it's time for you to get some closure.'

Closure. Closure from Hollie, closure from *Knight of Shadows*, closure from that whole part of his life. That did sound like a good idea. Everything had hovered over him for so long that perhaps one last trip to see everyone and be a part of that world was exactly what he needed. Maybe then he'd finally be able to move on.

Tate took something out of her bag, placed it on the coffee table, then walked out of the room. Once the door was closed behind her, Astin walked over to the coffee table to see what it was. It was a flyer advertising the premier of *Knight of Shadows*. In Barcelona.

THREE

Astin tugged at his seatbelt. Was it too late to back out? The plane hadn't taken off yet. There had to still be time. He reached for the buckle on his seatbelt. Tate, who was sat in the seat opposite him with Moxie on her lap, cleared her throat. Her expression was fierce.

'I can't do it, Tate. I'm sorry.' He unfastened his seatbelt. What was he thinking, travelling to Barcelona when Hollie was there? Liam had plenty of people around him. He didn't need Astin as well. He wasn't even on the same flight as them — he was taking his own private jet back later.

Tate had taken Astin home to pack as if she'd expected him to back out. Or maybe she'd just hoped to see Jack again before she left.

If he was on a normal flight he could've left already, but on a private jet — and one owned by Tate's dad at that — there were dozens of eagle eyes watching him. There was nothing but a small table separating him and Tate. Usually Maddy would be sat on the other side of the plane, but she'd stayed in Barcelona to help Hollie. Oh god. Hollie. What was he doing?

The pilot appeared from the cockpit. 'We'll be leaving in a few moments.' He noticed Astin and his seatbelt. 'If you'd like to put your seatbelt on please.' He flashed Astin a down-turned smile then returned to the cockpit.

Astin refastened his seatbelt and sunk into his seat. Was he really ready to see her again? No amount of books or music could distract him from the thought of seeing her again. Hollie wouldn't be happy to see him. Would he be happy to see her? Could he even handle seeing her? Just hearing her name was enough for him to feel like he'd hurt his back all over again.

Tate took her seatbelt off, removed Moxie from her lap, and placed her on Astin's. She circled in his lap a couple of times, then lay down and curled up. It was Tate's way of both helping him to relax and holding him hostage. Was that what he was? A hostage?

Was he overthinking it? He could've stood up to Tate if he'd wanted to. She was half his size.

He squeezed his eyes shut, then reopened them and turned to look out of the window. The plane began to glide along the runway.

*

By the time their plane arrived in Barcelona, Puddle of Mudd's *She Hates Me* was firmly stuck in Astin's head. Of all the songs. He tried to hum something else, but everything somehow turned into *She Hates Me*. Ugh.

The premier was in a couple of weeks. He should've waited until nearer the time to go to Barcelona. That would've given him more time to come up with an excuse not to go, too. Or to buy a one-way ticket to the middle of nowhere…

Maddy was waiting for them in arrivals, her severe features made even more severe by the blunt bob she'd had her hair cut into. She looked like an evil schoolteacher, but Astin knew better – without her, Tate wouldn't be able to function.

'Hey,' he said, kissing Maddy's cheek.

'Welcome to Barcelona,' she said.

'I'm still not sure this is a good idea,' he said with a sigh. He looked up through the window. It took up the top half of the building, exposing the bright sunlight outside. The weather may have been better than New York's, but his shitty mood had followed him. Would some time away help him to shake it off?

'Neither is arguing with Tate,' said Maddy, patting him on the shoulder.

He glanced over his shoulder at Tate, who was scurrying along behind with Moxie in one arm and her handbag in the other. Her poor bodyguard had somehow ended up with all her other bags. How was he supposed to protect her if he was playing pachyderm? No wonder her bodyguards never lasted.

'How are you, anyway?' said Maddy. Whenever people he hadn't seen for a while asked him that, he always assumed they wanted to know about his back. They were trying to be considerate; concerned; polite. To him, it was annoying. He wanted to forget that the accident had ever happened, but he also knew that that would never happen. Nobody would let him. If it wasn't someone he knew reminding him, it was a random well-wisher who remembered him from his modelling days and couldn't believe how well he'd recovered. He hoped being in

Europe would mean he was less well known. But then, when you modelled for a global company, the risk was always there. It was part of why he'd quit. That, and a great opportunity to start working on his stunt career had come about…

He shuddered. It had been Tate that had offered him that opportunity. Back then, he couldn't have been happier. Working as a stunt performer had been his dream. Until he'd had it ripped away by Lawrence Roskowski, the director from hell. Had Roskowsi been more responsible, Astin never would've slipped while doing a stunt. He never would've damaged one of his vertebrae so badly that he couldn't sit up for three months, then been confined to a wheelchair for another three. His back still hurt sometimes and he didn't have as much energy as he used to, but he was slowly returning to his old strength again.

Tate put her hand on his shoulder. He flinched. 'Astin, sweetie? Are you OK?' She narrowed her eyes in that concerned way that she always did. He forced his features to look neutral. Tate already had the upper hand; he'd fallen for her persuasive ways yet again. He wasn't going to give her any more leverage than she already had.

'Let's go.'

*

As usual, Hollie slept like crap. When she'd finally fallen asleep, she'd dreamed of the last person she'd wanted to think about: Astin. What was worse was that it had been a particularly dirty dream that her brain was still replaying. He'd walked into her room wrapped in nothing but a cerulean-coloured towel. His blue eyes had burned with desire as he'd pulled her up from her desk chair and into his naked torso. She'd placed her hand on his chest; his skin was warm under her fingers. He'd smelled of patchouli and citrus, just like he always had. He'd pressed her lips to hers, filling her with desire. Desperation burned inside of her.

No. No more replays! Her brain seriously needed a pause button.

She wasn't supposed to have dreams like that about Astin when she was going out with Santi! She needed coffee and stat. The sooner she got coffee into her system, the better she'd feel. She set the coffee machine up to do its thing while she went for a quick shower. She wasn't a huge fan of filter coffee machines, but it was early – she'd take what she could get. Nobody else was around, so her plan was to have a leisurely breakfast then go to the studio to get some work done.

Once she was dressed in skinnies and a puffball-sleeved jumper, she returned to the kitchen area and picked up the coffee pot to pour herself a hot drink.

The door to the apartment opened. Tate entered. Followed by the last person Hollie had ever wanted to see again.

'*Astin?*' The coffee pot slipped from her hand. It bounced off her foot and smashed onto the floor. She jumped up, hot liquid and broken glass searing her feet. 'Gah!' She jumped up onto the countertop and pulled herself across it to avoid the broken glass. She was so busy avoiding the glass she forgot about the sink and she fell, arse-first, into it. Her cheeks burning, she risked a glance to Astin and Tate. Tate was turned away, trying not to laugh. Astin was biting his lip. 'Do you need some help?' he offered.

'No. I'm fine,' she insisted through gritted teeth as she hoisted herself out of the sink, her arse soaking wet. Wet denim. Lovely.

She scooted along to the end of the counter, then hesitated. What next? The bottoms of her feet were burned and probably covered with broken glass. If she put weight on them, there was no telling what pain it would cause. But what else could she do? After a deep breath, she hopped off the counter. Her feet touched the floor and the pain of hundreds of needles shot through her. Her legs gave way. Astin, quick as ever, caught her and picked her up.

'Your back—'

'Is fine. Where's the bathroom? We need to get your feet cleaned up.'

'Second door,' she said, her teeth still gritted from the pain.

He carried her over to the door, which – of course – was shut. Hollie managed to open it while still in Astin's arms – which she was annoyed to find she still found comforting – then he propped her up on the edge of the bath.

The bathroom was so big that the bath was nowhere near the toilet, meaning that she had to balance on the very thin edge of the huge bath. With everything that had happened in the last few minutes, that was asking for disaster.

Astin didn't seem to agree, as he reached for the shower head, took it from its holder, and turned it on. Hollie wasn't ready, so she lost her grip and fell into the bath. It wasn't just her arse that was soaked any more – it was her whole bloody outfit. At least none of it was dry-clean only.

'Shit!' Astin reached to turn it off, but he just made the water run faster.

'Other way! Other way!' she cried. Literally cried. She'd had enough. Her cheeks were burning, her feet were burning, and all sense of dignity had vanished.

He turned the shower the other way and switched it off.

'Sorry,' he said, unable to look her in the eye.

'There are some chairs in the living room. I can sit on one of those then you can go do whatever it is you and Tate were planning to do.'

'She didn't tell you?'

'Tell me what?'

Astin stiffened. 'She invited me to stay.'

'Of course she did,' said Hollie, her hands curling into fists.

'I'm sorry, I thought she would've told you.' His shoulders slumped. 'If you don't want me here I can go.' He looked so sad. Like a puppy that needed a hug after something terrible had happened. She didn't want to be that person. Not when Liam really needed his friends. And it looked like Astin did, too. 'No, it's OK.' Famous last words? 'But I'd really appreciate that chair right now.'

'Yes! Right!' He scurried out of the room and returned a moment later with her computer chair.

'Not what I had in mind, but it'll do.'

'It means I can move you around easier,' he said.

He could move her around. Not that she could move herself. What was he trying to do? Win her around again somehow? Well, it wasn't going to work.

He helped her into the chair then turned the shower on again. Hollie reached for the controls and turned the temperature to its coldest setting. The cold water soothed the bottom of her feet, although the numbness would be an issue if she tried to walk. Keeping the shower over her right foot, she lifted her left onto her knee to examine it. 'Can you see any glass?' she asked Astin.

'We should get you to the hospital just in case,' he said.

'Hospital? Why do I need to go to hospital?' said Hollie, wiping at her feet.

'To get your feet looked at. Make sure there isn't any glass embedded in them.'

Hollie shuddered. The last place she wanted to be was a hospital. She'd have to wait forever to be seen, then get treated, probably have to follow up with some sort of treatment plan, and when she was done with all that she'd have to contact her travel insurance company. It was so much hassle. Why'd she have to drop the sodding coffee pot on her foot?

'He's right,' said Tate, sticking her head through the bathroom door.

'Go away,' growled Hollie. If Tate came any closer she was at risk of being impaled by one of Hollie's magenta fingernails. The coffee-pot-in-foot saga was all her fault anyway. 'I don't have time.'

'You don't have time to protect your feet so that you can walk again?' said Tate, lowering an eyebrow.

'I don't have time to piss about in A and E,' she replied.

'Short-term loss, long-term gain,' she said, disappearing out of sight.

'She's right,' said Astin.

'And who's going to take me?'

'I'll drive,' said Astin. Grr.

'Why?'

'Why what?'

'Why will you drive?'

'Why wouldn't I? Tate and I brought a rental car back from the airport so that it'd be easier to get around. I can call Fayth if you'd prefer.'

'No! She's job hunting. I don't want to bother her for something so silly.'

'All right. Let's get this shower turned off, get you changed, and get you to the hospital,' said Astin.

'Get me *changed*?' He was planning to undress her.

'Unless you want to go out in wet clothes,' he said.

She wriggled on the chair. Her jeans were soaked. But she was wearing skinny jeans. There was no way those things were coming off without a fight.

Astin turned the shower off, wheeled her back into her bedroom, then stood for a moment, as if thinking. 'How do you want to do this?' he asked. 'Those jeans look pretty, er, tight.'

He'd noticed her jeans were tight. What else had he noticed?

'We could cut them—'

'NO!'

Astin put his hands up in surrender. 'It was just a suggestion. I'm not sure how we're going to get them off your swollen feet, that's all. It's going to hurt.'

'I'll put a skirt on over the top, then you and Tate can pull my jeans off at the ankles.'

'If you're sure,' said Astin.

'I'm sure.' She knew it would hurt. But she also wasn't going to let anyone cut into her pink Levi's. It was her own fault. What difference would a little more pain make at this point?

While Astin went to find Tate, Hollie changed out of her wet jumper and into a dry blouse she'd thankfully left on the bed while trying to decide what to wear that morning. Even her bra was soaked through. What a great start to the day.

Tate helped Hollie into a skirt, then she and Astin sat on the floor ready to pull Hollie's wet skinny jeans off her.

'Last chance to change your mind,' said Astin.

'Leave her to it,' said Tate. 'I'd do the same.' She flashed Hollie a reassuring smile. It didn't make Hollie any less pissed off at her.

'Do it,' said Hollie. She'd already wriggled the jeans down to her ankles. It was time for the difficult part. She lay back, her eyes squeezed shut. Her feet burned as the tight fabric rubbed against them. She bit her lip. Fuck fuck fuck. That hurt a lot more than she'd thought it would. Then, relief. The scratching sensation stopped. Her feet were back to feeling sore and angry.

'OK?' said Astin.

'Uh-huh,' said Hollie, panting. 'Now what?'

'Now we get you to the car.'

'How?'

'The elevator.'

Goddamn modern technology.

Four

Hospital was exactly what Hollie had expected: busy and boring. She took a book but she was too distracted by Astin's presence to read. The chairs were so squished together that every time one of them moved they'd touch. And Hollie fidgeted a lot on a good day, let alone when she couldn't put her feet on the floor.

The worst part had been getting to the car. Astin had pushed her in her computer chair while Tate had held the doors open. Tate had then scurried off with Hollie's chair once Hollie was inside the car. She said she'd stay and hold down the fort with Maddy while Hollie was incapacitated. How convenient that that meant she was left alone with Astin. Not that it was all bad. He was quiet. She appreciated that. He seemed to understand that she didn't want to talk. Although talking a little distracted her from the sharp, stabbing pain and the searing burns. Goddamn it. Only she could burn and impale herself with a coffee pot.

Hollie shifted in the cheap, plastic chair. Her arse was going numb. How much longer would they be? How long had they even been waiting? 'Do you know how long we've been waiting?'

Astin jumped, as if he was surprised she was talking to him. Then again, *she* was surprised she was talking to him after what he'd done. Desperate times…

He checked his watch. 'A half hour.'

'*Half an hour*?!' Hollie echoed. 'You've got to be kidding me?'

'Nope.'

Hollie slumped farther into the chair. It was going to be a long day.

*

If Fayth had thought job hunting the first time around had been tedious, the second time was even worse. Thanks to Liam being accused of Trinity's death, Fayth's face was everywhere again as the villain in the Liam and Trinity Love Story. Some people just couldn't let it go, or accept that their relationship had been toxic.

That meant that not only did people recognise her, but they also assumed that she was difficult to work with. It was an impossible situation. She was running out of studios and galleries to visit.

When she reached the last one on the list, she didn't have any hope left. She'd walked from one end of Barcelona to another without any luck; to say she was exhausted was an understatement. Even in the comfiest shoes she owned her feet were killing her, but she was determined to tick the very last place off her list. If nothing else, she could at least say that she'd tried.

She squared her shoulders, tightened her ponytail – which she'd added hairspray to for once to ensure her curls did as they were told – then walked inside. An old couple stood at the counter, squinting over a computer screen. All around the room were photographs of graffitied memorials of the Spanish civil war. The photos had been edited to darken the backgrounds and brighten the memorials. She drew her attention back to the old couple at the desk. '*Hola!*' she said, trying to sound as chirpy as possible.

The old woman lowered her glasses and smiled. 'You wouldn't know anything about computers, would you?'

'What is it you need help with?' said Fayth.

The old man beckoned her behind the counter and pointed to the screen. 'Every time I paste this text into WordPress, it changes the formatting! I don't get it!'

Finally, all that time Fayth had spent updating the pub's website could be put to good use. 'Did you copy and paste the text from somewhere else?'

'Yes. Does that matter?'

'Sometimes,' she said. 'Hold on.' She had a quick look at the HTML, and there it was – random code that was changing how the text appeared on the page. After a few clicks and some deleting, she got rid of the code and fixed the page that the couple had been trying to update.

'*Gracias,*' said the old woman. 'By the way, what was it you actually came in for?'

*

Hollie had thought she was tired before. That was nothing compared to how she felt after the hospital. Her body refused to do as it was told and she was pretty sure she could sleep for a week (if she didn't have a shitload to do). The hospital had taken all the glass out of her feet and popped all of her blisters. The memory of that was enough to make her feel sick. The noise as each of them had popped…*shudder*. She'd been forced to hold Astin's hand as they did it. She'd needed someone to comfort her, and he was there. He hadn't said anything, not even when she'd turned his hand purple from her iron grip. He deserved some points for that.

The lancing of her blisters meant that her feet weren't nearly as horrible-looking as they had been, but they were still red, sore, and angry. The doctors had ordered her to rest. If only she could.

She also desperately wanted to bathe but couldn't bear the thought of walking any farther than she had to. The hospital had given her some crutches to use, but she preferred to walk on her blistered feet. Crutches were far too complicated.

Astin helped her as much as he could, but she wasn't going to let him help her into the bath. Technically he'd seen her naked before, but circumstances had changed. She'd have to wait until Fayth got back from job hunting. It was bad enough Fayth seeing her naked, but at least Fayth didn't have any ulterior motives. Hollie still didn't know what to make of Astin's looking after her, but then, it *was* his fault…partly, anyway. Most of it was Tate's. Who was still at the studio when they got back. Hiding, much?

Safely back in her room, Hollie reached for her phone on the bedside table, but it wasn't there. Neither was her laptop. Her phone was in her bag – which was over the other side of the room – and her laptop was on the coffee table in the lounge. Fuck.

Leaning forwards, she reached for the computer chair and pulled it towards her. Then she tried to manoeuvre herself into it, but instead she fell to the floor with a thump. For fuck's sake.

Astin ran in. 'Are you all right?'

'Marvellous,' she said, pulling herself back up onto the bed.

'What were you doing?'

'I forgot my phone and laptop.'

'You could've just asked.'

'I didn't want to bother you. You had a long flight and you've been running around after me since you got here.'

Astin shrugged. 'I slept on the plane.'

Why did everyone seem to be able to do that but her?

Astin disappeared, then returned with her laptop. He picked up her handbag from the other side of the room, then placed that and her laptop beside her on the bed. 'Do you want me to get you a coffee? It doesn't look like you'll be able to make one for a bit…'

'Very funny. It's fine. I'll be fine.' Her stomach disagreed. It let out a loud rumbling noise that she was fairly sure her nan heard back in England.

'I could get food if you'd prefer,' he said.

She sighed. Her stomach rumbled again.

Astin chuckled. She'd missed that laugh. It was such a warm laugh. What was going on with her brain? Why was it reacting like that to Astin? He was bad. Very very bad.

'I should probably eat something,' she said with a sigh.

'All right, I'll see what I can find.'

*

What a mess. Astin had been there less than six hours and already she couldn't walk and her stomach and heart were doing weird jigs. Hollie needed someone to talk things through with, but who? Fayth was still job hunting. Tate was in the doghouse. Liam was Astin's best friend and probably mid-air on his way back to Barcelona. That left Cameron or a family member. Talking about relationships with her family was weird, though, so she settled on Cameron instead. Would he be at work? Would he answer if he was at work? Desperate for someone to talk to, she rang him anyway. He answered after the second ring. 'I'm re-alphabetising stock. Please entertain me.'

'Astin is here.'

'Well now you have my attention.' She imagined him sat cross-legged on the floor of the stockroom, an eager expression on his chubby face.

Hollie filled him in on everything that had happened. The sound of CDs clattered in the background as she spoke.

'I don't know whether to laugh or cry,' said Cameron. 'How's your ego?'

'Not nearly as bruised as my feet or my arse. I don't think.' It was hard to tell. Everything hurt.

'Are you going to let him stay?'

'"Let him?" This isn't a dictatorship.'

'Then why did Tate invite him without asking any of you first?'

'You have a point,' said Hollie. Why *did* Tate think it was acceptable to invite someone to stay without asking? Someone who happened to be Hollie's ex-boyfriend and who'd had a major attitude problem the last time she'd seen him? 'He looked so broken. I couldn't kick him out.'

'Broken how?'

'Like…depressed. Maybe he needs a friend just as much as Liam does right now,' said Hollie.

'You're a nicer person than me,' he said. He lowered his voice. 'I've got to go. Someone's coming. Keep me posted!'

He hung up. Hollie lay back on the bed, her feet still throbbing. She had so much to do. She didn't have time to relax...but she found herself lying back and falling asleep anyway.

The next thing she knew, someone was tapping on her bedroom door. She opened an eye to see Astin standing in the doorway, a bag in hand. 'Sorry for waking you up. I didn't want your food to go cold.'

'It's fine,' she said, sitting up. 'I didn't intend to fall asleep.'

'You must've needed it,' he said, entering the room and putting the bag on the bedside table. Without saying anything else, he turned around. He'd done all that for her and wasn't even going to stay and eat it with her? That felt wrong. 'Didn't you get anything?'

'I was going to eat it in my room,' he said.

'Do you want to...stay?' The last word almost pained her to say, but she wanted it. She wanted him there more than she liked to admit.

A small smile flashed across his face. It vanished almost immediately. 'Um, if you're sure.'

She nodded.

'I'll just go get my food.' He left her alone to dig into her bag of food. A ham and cheese baguette. A vanilla latte. And churros. Yum.

He returned with his own bag of food and sat on her computer chair while they ate. It was a little awkward, but not as awkward as it could've been. They fell back into each other's company almost as easily as they had the first time they'd met. Almost like she hadn't told him to fuck off and never speak to her again. Almost like she hadn't ignored his text telling her he'd always be there for her...

What a mess.

Was she really prepared to let him back in after what he'd done? But could she really cut him out when he looked so sad? When his words were so measured, so mumbled, that sometimes they were barely audible? She knew the subtle signs of depression all too well. It was highly unlikely he'd even acknowledged his mental state to himself, but the slow movements, the hunched shoulders, the sadness in his eyes...it was all there.

'How have you been lately?' she asked without thinking. It wasn't even her place to ask, for god's sake.

He shrugged. 'You know.'

Talk about dodging the question. She could probe, but what was the point? He'd never been one for talking about his problems, and it was none of her business. Not any more.

Astin munched on his food for a few moments. Then he broke the silence: 'I apologised to Cooper.'

'Oh?' said Hollie. She tried to hide her excitement. Cooper was Astin's adorable younger brother. Astin had been a total dick to him, too.

'He said he's forgiven me. He even…he even stood up to my mom, which he's never done before.'

'Wow, what'd he say?'

'I went to stay with a friend in Texas and I didn't visit my parents. When my mom found out she came over while I was at my grandparents' place. Coop told her to leave me alone and said he didn't blame me for not wanting to talk to her. She stormed out in a rage.'

Hollie forced back a laugh. It sounded like Astin's mum had got exactly what she deserved. Hollie hadn't met her, but she'd heard plenty from Astin and Cooper about what she was like: bad-tempered, selfish, and controlling. How Astin and Cooper weren't shrivelled psychological messes she'd never understand.

'Wow. How is he now?'

'Older. Cheekier. Wiser than me.' Astin gave a small laugh.

'He was always wiser than you,' said Hollie with a wry grin.

'Yeah, I'm starting to think that.' Astin sighed. 'Sometimes you have to be with parents like ours.'

Hollie hadn't had parents as bad as Astin's, but her dad had left when she was young. As an only child, she'd spent most of her life surrounded by adults. Even as a kid she'd had no idea how to act as a kid. Since Astin was away so much, she had a feeling Cooper felt exactly the same way.

Hollie finished her baguette and dug back into the bag for some churros. Sugar fell over the bedspread as she fished them out, but she was past caring. She'd sort it later. She held out the bag and offered one to Astin.

'They're for you,' he said.

'And I'm offering one to you,' she said.

'Thanks.' He reached out, took one from the bag, and bit into it. 'Churros are so much better in Spain.'

'Yeah. I'm never eating English ones again.'

'Those things y'all serve aren't even proper churros,' said Astin.

Y'all. It always made her giggle when he said that. This time, she suppressed her giggle. It wasn't the time to be laughing at his Southern dialect.

'Nope,' agreed Hollie, taking a bite of one. Her mouth was filled with crisp sugar and fried batter. Damn, churros were good.

*

Hollie was finishing off a bag of churros when Fayth walked in. Except Hollie wasn't the only one eating churros. Astin was sat in her computer chair, eating churros and *talking to her*! What had happened while she was out? What had she missed? 'Astin! When did you get here?'

'Round about the same time Hollie injured herself with the coffee pot.'

Fayth turned to Hollie. 'You did what?'

Hollie blushed. 'Long story. Short version, I can't walk. Could you help me into the bath before Santi gets here please?'

'Sure.'

'I'll go get the water running,' said Astin, getting up and leaving them alone. He was running her a bath! What did *that* mean?

Fayth took his spot in her computer chair. 'What am I missing? Why didn't you text me?'

'A lot, and I didn't want to bother you. I wanted you to focus on your job search. Did you find something?'

'Yes. Now back to you. What happened with your feet?'

'Oh, you know. Saw Astin. Shock made me drop the coffee pot. It smashed to pieces. Burned my feet. Jumped on a few shards of glass. Hurt like a bitch. Ended up in hospital. They've lanced the blisters, but I've got to have someone come out and change the dressings for the next few days while they heal.'

'Sounds like I missed a hell of a lot.'

'Oh, you have no idea.'

*

It just so happened that the day that a) Astin arrived and b) Hollie dropped a coffee pot on her feet coincided with a rare night she'd given herself off to spend with Santi. Since that couldn't happen any more, he insisted on joining her at the apartment. Hollie wasn't keen on the idea given the presence of Astin, but she did want to see him. It was about time her actual boyfriend looked after her rather than her ex-boyfriend.

Hollie was just rousing from sleep when she heard a faint knocking at the front door. A moment later, Santi's voice: 'Hello?'

'Hi, I'm Astin.' Hollie pictured him holding out his hand to Santi. She wasn't sure if Santi would shake it or not. Was he the jealous type? She didn't know him well enough to be sure.

'Astin?' said Santi. From the tone in his voice, it was clear that he remembered Hollie mentioning him. How many bad things had she said? Oh god.

'Tate invited me. It's a long story. Did Hollie tell you what happened?' said Astin.

The door closed. Their voices grew louder.

'Yes. How is she?'

'She's been asleep the last couple hours.'

'Good. She never seems to get enough sleep.'

Astin scoffed. 'That's nothing new.'

Hmph.

'Hollie?' called Santi through the door.

Hollie shuffled up in bed and flattened her hair. 'Come in.'

Santi walked in, a takeaway coffee cup in his hand. Hollie smiled. He had on a crimson jumper. Surprise surprise.

Wait, where did Astin go?

Ugh. That was *not* something she was supposed to be thinking. He'd likely gone off to do his own thing so that she could spend time with her boyfriend. Which made perfect sense.

'How are you feeling?' he asked, walking over to her then kissing her cheek.

'Fine until I try to stand.'

'Thought this might cheer you up.' He handed her the takeaway coffee cup.

'Bless you.' She took the coffee from him with one hand, then used the other to pull him back towards her so that they could kiss properly. His warm, soft lips pressed against hers. Mmm. He tasted like paella.

'Do you want my help with anything while I'm here?' he offered.

'Like what?'

'Do you need any help in the bath or shower? How are you going to get to and from there if you can't walk? How have you gone so long without going to the toilet?'

The cheek! She didn't pee *that much*. 'I've been crawling,' she said, only half-joking.

'Didn't your friends help you?' There was a hint of bitterness in his voice.

'On and off. I don't want to rely on them too much. I changed into a skirt to try to make life easier.'

'Let me help,' he said, giving her his warmest smile. How could she say no to that?

'All right. But after coffee.'

'Very well,' he said, sitting in her computer chair.

She sipped the coffee. Her tastebuds filled with vanilla and coffee and – 'Is this decaf?' It was definitely less bitter than usual.

Santi smirked.

Hollie glared, but she was secretly glad. She really did need to cut down on her caffeine intake. She had done for a while, but given how busy she'd been lately she'd needed something to keep her going, and that something had been caffeine.

FIVE

Hollie crawled out of her room and across the living room. The flooring was smooth and cold underneath her hands, but at least Fayth had mopped the floor the night before, so she knew it would be relatively clean.

Liam looked down at her from the kitchen, his brow furrowed. 'How are you feeling?'

'Well my feet look like Mr Blobby's and they feel like someone's trying to stab them with needles whenever I walk. But other than that I'm peachy.'

'Who's Mr Blobby?' he said, turning over some bacon in the frying pan.

'The character of nightmares.'

'He was a creepy character in a bunch of '90s TV shows,' said Fayth, emerging from their room in her fluffy green dressing gown. 'Some poor sod dressed in a pink suit with yellow spots on.'

'That *does* sound creepy,' said Liam. He turned back to Hollie: 'You know, we could've brought you breakfast. You didn't have to crawl for it.'

'I'm bored! I don't want to lie in bed all day!'

'But you can't walk,' he reminded her.

'So get me a wheelchair,' she said.

'Or you could just stop being a baby and do what the doctor says for once,' said Fayth.

Hollie narrowed her eyes. Why didn't she get it? She didn't have time to rest! 'I have an outfit I need to finish back at the studio.'

'How do you plan to do that?' said Fayth.

Hollie fluttered her eyelashes. 'I was hoping someone would go pick it up for me.'

'That someone being me?'

'Or Liam. Or Tate.' Hollie shrugged. She manoeuvred so that she was sat cross-legged on the floor.

Fayth sighed. 'You should be resting, not sewing.'

'But I need to finish this outfit. I'm almost done! I'm not going to be able to rest until it's finished and you know it.'

Fayth sighed again. 'I do know it. All right, I'll get it for you after breakfast.'

Hollie beamed. 'Thank you!'

'Provided you go back to bed and stop crawling around, that is.'

'But crawling is fun.'

Fayth lowered an eyebrow. 'Right.'

'It is! You should try it!'

'What happened to little miss I'm-not-putting-my-hands-on-that-because-I-don't-know-where-it's-been?' said Fayth.

'She lost the use of her feet,' grumbled Hollie.

'Temporarily,' said Liam.

'But how long is temporary?' sighed Hollie. 'My feet are freezing and I can't put any socks on.' She tucked her feet underneath her to warm them up. Pain shot through her. She shuddered, twisting so that she could sit cross-legged again.

'Doesn't the dressing keep them warm?' said Liam.

'Not as much as I'd like,' said Hollie.

'Why can't you wear socks?' said Fayth.

'My feet are too swollen. None of mine fit.'

'Mine might,' said Liam. She glanced at his socks. They were red and black striped, and made out of really thick wool. They looked super snug.

'How big are your feet?' said Hollie.

'Big enough, I think,' he said.

'You know you've walked right into a joke?' said Hollie.

'Yes. I'm hoping you're mature enough not to make it,' he said.

'Only because I want your socks.'

'Your maturity is appreciated,' he said.

*

'Morning!' chimed Tate as she walked into Hollie's room. Why was she in such a good mood? It was as if she'd done nothing wrong. Like she couldn't acknowledge when she'd hurt someone else. What the hell was wrong with her?

Hollie was perched on the end of the bed, her feet freshly bandaged. The nurse had said they were making good progress, but she'd need a couple more dressing changes. Her freshly dressed feet were wrapped in two pairs of Liam's socks to try to keep them warm. She was pretty sure they were expensive –

possibly handmade – socks. If buying fancy socks wasn't a sign someone had money, she didn't know what was.

Fayth had taken the rental car to pick up a mannequin like Hollie had asked. That meant Hollie could take out her pent-up aggression on the mannequin instead of someone that was giving her money. It was better than nothing.

'What's up with you?' said Tate as Hollie stabbed the mannequin through the playsuit it was wearing.

Tate was *not* that stupid. She knew exactly why Hollie was pissed off. Hollie ground her teeth so hard she could hear herself doing it. She needed Tate. She couldn't antagonise her. As much as she wanted to.

Tate sat in Hollie's desk chair and spun around a few times. Sometimes it was like working with a child. When would she grow up and realise that the world didn't revolve around her? The old chair creaked every time it got to a certain point. It was like nails on a chalkboard. Hollie couldn't take it.

'Would you stop that!'

Tate stopped spinning and stared at Hollie with her eyebrows raised, as if waiting for her to talk.

'You invited my ex *to live with us*. Why do you think I'm pissed off?'

Tate sighed. 'You seemed to be getting along fine yesterday.'

'That's. Not. The. Point!'

Tate cocked her head. 'Then what is?'

'You went behind my back! That's not cool!' Hollie stabbed the mannequin with another pin.

'Would you have said yes if I'd asked?'

'No.'

'Exactly.'

'Exactly what? Why is he even here?'

'Liam needs a friend right now,' said Tate.

'He's surrounded by them.'

'He needed a male friend.'

'What difference does that make?'

'The same difference it would make to you if Fayth wasn't around.'

Hollie turned back to the mannequin and pinned some more of the playsuit she was working on into place.

'Astin needed his friends, too,' said Tate.

'He has friends all over the place.'

'It's not the same and you know it.'

'So, what, I'm just supposed to deal with him living in the same apartment? Why can't he move to a hotel?'

'If I recall, he offered, and you said no.'

How did she know that? Hollie jabbed another pin into the mannequin. She turned to Tate, burning with rage. 'You knew I wouldn't be able to kick him out. He looks like a lost puppy. The guy is so broken you could break him by saying boo.'

'If you hate him so much, why didn't you?'

'You know I'm not that much of a bitch.'

'Then that's on you, not me,' said Tate.

'I can't even,' said Hollie. She closed her eyes and took a couple of deep breaths. In…Out…In…Out. She opened her eyes. 'You intentionally put me in that horrible position. And you don't even care. You don't even fucking care.'

'Maybe one day you'll realise that I didn't do it to hurt you.'

'Just because you can't fix your own relationship that doesn't mean you need to try to fix everyone else's!'

Tate's eyes widened. 'Wow. OK. That was uncalled for. Jack and I are fine, thank you. And, for the last time, I brought him here to help Liam. Anything that happens between the two of you is on the two of you.'

Tate walked out without another word.

*

The old couple that ran the gallery Fayth had helped offered her the chance to work there for two days a week. It was just what she was looking for.

Francisco and Ramira had been together for forty years and married for thirty. They were adorable. And they didn't make Fayth wish for her old life like seeing old couples together once had. She didn't care if she and Liam never got married. What mattered was that they were happy together. And – Trinity aside – they were.

Working for two days a week meant that she had money coming in but could also spend time with Liam exploring Barcelona. It was such a beautiful city with so many great photo opportunities. Since it was February and it wasn't overly sunny, it was also a great time to take photos. She'd made Liam pose in a couple, but those ones were just for her. They were her way of documenting the time she spent with her boyfriend.

Of course, she'd love to spend time with Hollie too, but that wasn't going to happen. Whenever Fayth suggested going out to do something, Hollie would say she was too busy. Barcelona was a city Hollie had always wanted to visit, yet she refused to explore it because she was too bloody busy working. When would she come up for air?

While Fayth liked helping people, she wasn't much of a problem-solver. It was something she needed to work on. Whenever she had an issue, she always went to Hollie for advice. She was great at giving it. She always knew what to do. Except when it came to herself, it seemed.

Sighing, she returned to the editing she was doing on the gallery's website. Since the ancient computer was on the reception desk, that also meant that she was on reception and till duty too, but she didn't mind. Whenever she struggled to communicate with someone, there was an intercom that connected her to Francisco and Ramira so that they could come and help.

Francisco and Ramira gave her more freedom than Regina had; they trusted her judgement, and that meant a lot. It was also nice that most of the people who came into their gallery were slightly older, meaning they were less likely to recognise her as Liam York's girlfriend.

Most of them, that was.

'Hey, aren't you Liam York's girlfriend? Why are you working here if he's got all that money?'

Fayth looked up from the computer. Standing on the other side of the counter was a twenty-something female wearing too much eyeliner.

'How may I help you?' said Fayth, trying to forget her question and remain as polite as possible.

'Who's in charge here? I'm interested in exhibiting my photography.'

Fayth noticed she had a portfolio under her arm. Feeling empathy for her situation – even if she hadn't liked how she'd started the conversation – Fayth pressed the intercom button on the desk and called Francisco from the back office. He emerged a moment later, flattening his unruly grey hair. He took the woman off to explore the gallery and talk, leaving Fayth to seethe at how she couldn't go anywhere without being recognised as Liam York's girlfriend. She loved Liam, but she wished that people would see her as more than that. Was it really necessary for her whole identity to be tied to him?

'*Gracias!*' said Francisco as the woman walked out five minutes later. He turned to Fayth. 'I hear you're famous.'

For the love of *Highwater*. Fayth sighed.

'Oh don't worry, I don't care. I have no interest in that celebrity schtick,' he said, a twinkle in his hazel eyes.

'Thank you,' said Fayth. He had no idea how much it meant to her to hear him say that.

He scoffed. 'For what? Being a grumpy old man?'

'You're *far* from grumpy,' said Fayth.

Francisco smiled. 'You say that now. There's still time for you to change your mind.'

Fayth laughed. 'Is she going to showcase here?'

'I said I'd let her know. I want to do some more research first. That's part of why I have that thing.' He gestured to the computer. 'If they have a following, it brings people in here, you know?'

Fayth nodded. That was good marketing.

'Have you ever exhibited your photography?'

'Just once,' said Fayth, 'back in New York. It was part of a class that I did when I was over there.'

'You should do one while you're here in Barcelona. I know this great gallery.' He winked.

*

'Hey,' said Astin, poking his head through Hollie's bedroom door. 'I'm going to the store. Want anything?'

Hollie's concentration was broken. She shifted on the edge of the bed, moving too far forwards and slipping. Her head fell into the mannequin's stomach. It rolled away. She face planted the floor. How many more times could she make an arse of herself in front of Astin before she died of embarrassment?

Astin ran over and helped her up. If she carried on, she'd have no dignity left.

'Thanks,' she said as he helped her back onto the bed.

'Are those Liam's socks?' he said, noticing her very toasty toes.

'Yeah. They're the only things that will go around my swollen feet right now. They're super soft. I need to find out where he gets them from,' she said.

'I think he has them custom made somewhere,' he said.

Hollie chuckled. 'Of course he does. Still, they're lovely and soft. Totally worth it. Cheap socks just roll down your ankles and let them get cold.'

'If you say so.' He turned to the mannequin. Luckily Hollie's fall hadn't done anything to the mannequin – it was on wheels, so it had just moved a few feet away when Hollie hit it. And there'd been no pins in the section she'd hit. Phew. 'Is that what you're working on right now?'

'Yeah. I'm not sure if I'm going to keep the shoulder detail yet.'

'Why not?'

'Do you think it's too much?'

'No. It's made from recycled carrier bags, isn't it? I assumed it was a statement on our consumerist society,' he said with a shrug. How did he get that so easily? Santi had said it looked silly.

'You think it works?' she asked.

'Yeah. It makes the design more unique. The black jumpsuit would look great, don't get me wrong, but anyone could design a black jumpsuit. A shoulder made out of pleated plastic bags? That's what makes it Hollie Baxter's.'

Santi had thought it was too over the top. But Astin knew the industry. He knew how important it was to stand out in an industry where everyone was constantly vying for people's attention. And he knew exactly what she was trying to achieve within seconds of walking into the room. Maybe it was worth giving him a chance, even if it was just for another opinion on her designs…

Six

Astin pulled the quilt over his head. It was past lunchtime but he didn't care. He was living with someone that hated him, and the premier for *Knight of Shadows* was in a few hours' time. He couldn't go. He just couldn't. Why had he ever thought it was a good idea? Going was a bad idea. A really bad idea. It didn't matter if Tate thought it would be good for him. It was his life, his decision. The sooner he moved on from that film, the happier he'd be.

Wouldn't he?

He turned over and screamed into the pillow.

Liam burst in. When he saw that Astin was fine, he said: 'Sorry, thought someone was trying to suffocate you. That or you were masturbating, but I didn't think it'd be that 'cause if you were doing that you'd try to be quiet or in the shower.'

Astin sighed.

'Nervous about later?' He perched on the end of the bed.

'Is it that obvious?'

'I mean, I get nervous going to premiers without all the shit you went through.'

'Why?'

'All that attention. Plus seeing the cast and crew again. There's always some sort of drama people try to drag you into. I try to stay out of it, but sometimes…' He shrugged.

'This time, *I* was the drama,' said Astin.

'Have you spoken to anyone since it happened?'

'I did initially, but they slowly stopped reaching out. I haven't spoken to any of them in months.'

'Do you want to?'

'Do I have a choice if I go?'

'Not really. Why didn't you go to the New York premier?'

'It would've been bigger. Plus I would've had to go on my own.'

'I would've flown back to come with you.'

Astin sighed. 'I never should've come here, should I?'

'It depends what you want to get out of being here.'

'I had nobody in New York. Y'all are here.'

'Jack was there.' Liam said his name through gritted teeth. While Jack was Astin's flatmate, he and Liam had a long and complicated history. Liam was a recovered addict while Jack had only recently joined that category. Most people still believed he'd relapse again. So far, though, he'd been clean for almost a year. That didn't mean he was any better at dealing with emotions, though.

'He didn't get why I was so worked up about going. If I go, I need someone that gets it,' said Astin.

'Empathy never was his strong point.'

'Or emotions in general,' said Astin with a laugh. 'What time is it?'

'Lunchtime. Didn't you say Jack's flight gets here about three?'

'Yeah.' While Jack wasn't the best at moral support, he meant well. And the more moral support he had, the better he'd feel. Then again, with Jack there, it would make Astin the odd one out. Tate would be with Jack, Fayth would be with Liam, and Hollie would be with…*him*. Astin tensed his jaw.

'I was about to go for a jog. Wanna come? It might clear your head a bit,' said Liam.

'Sure. It's not like I can feel any worse.'

*

'Ready to go?' called Liam through the door.

Astin flinched. 'Just a minute.' He walked over to the mirror in the corner of his room. It didn't matter how many times Tate told him he looked good – he still felt self-conscious in his navy suit. Even the world's most expensive label couldn't protect him from himself. He adjusted the collar on his sky blue shirt. It would be his first (semi) public appearance since the accident. He'd got out of doing the red carpet, so that was something. He couldn't avoid the people he'd worked with on the film, though. He'd wanted to. Really wanted to. But too many people to count had reminded him how therapeutic it would be. He blamed that film – and its director, Lawrence Roskowski – for everything that had gone wrong in his life. Would seeing them one last time really allow him to close the door on that chapter of his life?

When he'd first considered going a few months earlier, he'd thought Hollie could sit beside him and comfort him. He hadn't expected her to have a date. He'd expected her to be too busy with work to have any time for relationships. He'd read her wrong.

Again. Had he ever known her, or did he just know the image of her that he'd created in his head?

He smoothed over his gelled back hair, straightened his blazer, and went into the living area. Everyone was already there. Well, everyone important. Santiago was missing. What a shame.

Hollie sat on the sofa, giggling with Fayth. She was pretty when she laughed. From what Liam and Tate had told him, she didn't laugh much any more. It almost seemed like Tate blamed him for that sometimes. Did she?

Then again, she was probably right to. How Hollie hadn't kicked him in the balls he didn't know.

She wore an understated but tight-fitting teal dress. Damn, she knew how to draw attention to her figure. Sigh.

Her feet were covered by ankle boots. They'd mostly healed but she obviously didn't want to risk heels yet. He didn't blame her. Those cuts and burns on her feet had looked painful. How she could even walk he didn't know.

'Let's get this over with,' said Astin. How good or bad her feet were wasn't his problem. He needed to remember that. Even if her dropping the coffee pot had been his fault.

'It'll be over before you know it,' said Tate, squeezing his shoulder.

'Yeah, or you can just hide out in the bar until it's over,' suggested Jack.

Everyone turned and glared at him.

'What?' He looked to Tate, then Liam. 'Are you both telling me you watch your movies *every* time you go to a premier?'

They both looked away.

'Exactly,' said Jack.

'Shall we get going?' said Fayth.

'Yeah. Santi should be here any minute,' said Hollie.

Oh great. Not only was he going to the premier, but he was travelling with them too. Nobody had told him that. Shouldn't it have been his decision, since they were going for him? Oh well. If it made Hollie happy.

Hollie's Latin Lover was waiting for them outside. He wore a jumper over a shirt with a pair of chinos and brogues. Tate was right – he did wear the same thing all the time. That would drive Hollie mad. She could barely handle wearing the same pair of shoes two days in a row, let alone outfit recycling. What had made her choose someone like that?

Santiago introduced himself to Jack then greeted everyone with air kisses. Except Astin. Why was that? Some sort of underlying motive? He gave Hollie a long, lingering kiss. Astin's stomach turned. Why? Why do that in public?

He carried on walking, unable to watch their PDA. Fayth and Liam fell into step with him.

'You sure you're all right with this?' said Liam.

'Do I have a choice?' said Astin.

'Not really,' said Fayth.

'Thanks. Y'all are really helping.'

'Don't worry. We'll dose you up with vodka and you'll be fine in no time,' said Fayth.

He didn't drink much because alcohol gave him migraines, but given the situation... 'A migraine is better than watching that all night. I'm in.'

Two black Rolls-Royce Cullinans waited for them just outside the doors with sharply dressed chauffeurs holding the doors open for them. Astin, Tate, and Jack got into one, while Hollie, Fayth, Liam, and Santiago climbed into the other.

*

In hindsight, going to her ex-boyfriend's film premier with her new boyfriend probably wasn't a great idea. Hollie hadn't come up with a way to get out of it, though. Everyone else was going, so she could hardly say no. But since she and Santi were an item, not inviting him didn't seem like an option either. Catch-22, much?

And OK, a part of her enjoyed seeing Astin seethe when he saw her with Santi. It was his fault they'd broken up. If he hadn't been such an arse, they might've still been together.

But then, would they?

Had the accident just caused him to reveal who he really was sooner? Was the incorrigible Astin the real Astin, or was it the one she'd met in New York? Or was it someone she didn't even know yet? The version she'd spoken to as little as possible since he'd joined them in Barcelona was different to the one she'd known in New York or England. There was a darkness to him that hadn't been there a year ago.

The Rolls-Royce pulled to a stop at some traffic lights. Hollie turned and glanced at the car behind them. She could see Astin's shape in the window, his face solemn. Why was he torturing himself by going to the premier of a film that had ruined his life? Why was he risking running into people like that again? Especially when he was suing the director for negligence? Wouldn't that make things awkward?

Santiago squeezed Hollie's knee. She flashed him a smile. It was going to be a long night.

*

Hollie hated to admit it, but so far, *Knight of Shadows* wasn't as bad as she'd hoped. Roskowksi was a dick, but he was a good director. She was on her edge of the seat because of the action, and the anticipation at seeing what had happened to *that* scene. The one where Astin fell. Then it happened. The character's hand slipped from the wall. It was only a second, but Hollie knew that shot all too well. She'd played it on repeat after Astin's accident. The filmmakers had used the shot of him losing his grip mid-stunt and falling backwards. They hadn't included the camera crane or crash mat he'd hit, of course. They'd CGIed the rest – badly – to show the character hitting the ground. But he was a superhero. He survived. If Astin had fallen like that, he wouldn't have.

Astin pushed past them and stormed out of the auditorium. She wanted to go to him, to help him in any way that she could. The footage of Astin slipping down that wall still haunted her. Seeing the clip used like that, she couldn't even begin to imagine how Astin felt.

She followed him out, ignoring the piercing pain in her feet as she walked. They were almost healed, but they still weren't happy when she used them too much.

He wasn't in the lobby or the foyer. She sat down at the bar and tried to look casual. She could just pretend it was a loo break if he didn't show up. Actually, she could do that anyway. Nobody would question it if she told them her IBS was playing up. Astin leaving at the same time was just a coincidence.

She stared down at the chequered floor and started counting the black floor tiles. One, two, three…what was she doing? Why had she thought chasing after him was a good idea? Four, five, six…maybe she should go back inside. The film wasn't too bad. She couldn't fully enjoy it because the director had been partly responsible for her breakup with Astin. He'd turned up unannounced at their hotel to talk to Astin about how Astin was suing him. Hollie had told him he couldn't speak to Astin, but he'd weaselled his way into the suite anyway. Astin had blamed her, and everything had crumbled from there. If he hadn't turned up unannounced, would they still be together?

Astin was lucky his injury had been temporary and that he'd mostly recovered. His desire for revenge, though, was still ongoing.

He was suing the film's director for damages. But what difference would that make? It wouldn't bring his stunt career back and it wouldn't fix their relationship. What purpose did it solve? He had to have a reason other than revenge, didn't he?

'Hollie?' said Astin.

She flinched. 'Hi.'

He walked towards her, reentering from outside. His eyes were red and puffy. 'What are you doing here?'

'I came to see if you were OK.'

'I'm fine,' he said, his voice wobbling. 'I just went outside to get some fresh air.'

'Are you sure? I mean, wasn't that clip—'

'Yeah. It was me.'

'Shit.' Hollie reached out to touch his arm, then retracted it. No. Touching Astin was *bad*. Very bad. What was she even doing comforting him? 'What is *wrong* with Lawrence?'

'How long have you got?' said Astin with a small laugh.

Hollie laughed back. It felt good to laugh. She didn't do it often lately. Being around Astin, she seemed to laugh a little more than she used to. But it wasn't supposed to be him making her laugh. She had other people for that. 'I should get back.'

'Oh. Yeah,' said Astin, his voice falling.

'Are you going to stay out here?'

'For a bit, yeah.'

'OK.' She headed back to the auditorium. The temptation to stay and talk to him, to distract him, was strong. But she couldn't do that. The more time she spent around him, the more likely she was to lower her guard. And as soon as she did that, he'd be back in her heart.

*

After the premier, they hopped back into the Rolls-Royces and headed to the afterparty. Nobody really seemed in the mood to go after discovering Astin's accident had made it into the final cut, but Tate had used the last amount of enthusiasm she had to convince people. Even she looked disheartened. What did that say?

The afterparty was in a curved building overlooking the harbour. Hollie couldn't fault their choice of venue, even if their choice of director left a lot to be desired.

The seven of them hopped into the elevator and went up in silence to the 26th floor. As they walked through the doors, they were greeted by champagne, entrees, and hors d'oeuvres. Liam reached out to grab a glass of champagne, but retracted his hand before he'd touched anything. Hollie and Fayth exchanged confused glances. What was that about?

Hollie grabbed some nibbles from one of the trays. Whatever it was, it was bitter and salty. Seafood? She forced it down, then grabbed some orange juice from a passing waiter and put the half-eaten whatever it was into a napkin. The orange juice didn't help remove the taste much. Ugh. She'd been so busy trying to get rid of the vile taste she hadn't even realised she'd lost everyone. They'd been absorbed into the crowds and she hadn't even noticed. But for once, she didn't care.

Hollie settled into a seat by the window. With its central bar, intense lighting, and view overlooking the water, it reminded Hollie of the hotel where she and Fayth had first met Liam. It had the same feeling of opulence. And probably, as far as Fayth was concerned, inadequacy. Or did it? This time Fayth wasn't in a duffel coat and she wasn't recoiling into herself. She was wearing a jumpsuit Hollie had made for her that actually showed off her (amazing) figure instead of hiding it. Gone were the frumpy clothes that anyone could pull off. She had on something that hugged and disguised all the right places. She looked like she belonged. And this from someone who, just 13 months earlier, had believed she'd never fit into a world like that.

Hollie always pretended she fitted in everywhere she went, but she always felt like an outcast when she wasn't with her friends. People didn't care for overly ambitious twenty-something females. They insisted that you should go away, get some life experience, then start your business. But why wait? She had the idea. She had the ambition. Sure, she had a lot to learn, but why couldn't she learn it as she went? What was so wrong with that? Why did she have to learn by working for other people first? She'd have to do just as much grafting working for herself as she did working for someone else. The only difference was that the risks were higher and the potential payoff much higher, too.

Hollie leaned forwards and rested her elbows on the table. The Mediterranean sea lapped at the edges of the sand. It was too dark out to see if anyone was on the beach. A part of her wished she was, though. She'd always found water soothing. The sound of it as it lapped against the shore. The gentle caress of it against her skin. The smell of salt. She really needed to move to the seaside.

'Hollie, have you got a minute?'

The hairs on the back of Hollie's neck pricked up. She hadn't heard that voice in months, but she had no doubt about whom it belonged to. She turned, and, just as predicted, Lawrence Roskowski stood before her. His hair still looked like a poodle and he still wore suits that washed him out and didn't fit. You'd think working in Hollywood someone would have told him, but apparently not.

'I don't, actually.' She stood up. So much for enjoying the view and some (sort of) alone time.

'It won't take a minute,' he insisted.

'Why should I spend my time listening to someone who doesn't listen to me?' Her hands curled into fists, she began to walk away. Lawrence put his hand on her arm.

She removed his hand and turned back to him, her face hard. 'Don't touch me. Don't talk to me. Don't ever come near me again.'

'But—'

'You heard her,' said Astin, appearing from the crowds. 'You've done enough damage.'

'*I've* done enough damage? You're suing me!'

Unbelievable. He put a guy in a wheelchair and *still* couldn't accept responsibility.

'Have you ever once acknowledged that what happened on the set of that fucking film was your fault? Will you ever grow a fucking pair? You're unbelievable, you know that? Everything has to be your way, and you'll keep badgering people until it is,' said Hollie.

'My fault? I wasn't the one that slipped,' said Lawrence.

'Oh my god, I can't listen to this,' said Hollie. She walked away, and this time, Lawrence didn't try to stop her. Astin caught up with her just as she set eyes on Santi. He was standing at the far end of the room, staring out at the sea with a glass of champagne in his hand.

'Thanks,' said Astin.

'For what?' said Hollie.

'What you said to Lawrence.'

'I was just saying how I felt.' She could've said a lot worse.

'I'm not suing him any more, by the way. Not that I've told him that yet.'

'What? Why not?'

He'd been so hellbent on revenge a few months ago dropping the lawsuit had been inconceivable. What had changed his mind?

He stuffed his hands into his pockets. 'What's the point? It won't fix anything, it'll just drag out the pain. He's got no money. He hasn't got anything I want. It's time to move on, don't you think?'

'Yeah.' What did he mean by moving on? Did he mean moving on from the accident, or moving on from each other, too? Was he no longer interested in her? Did he not want to get back together any more?

What was she thinking? She wasn't available anyway.

Santi made his way towards them. 'Hollie, can we talk?'

'Um, sure,' she said. 'Excuse me,' she said to Astin. She and Santi left the crowded room and went into the corridor to talk. 'What's up?'

Santi stared back through the door for a moment, a look of sadness on his face. Oh no. He turned back to her. 'I can handle coming second to your work, but I won't come second to a guy who treated you like he did.'

'What are you talking about?'

'I'm not blind, Hollie. Everyone knows where you went when you walked out of that film. Don't deny it. Liam was about to go too, but Fayth stopped him. Why would she do that?' He paused and took a deep breath. She knew where the conversation was going, but she didn't have anything to say in response. 'All your friends are rooting for you to get back together with him, and you know what? I don't get it. You said it yourself – he hurt you. I'm right here, and I would never, *ever* treat you the way he did. But you don't want me, do you?'

Her eyes filled with tears. 'I…' was all she could croak out in response. He was right. About everything. 'I'm sorry,' she whispered.

He sighed. 'Me too.'

She didn't stop him from leaving. Her heart didn't break as he walked away, nor did she think he'd made the wrong decision. As much as she liked him, she could never love him. There was a fire to her relationship with Astin, and she was drawn to that. With Santi, everything was so plain and simple. He didn't push her or challenge her, or make her want to be better. He'd never complement her in the way that Astin did.

But then, Astin had said that he wanted to move on. Did that mean from their relationship, too?

Most of their relationship had been spent in London, after the accident. It made sense if he wanted to move away from that, too. If that was the case, she didn't blame him. How could she? It was a painful period in his life, and it *was* time he moved on from it. His childhood dream of becoming a stunt performer was over; he needed to find a new path and not be tied down by his old life.

She almost went over to him to ask, but then Santi's words echoed in her mind: *he hurt you*. He'd hurt her so, *so* badly, and she wasn't even sure if she'd fully recovered yet. How could she ever forgive him for that?

Unable to face anyone, she went into the toilets and locked herself in a cubicle. Was she supposed to be crying? What was wrong with her? She'd had a panic attack after breaking up with Astin. After breaking up with Santi, she felt like a noose that had been holding her back had finally been cut free. She was a terrible person. And so not in the mood to party. She texted Fayth to tell her she was leaving and not to worry, then grabbed a taxi and headed back to the apartment. She needed to be alone.

Except when she got back, the lights were already on. Her anxiety decided someone had broken in. She forced common sense to the foreground and called out, 'Hello?'

There was no one in the main living area, but the light in Astin's room was on. Against her better judgement, she went over to it and knocked. 'Astin?'

'Hollie?' Feet shuffled against the carpet, and a few seconds later, he opened the door. His hair was unruly and he'd changed into pyjama bottoms. He covered his top half with the door. Since when was he embarrassed about being semi-naked? And how had he beaten her back? 'What're you doing back?'

'Oh…I…I wasn't feeling well,' she said. Not a total lie. But she couldn't bring herself to tell Astin about being dumped. That risked getting into the reason why, and that was a path she wasn't ready to walk down.

'Neither was I,' said Astin.

'Well I'd better leave you to get some rest. I hope you feel better,' she said.

'Yeah. You too.' He closed the door.

Hollie went into her own room and lay back on the bed. How obvious were her feelings for Astin? If Santiago – whom she hadn't even known for that long – could tell, did that mean that everyone they were living with could too?

Oh god.

Acting never had been her thing.

SEVEN

Astin tossed a used condom into the bathroom bin and splashed water over his face. When he returned to the bedroom, Martha was getting dressed. *Martha?* Why was his teenage girlfriend there?

'What're you doing?' he said.

She pulled on her t-shirt and turned to face him. 'I like you, Astin, but I'm not expecting anything. I know your heart is somewhere else.' She flattened her mousy hair then resumed getting dressed.

He sunk onto the bed and pulled the covers over himself. Was he really that transparent?

'If you care about her that much, you should go get her back,' she said, tying her shoelace.

'It's not that simple.'

Martha turned to face him, tucking her leg underneath herself. 'Do you love her?'

He pulled the duvet tighter around himself.

'What was the last thing she said to you?'

'To fuck off out of her life.' The words played in his head like a demented lullaby every night.

'I see,' she said. 'So you're respecting that?'

'I texted her and apologised; she never replied.'

Martha ran her hands through her scraggly hair. 'Then I hate to say it, but maybe you need to move on.'

'I wish I could,' he said with a sigh.

'If you love her that much, why don't you reach out to her again, now that the dust has settled?'

'No, she made it clear how she feels,' said Astin.

'We all say things we regret in an argument.'

*

Astin sat up in bed. Why was he having sex dreams about his ex-girlfriend?!

He sunk back into bed. Oh. They weren't dreams. He *had* slept with Martha, back when he'd stayed at his friend's house in Texas. And she *had* told him to go back to Hollie. Was she right? Was Hollie lashing out at him because she still had feelings for him? It wasn't like he could ask her. She'd never tell him. And there was no way Fayth would. But Tate seemed to believe there was still something there, or she wouldn't have kept interfering. Then again, Tate interfered with everything.

He rubbed his burning eyes. The sun seeped in through the cracks in the curtain. Fuck, that was bright. The rain was hammering against the window, too. He closed his eyes. Why had he drunk a whole bottle of bourbon to himself? He was supposed to know better. He was supposed to not fall into the same traps as Liam or Jack. And yet there he was. Self-medicating. That wasn't who he was. That wasn't who he wanted to be. He wouldn't end up like his friends. He couldn't.

He had to fight. He had to get better.

Just as soon as he slept off his migraine.

He pulled the covers over his head as Fayth and Liam started talking outside his door.

'Have you heard from Astin yet?' asked Liam's muffled voice. 'I saw him grab a bottle of bourbon before he left.'

Damn, he thought he'd been subtle and nobody had noticed.

'Think we should take him some aspirin?' added Liam.

Why did people have to talk so loudly? The sounds of their voices went through him. He didn't just hear them talking, he felt it. Now he remembered why he avoided alcohol.

But aspirin sounded good. People continuing to talk right outside his door did not. If they carried on, he was pretty sure his head was going to explode. He'd desperately needed a drink after seeing Hollie with Santiago and his failed stunt on screen for the whole room to see. At the time, he'd thought the hangover would be worth it. It wasn't. It had been so long since he'd had a drink that he'd blocked out how horrific the migraines he had after drinking were. Why had he been so stupid and masochistic?

'Nah, leave him to rest,' said Fayth. 'He'll come out if he wants something.'

A woman who spoke sense. He knew there was a reason he liked her.

They fell silent, then a few moments later he heard the front door close. Peace. Finally.

He grabbed his sunglasses from the bedside table and pulled them on before opening his eyes. It didn't do much to help him with his sensitivity to light, but it was better than nothing. He'd go into the kitchen, get some water, then return to his room where he had painkillers. After that he'd fall back to sleep and hopefully wake up feeling better.

That was the plan, anyway.

He rolled over and forced himself to sit up in bed. Fuck, his joints were stiff. Had someone switched his muscles out for lead overnight? He took a few deep breaths, focusing on the areas that were the worst. Breathe in to the pain. Breathe the pain out. Breathe in to the pain. Breathe the pain out. That's what one of his physiotherapists – who'd also been a yogi – had taught him. It helped, a little. But not nearly enough. He didn't usually take painkillers. But he needed something to pacify the pain. The night before had been about pacifying the emotional pain. The morning after was about pacifying the physical pain.

He grabbed the empty bottle of bourbon and stumbled into the living area. When had he become so uncoordinated? Was he still a little bit drunk?

Hollie was in the kitchen, making coffee. He'd assumed she'd already be at work. She was usually long gone by 9am. Was she treating herself to a day off?

'Don't drop the coffee pot. I don't think I'll be fast enough to catch it this time,' he said with a small laugh.

She flinched, then turned to look at him. Her eyes were red and puffy as if she'd been crying. 'I'll try not to,' she said meekly. No sarcastic comment about the sunglasses? Something was wrong.

'Are you all right?' he asked as he put the bottle into the recycling bin and grabbed a glass from a cupboard.

'Fine,' she said, pouring coffee into a cup.

There was no point in probing. If she wanted to tell him she would. But really, it wasn't any of his business. They lived together, but it wasn't like either of them had had a choice. Or had they? Had they both used Tate as an excuse when really they both wanted to be around each other again?

He filled the glass with water from the tap. An awkward silence filled the air, but he had no desire to fill it. They were exes. Things were bound to be awkward.

She sipped the coffee. She hadn't even put any milk in it. Damn, she must have needed the caffeine hit. She hated the taste of strong coffee.

'Santi and I broke up last night.'

Astin tightened his grip on his glass of water. Internally he was delighted. If he showed that externally, he'd look like a dick. 'I'm sorry.'

'Are you?' she said. It almost sounded like she was baiting him.

He threw the question back at her. 'Are *you*?'

She gave a meek laugh, staring into her coffee. 'Not for what I should be.'

What did that mean? He didn't get a chance to ask. She and her coffee went into her room and closed the door. While he was pleased she was single again, he felt guilty, too. He wasn't superstitious, but he had wished for them to split up. Did that make him a bad person? Did he even deserve to get her back after everything he'd said and done? Of course he didn't. To say he'd been a dick was an understatement.

He drank the water, filled his glass back up, then returned to his room. After taking some painkillers, he took a moment to look out of the window. It was raining outside. Hard. The rain bounced off the buildings all around, drenching people as they hurried to get out of the rain. Was that why Hollie had opted to stay in, or was it because of Santiago? Why couldn't he get her out of his head? Why did she haunt him no matter what he did? He slammed his empty glass onto the windowsill. The rain came down harder, heavy winds blowing the trees outside the window. He opened it. The wind swooshed as the rain hammered on the rooftops. Thick, dense rain flew past the window. It was soothing to know that no matter what was going on inside his head, some things would never change.

*

Astin's head was still pounding when he woke up, but the pain had lessened enough for him to be able to shower. The warm water against his skin massaged his throbbing forehead, offering him a little more comfort. After making himself a coffee – still wearing his sunglasses – he sat down at his laptop. He was curious to see the reviews for *Knight of Shadows*. A part of him wanted it to do badly because of his hatred of Roskowski, but if it did, his accident was for nothing.

He opened some of the big review sites. It was pretty unanimous: they loved it. They loved the characterisation, the plot, the direction…

He slammed his laptop shut and leaned back on the sofa. Not one of the reviews had mentioned that that damn film had nearly killed him. Did they care about that? Did it matter to them at all?

Hollie walked out from her room, still in her pyjamas. Her hair was ruffled as if she'd just woken up.

'Hey,' said Astin.

Hollie jumped. 'Oh. Hi. I didn't realise anyone else was in.'

'Just me,' he said, flashing her a small smile.

'Do you want a drink?'

'Just water please,' he said.

She nodded, went into the kitchen, and turned the kettle on. She poured him a glass of water then handed it to him. His fingers touched hers as he took the glass from her. Her skin was dry but touching her still gave him goosebumps. She flinched, pulling her hand away.

'Thanks,' he said.

She went back into the kitchen to finish making her drink. He wanted to talk to someone about the reviews, but was Hollie really the right person to discuss it with? But who else did he have? She understood more than anyone else what that film had done to him…

'Have you seen the reviews for *Knight of Shadows*?' he asked casually, propping his feet up on the coffee table.

'No,' said Hollie. 'What do they say?' She sounded at least a little curious. That was a good sign, right?

'They love it,' he said with a sigh.

'You almost sound disappointed,' she said as the kettle finished boiling.

He sighed. 'If it did badly it was all for nothing, but if it does well…' He shrugged.

'Roskowski won't get far with his victim-like attitude,' said Hollie. 'They'll eat him alive.'

'You think?'

'Look at what happened to Trinity,' said Hollie.

He sighed. 'Yeah, I guess you're right. Is it bad that I haven't moved on yet? That I'm still bitter about what happened?'

'No,' said Hollie, wrinkling her nose. She was cute when she did that. 'I'd still be pissed off, too. I mean, he did…' 'Cause their break-up. 'I'd better get back to work, anyway.'

'Are you sure you're up to it? After last night? How are you feeling after it, I mean?'

Hollie shrugged, avoiding eye contact. 'Doesn't matter how I feel. I have other things to worry about.'

EIGHT

Whenever Fayth was at work, Liam either exercised, slept, read, or gamed. It was kind of pathetic existence, really. He'd never had so much downtime before. His agent was trying to find him some auditions, but so far nothing had come about. Had he been blacklisted because of what had happened with Trinity? It hadn't even been his fault. But then, did that matter in Hollywood?

He was in the middle of a trainer battle on the latest *Pokémon* game when his phone rang. Rolling over in bed, he answered it without even looking at the caller ID. He really needed conversation. 'Hello?'

'Hey Liam.' It was Jim.

'Hey, what's up?'

'So I just spoke to the producers of *Sea of Dogs*…'

'They dropped me, didn't they?'

'I'm so sorry. They can't risk the bad press. It's a kids' film, you know?'

'But why wait so long? Why didn't they recast right away?'

Jim sighed. 'They weren't going to initially, but during the test screening…well, some of the parents complained. They said using you set a bad example.'

Liam punched the pillow beside him. People had complained about him! They couldn't even see his face! How could he set a bad example when they couldn't even see him? 'Who have they replaced me with?'

'No one yet.'

'So maybe we can re-convince them!'

'I'm sorry Liam, I really am.'

'Have you heard about any other roles?'

'I did get this one call. It's a spy thriller.'

'Who's involved?'

'I only know the casting director. He's an old friend from college. I can arrange an audition if you'd like?'

'Yes! Yes. Please do.' He was so desperate he'd take almost anything. And a spy thriller didn't sound so bad. It was something different. That was what he wanted, wasn't it? Maybe being seen as a potential murderer would mean people stopped hiring him for the pretty-boy roles.

'All right. I'll make a call.'

*

Liam spent the next few days reading over the script. It was by an unknown writer, but it was pretty good. Liam was confident he could bring something special to the protagonist. It could be the role he'd been after for years to shake his pretty-boy image! It was edgy and artistic and just downright perfect.

The auditions were held in some dingy offices on the outskirts of Barcelona. Was it an indie film? It had to be if they were casting in somewhere so…characterful. The smell of damp hung in their air, and Liam had to hold his breath to mask it as he and Wade made their way down the corridor to find a seat. It was full of other guys around the same age. They all looked a little bit different, but they all looked tougher than Liam. That didn't matter, though. He could look tough if he needed to. He squared his shoulders and sat down at a seat close to the exit. Wade sat beside him.

Liam flicked through the script again. He was reading the opening scene where the main character is introduced. It started off with him helping a young girl escape her abuser by murdering him. After that, the character's morals became increasingly blurred.

He read the script over and over, rehearsing in his head different ways to read the dialogue and different body movements he could do to try to convey more meaning into the words. By the time his name was called, there was only him and one other guy left waiting.

'Good luck,' said Wade as Liam stood up.

'Thanks.' He wouldn't need it, though. He'd ace his audition. He loved auditioning. They never fazed him.

Three casting directors sat at a table in the small room. An X was on the ground in front of them, between their table and a white backdrop. A camera to the side of their table was set up but not recording. Had they forgotten to hit record? Were they out of memory?

Liam stood on the X.

'Name?' said the woman on the left. Was she the person Jim knew? He didn't recognise anyone in the room.

'Liam York.'

'Age?'

'26.'

'Please read the opening monologue on the first page, starting with "This is how…"'

Liam nodded. '"This is how I went from being a police officer to a spy. It started out as a normal day. I got a call to—"'

The guy in the middle held up his hand. 'Thanks Liam, that's enough.'

'But I didn't get a chance to—'

The man in the middle continued. 'I'm sorry Liam, I only agreed to this as a courtesy to Jim. We've been friends for a long time and I owed him a favour.'

Liam's jaw fell. 'That's all I am to you? A pity audition?' Had he really fallen that far down the food chain?

'Why don't you take some time off, let this all blow over? I'm sure in a year's time nobody will remember any of it.'

'How dare you invite me to this, waste my time, then try to give me life advice? How about you should've had the gumption to tell him you didn't want to meet with me instead of wasting my time? How about that?' He stormed out of the room. How fucking dare they? Liam was so distracted when he left that he forgot to stop for Wade, but Wade managed to catch up with him on the stairs anyway.

'Fucking time wasters,' grumbled Liam.

Wade remained silent.

'They met with me out of courtesy. Courtesy! Is that all I am now? A pity audition?'

They left the building. Liam continued to stomp down the street, but Wade managed to stay in step. It helped that he was well over six foot tall so could easily keep up with just about everyone.

Liam continued ranting to his bodyguard as they grabbed a taxi and made their way back to the apartment. As they were driving down, Liam spotted something. 'Stop!' The taxi driver pulled over. Liam got out. There was a hairdressers' salon. That would be one way to shed his pretty-boy image. Would people take him seriously then?

NINE

Hollie, Fayth, Astin, and Tate leaned over the table in the studio, studying plans for the fashion show. They were working out what order to show the outfits in, and which songs Tate should sing. They'd spent all morning working on it, and Hollie's head was starting to hurt. She used to be a huge fan of Tate's music, but after spending all morning flicking from one track to another and back again, she couldn't stand to listen to them any more.

Just as they were about to take a break, Liam walked in wearing an 'I ♥ Barcelona' beanie hat. Hollie forced her facial expression to remain neutral. Liam's fashion sense was terrible, but the only reason he'd wear something that ghastly was if something had happened to his hair.

'Nice hat,' said Astin.

'It's not a fashion choice,' mumbled Wade.

Liam shook his head.

'What's wrong?' said Fayth.

'You'll have to show them eventually,' said Wade.

His head lowered, Liam pulled off the beanie. His thick, floppy hair was gone. It had been replaced by some sort of Elvis quiff that had only slightly been squashed by the hat. Fayth, Astin, and Tate stepped forwards, mouths agape. Hollie turned back to the table and tried to focus on the plans.

'It looks like a penis on your head,' said Fayth, laughing.

'What on earth made you want *that* for a hairstyle?' said Tate.

'It wasn't intentional! He just…he didn't get what I wanted.' He sighed.

Hollie remained silent. She knew what a poor haircut could do to someone's confidence, no matter how people tried to console you.

Tate flipped her rose gold hair over her shoulders. 'Well you can't go around like *that*.'

Because saying that was helpful.

'It'll grow out,' said Astin.

'And in the meantime I have to have *this* on my head?' said Liam. He stormed into the bathroom. If he hadn't been such a good actor, he probably would've started crying in front of them.

'I'll go,' said Hollie. The others had no idea what it was like. Well, Tate did, but she was more image-obsessed than anyone else. She'd just berate him for being an idiot. Hollie had made plenty of bad fashion choices in the past and been bullied for them. She knew how he felt. She knocked on the bathroom door. 'It's me,' she said. 'Are you peeing or just avoiding people?'

'Both,' said Liam as the toilet flushed.

'They think they're being harmless. We both know shit like that hurts,' said Hollie.

Liam opened the door slightly. Hollie forced her gaze away from him. He'd always been known for having great hair. His haircut was even called The Liam. And now The Liam had been replaced by one of the most horrific haircuts Hollie had ever seen. Who'd cut his hair? The Blind Barber?

'When I was at school, I wanted my hair like Tate's. She had it long at the time, with lots of layers. I showed my hairdresser a photo, and instead of making my hair look like hers, she cut my waist-length hair into a shoulder-length mullet.' Hollie shook her head. Since then, she'd been *very* careful about who touched her hair. 'Everyone picked on me for it. But after a few months, it grew out. You know what made it even worse though? A few months after that, mullets were *in fashion*. In. Fucking. Fashion. All the girls in my class – including the ones that had picked on me for my hairstyle – now wanted their hair cut exactly how I'd had it a few months earlier. Bloody hypocrites. The boys still didn't get it. They teased the girls just like they'd teased me. But the girls didn't care because they were following fashion.'

'Sheep,' mumbled Liam. He stepped aside so that she could join him in the bathroom. She closed the door behind herself so that the others couldn't eavesdrop.

'Yeah. After that I vowed never to follow fashion, but always to wear pieces I'd never regret. My point is, I get why you're upset. Difference is, you can always go shorter with your hair. I lacked the confidence and money to cut mine any shorter or get extensions. But you…'

'You think I should go even shorter?'

'If you're going to change your image, go big or go home, right?' Hollie cocked her head to the side, studying Liam's face shape. 'Instead of having something like that, you could try something like a shorter version of Luke's.' She took out her phone and showed him a picture of Luke Andrews, Cameron's boyfriend. His hair was unnaturally pouffy. How it stayed up all day she didn't know. It defied gravity. 'Not this big, obviously, but just a bit of volume on top would bring out your cheekbones in the same way that the floppy hair did. It would really balance out your features and big forehead.'

'Fivehead,' corrected Liam.

Hollie held back her fringe and put her palm against her forehead. Her forehead was so big her whole hand fitted between her hairline and eyebrows. 'Join the club.'

Liam leaned against the door. 'What have I done?'

'Cut your hair,' said Hollie.

He stared at her blankly, shoving his hands into his pockets. 'What am I doing, Hollie?'

'Going through an identity crisis,' she said.

'I already had one of those,' said Liam.

'Yeah, well, everyone sheds their skin once every few years.' She ran her hands through her hair. Seeing her reflection in the mirror made her realise how much she missed being a redhead. Sure, brown hair suited her skin tone, but did it really suit her personality?

'Thinking of getting a makeover too?' said Liam.

'Just missing my red hair, that's all. Anyway, back to you. I might be able to fix it. If you trust me with a pair of scissors, that is. Or you could go to another salon if you'd rather get it done by a professional.'

'It can't get any worse than this, right?' Liam went over to the mirror and studied his reflection. He lowered his head, as if he was unable to look at it for too long.

'Thanks. I think. I don't have the right scissors though, so we'll have to get those first.'

'You own like a dozen different pairs.'

'And if I catch you using any of them for the wrong purposes I will hurt you,' said Hollie, narrowing her eyes into a death stare.

'Scissors are scissors.'

Hollie narrowed her eyes even more.

'Aren't they?' he almost squeaked.

'Nope. Different blades and shapes and stuff. Plus I'm left-handed. Anyway, is Ola free to go shopping for scissors?'

'No, it's her day off.'

'OK, let's send Astin.'

'Why Astin? Why not Wade?'

'Out of everyone here, he's the only one who doesn't really need to be here. Plus his Spanish is the best.'

'Is that it?'

Hollie shifted positions, staring at the floor.

'Is he bothering you?'

'No, it's not that. Having him around is confusing, you know? And he's the best person to help, really.'

'All right,' said Liam. He pulled her into a hug. 'Thanks. You know I'm here too, right? Just because I'm friends with Astin that doesn't mean I'm not still a good listener.'

Hollie rested her head on his chest. 'Thanks.'

'Have you found a portal to Narnia or something?' called Fayth from the other side of the door. 'You've been in there for ages.'

Hollie opened the door. 'Where's Astin? We need him to run an errand.'

'Why me?' said Astin, appearing at the door too.

'You speak the best Spanish,' said Liam.

Hollie pulled up a photo on her phone of some hairdressing scissors. 'I need something like this.'

'Where do I find those?'

'There's got to be some sort of beauty supply shop around here,' said Hollie.

'Can't you just order them online?' said Astin.

'No!' said Liam. 'And I'm not trusting anyone else near me with scissors.'

Hollie raised an eyebrow. 'But you're trusting me?'

'Desperate times,' said Liam.

Hollie nudged him. He smirked.

*

Astin was only gone a couple of hours, but Liam spent the entire time wearing the beanie and pacing the small space while he waited. Hollie tried to give him stuff to do, but every time she did he either got confused or lost his patience, so she left him to pace. He wouldn't leave the office, so Fayth gave him her earphones and he deafened himself with the Foo Fighters while the rest of them put together outfits for the fashion show.

'The shoes don't go,' said Liam, pulling out one of his earphones.

Hollie turned to face him. She hadn't even thought he was paying attention. 'Why don't they?'

'The lines are wrong,' he said, joining them at a mannequin in the corner of the room. 'The dress is all sharp edges and points, then the shoes are all curves. It doesn't work with the lines you've created.'

Hollie stepped back, placing her hand under her chin. It was a v-neck dress with a drop hem. And the curved toe of the shoes did *not* work. 'You're right. You're totally right.'

'Damn it,' said Tate, stamping her foot.

Fayth turned to face Liam. 'Since when are you good at fashion?' Liam was notoriously bad with fashion. The only reason he was well-dressed most of the time was because someone else chose his outfits for him. That, and it's hard to go wrong when your whole wardrobe compromises of shirts, jeans, and chinos.

'Since the line thing is an art thing, not a fashion thing. Why don't you try the kitten heels you discarded from the last one?' he suggested.

Hollie clapped her hands together. 'Yes! Where did we put them?'

Tate scurried over to the pile of shoes at the other end of the room. 'Got one!' she said.

The door opened and Astin entered carrying a paper bag. Hollie's heart skipped. Being around him was so confusing. Why did he have that effect on her? Why couldn't she just let him go?

Because love wasn't that easy.

No. She didn't love him.

She couldn't love him.

And yet…

'I think these are the right ones,' he said, handing Hollie the bag.

'Damn it, where's the other shoe?' cried Tate.

Everyone turned to look at her. She was surrounded by shoes, and she'd somehow managed to get a heel stuck in her extensions. Hollie stifled a laugh. Fayth shook her head and retrieved the shoe from Tate's hair. Tate took the shoe from her friend. 'There it is!'

Everyone laughed.

Hollie peered inside the bag and took out the scissors. 'Yep, they're the ones. Oooh you got a razor too.'

'The woman in the shop said you might need it when I described the style to her.'

She smiled, meeting his gaze for just a second. 'Thanks.'

Astin gave her a small smile.

'Right, shall we get this sorted then?' said Liam, taking his hat off and pointing to his hair.

*

So that she could concentrate, Hollie sent everyone else out to search for some food. There was nothing worse than other people hovering around when she was trying to concentrate. To protect the bathroom floor – and make cleaning up easier – they'd put some towels down then placed a chair on top. When he sat on it, Liam was too short to see his reflection in the mirror above the sink, which was probably a good thing because it would mean he couldn't see if she fucked up. 'I hope you realise I don't cut hair very often,' she said, holding the scissors above Liam's head.

'I hope you realise I'm beyond caring at this point. It can't get any worse than it already is,' said Liam.

'Noted.'

Liam had already washed his hair, so all the product had disappeared. His quiff hung limply and sadly to the side. Hollie took the longest part in her hand and chopped. Liam exhaled. 'You have no idea how glad I am that that's gone. I felt like I had a penis on my head.'

Hollie giggled. 'Don't make me laugh! I need to keep my hands steady!'

'Sorry,' said Liam.

'Are you sure you want to go with the style we discussed? This is your last chance to change your mind,' she said as she combed through it.

'What are my other options?'

'You could have something short and simple, like Astin had when I first met him.' Like when she'd forgotten everything around them because she was so hypnotised by him. Like when he'd been charming and funny and completely different to the person she'd ended up living with.

Stop. Stop thinking about Astin!

Liam ran his hand through his hair.

'Stop that! I'm trying to get it to sit how I need it to,' said Hollie, swatting his hand away.

'Sorry,' he said, trying to flatten it back to how it was. 'I like the style we discussed.'

'All right then. Slightly pouffy hair coming up,' she said. 'Hopefully,' she added quietly.

*

Fayth poked her head through the studio door. 'Is it safe to come back in? I have tapas.'

'It's safe,' said Hollie. She was staring at the mannequin again. A purple necklace had been added since Fayth had left an hour ago.

Fayth, Astin, Tate, and Wade reentered carrying food.

'Where's Liam?' said Fayth.

'Here,' said Liam, rounding the corner from the kitchenette carrying a mug of tea.

Fayth's eyes widened. Whoa. He'd been hot before, but with his new haircut, his lost puppy appearance had been replaced by something very grown up. He wasn't a pretty boy any more. He was a *very* pretty man.

Liam grinned. 'You like?'

'I mean, yeah,' said Fayth, swallowing. 'It looks nice.'

Tate shook her head. 'You look hot,' she said flatly. Of course Tate would be comfortable saying that to one of her oldest friends. 'And you look more grown-up.'

'Hollie did a really good job,' said Astin.

'Did you expect anything else?' said Hollie, raising an eyebrow.

'No.'

A tangible silence hung in the air as Hollie and Astin locked eyes. For goodness' sake. They needed to hurry up and get back together. The tension was driving her nuts.

'Anyone want food?' said Wade. 'I'm starving.'

'Yes. Food. Let's eat,' said Astin.

TEN

Fayth and Liam went out that night to end an emotionally draining day on a high note. When they returned to the apartment a couple of hours later, there were dishes in the sink and the TV was on, but there were no signs of anyone. Where were they?

'Hello?' called Fayth.

'In here!' replied Tate.

Fayth and Liam followed the sound of her voice and found her and Hollie leaning over the bath. Tate had the shower in one hand, and she was washing dye out of Hollie's hair with the other. Hollie gave a half wave, using her other hand to cover her face from the water.

'Going back to red?' Fayth asked.

'Yup,' said Tate, grinning.

'Cool,' said Fayth. Hollie going back to being a redhead was a sign she was almost back to feeling like herself again. Fayth had no idea what had changed, but she didn't care. What was important was that Hollie was ready to pull herself out of the doldrums.

'We've gone for a purpley red,' said Tate.

Hollie cleared her throat.

'Oh and there are some pink streaks underneath too,' added Tate. 'We wanted to go for something different without going too crazy.'

'That must've taken forever,' said Liam.

'Yeah. Getting Hollie to sit still for that long was a challenge,' said Tate with a wink.

Hollie kicked her.

Tate flicked the shower head so that the water went into her eyes.

'Oi!' squealed Hollie.

Tate giggled.

*

Astin's Spanish was rusty, but he hoped that that and his English would be enough to get some answers from a doctor. He hadn't been for a check up since leaving New York, and he needed one to see how his back was healing. He was exercising more and more and feeling stronger and stronger, but he didn't want to damage his back by doing too much. Mentally, he didn't think there was such a thing, but he knew that if he pushed his body too far it wouldn't be just one step back, it'd be one thousand.

The doctor called his name. He went into the office and sat down, clamping his hands between his knees.

'*Hola*. I'm Dr Fry. Your notes say you're here for a check up,' she said, lowering her glasses as she skimmed the computer screen in front of her. 'I spoke to your doctor in New York and I've read your notes, and it seems you've made an impressive recovery.'

'Thank you,' he said.

Dr Fry checked his weight, blood pressure, oxygen levels, pain, strength, and so many other things that he lost track. When they were done, she sat back down and gestured to the seat beside her desk. 'There's still a lot of tension in your upper body, but I have a feeling not all of that is to do with your injury.'

'What do you mean?'

'You've recovered especially well, but it sounds like you're still being hard on yourself. Forgive me for saying this, but you seem low. Have you spoken to someone about everything you've been through in the last few months?'

'You mean like a therapist?'

The doctor nodded.

'No.'

'I really think that would help your physical and mental recovery.'

'You do?'

'You're holding a lot of tension in your shoulders. You can exercise to loosen them up, but that doesn't fix the problem. The problem is whatever is affecting your mental health.'

Astin sighed. Where to begin? 'I was offered counselling when it first happened but I turned it down,' he confessed.

'May I ask why?'

'I didn't think I needed it.'

'And now?'

'I underestimated the toll it would take on me, physically and mentally.'

Dr Fry took out a piece of paper from a drawer and scribbled something onto it. She passed it to Astin. 'These are an online counselling company with therapists from around the world. You can talk to them any time, anywhere. If you need to talk to someone, they may be just what you need.'

'Thanks,' said Astin, pocketing the paper. 'Can I ask you one more question?'

'Go on.'

'There's this thing that I've wanted to do for a long time. I want to know if my back will stop me.'

The doctor narrowed her eyes. 'What is it?'

*

Hollie rubbed at her eyes. God, they were sore. It felt like someone had poured vinegar into them. She flicked on the kettle and reached to get a mug out of the cupboard. There was still loads to do, but with her eyes so sore she could barely see straight. It'd have to wait until morning.

'Helping Liam like that was really nice of you,' said Astin.

Hollie jumped. The mug she'd grabbed slipped out of her hand and flew towards the floor. Astin reached out and grabbed it, catching it just before it smashed.

'Nice reflexes,' said Hollie.

'Nice hair,' he said, handing her the mug. His fingers grazed hers. Her skin tingled. She jerked her hand away. 'Thanks. Do you want a drink?' she asked.

'Have we got any green tea?'

'I think so,' said Hollie. She didn't understand the fascination, but Astin and Tate were big fans. She opened another cupboard and found a box.

'What did you say to Liam yesterday, by the way? He doesn't usually calm down that quickly,' said Astin, leaning against the worktop. He had on his gym gear. Surely he wouldn't be exercising so late?

'Just that I knew how he felt,' she said with a shrug. 'And that it's just hair. But it turned out for the best anyway.'

'Yeah, it suits him,' said Astin.

Hollie rubbed at her eyes again.

'Sore eyes?'

'Yeah,' she said, holding them shut for a few seconds. The relief was glorious.

'Early night?'

'You offering to come with me?'

The words were out of her mouth before she could stop herself. What was she doing? She reached for the kettle as it finished boiling, unable to look at him.

'I only join people who invite me,' he said.

'So you really are a vampire?'

'Depends what kind you're thinking of,' he said.

She passed him his green tea.

'Thanks,' he said.

'The kind that goes out exercising at nine o'clock at night,' she said.

'I'm just going to do some yoga before bed, that's all. It helps keep me flexible.'

That was not an opportunity to flirt. That was not an opportunity to flirt.

Hollie bit her lip. Then she realised that that could also be construed as flirting, and stopped herself. 'How's your back these days?'

'Mostly fine,' he said. 'It has its moments. I know it will never be the same,' he said with a sigh. 'But I've got something to work towards now at least.'

'What's that?' Hollie asked.

'I'm going to climb El Capitan. The Dawn Wall way.'

Hollie stared at him. 'As in that really high, steep mountain that the Mac operating system was named after?'

'That's the one.'

'But why?'

'I want to push myself. I want to prove to myself that I can still do stuff.'

'But climbing El Capitan *the Dawn Wall way*? Don't you have to, like, pitch a tent on the rock face so that you can sleep because it's so tall you can't climb it in a day?'

'Yep.'

He sounded so casual about it, like he was talking about walking from one side of Barcelona to the other.

'That doesn't bother you?'

'I like a challenge.'

It wasn't her place to tell him it was dumb, or dangerous, or any of that. Not any more. Not to mention that doing so wouldn't make any difference anyway. If anything, the more dumb and dangerous it was, the more it would spur him on. And after the accident and how horrid he'd been, he was desperate to prove himself to everyone. It had never occurred to her that he had something to prove to himself, too.

ELEVEN

Even after everything that had happened, Liam was determined to make Valentine's Day special. If anything, recent events had made him *more* determined. He'd got Ola to pick up Fayth's moped and park it outside their apartment so that he could wake her up with breakfast in bed. Unfortunately, she woke up before him and surprised him with a full English breakfast in bed instead.

'Thank you,' he said, kissing her.

She pointed to his bedside table. On it was an envelope. He opened it. Inside was a card with a handwritten poem inside.

Your espresso-coloured eyes that know too much;
The way you listen so intently, it's like you're hanging on my every word.
Your dry hands in the winter, comforting against my skin.
The French toast you make me in the mornings,
hiding that you burned the first slice.
That twitchy foot you get when riding your Ducati.

'I didn't know what to get you…' she began.

He pulled her into him, almost knocking the food over. It was a beautiful, romantic poem and he loved it. He loved reading romantic lines but he sucked at writing them.

'You really like it?' she said, her eyes lighting up.

'I really love it,' he said, kissing her. 'And you. I love you too.'

She grinned.

*

After breakfast, they got dressed, then Liam took a blindfolded Fayth downstairs. Parked right outside, just as Ola had promised, was Fayth's custom moped. It had a green bow wrapped around it. That must've been Ola's doing, because he'd never put a bow on anything in his life.

Liam pulled the blindfold from Fayth's eyes. 'I remembered you saying you wanted to learn to ride a bike but you couldn't, so I thought this would be a good way for you to get around the city. I booked you some lessons for later, too.'

Fayth ran her fingers over the green metal, a huge grin on her face.

'This is amazing,' she said. 'You shouldn't have.'

'Why shouldn't I?' he said.

'It's too much. I only gave you a poem.'

'It's not how much money you spend that counts. It's the sentiment behind it. Now, shall we take this thing for a spin?'

*

Astin had the apartment to himself for most of Valentine's Day, so he spent it reading *Frankenstein*. It didn't do much to make him feel better, but it distracted him for the day, which was what he needed. Especially given the year before he'd been with Hollie and everything had been (almost) perfect, distance aside. So much had changed in so little time.

By the time he'd finished reading, it was dark outside. He checked the clock. It was close to midnight.

'Hey!' said Fayth, a huge grin on her face as she walked in the front door. Liam followed, smiling too.

'Good day?' said Astin.

'Amazing!' said Fayth. 'I should've learned to ride a moped sooner! We went to a flamenco show after my lessons then met up with some of Liam's friends for drinks. I haven't had that much fun in *forever*. Is Hollie around? I want to tell her about it!'

'Haven't seen her all day,' he said. 'She was pretty tired last night so I think she went to sleep early. Maybe she's working late to make up for it?'

Fayth frowned. 'She wouldn't still be at the studio this late, would she?'

'Wouldn't she?' said Astin. She'd worked well into the early hours of the morning when they'd lived together. The closer it got to the fashion show, the more likely she was to repeat the same patterns.

Fayth took out her phone and rang her. 'Hey Bea, where are you?' She paused. '*Still?* It's almost midnight.' Pause. 'You can't sleep there! Come on, Bea. We—' She turned to Astin and Liam. 'She hung up on me.'

'Do you want to go get her?' said Astin. He hated the idea of her sleeping in that cold studio on her own.

'Yeah, I think we should.'

'Do you need me?' said Liam.

'No, you get some sleep,' said Fayth. She kissed him.

Astin grabbed a jacket and his keys from by the door. 'Do you know where Tate's studio keys are?' Tate was out with Jack, so she wouldn't be back until late. If she was back at all. Tate would also be all for stopping Hollie from sleeping at the studio.

'Found them,' said Fayth, picking them up from the coffee table.

'Awesome. Let's go.'

They headed downstairs to their rented Renault Clio.

'I'm worried about her,' said Astin.

'Me too,' said Fayth, 'but what can we do beyond what we're already doing?'

'Nothing,' he said. 'Not until she acknowledges that she needs it.'

The studio door was locked when they got there, but luckily Hollie hadn't left her key in the door like she sometimes did.

The floor of the studio was littered with paperwork. It looked like there'd been an explosion. 'I thought Hollie's room was bad,' said Astin. He wanted to tidy up, but he knew that the repercussions of that would be even worse than the consequences of what they were about to do. While it looked a mess to everyone else, to Hollie, it was a perfectly organised system.

The paperwork all faced in the same direction – further signs of her organised chaos. It also guided their gazes to Hollie. She was curled up under her desk – the only spot of floor not covered by paperwork. She looked cute. And utterly exhausted.

'How do you want to do this?' said Astin.

'Let's not wake her up – she needs the sleep. I'll carry her downstairs.'

'I'll carry her,' said Astin.

'No. I don't want to risk your back. She's not heavy anyway.'

'My back is fine.'

'And I'm still not risking it,' said Fayth. She shot him a warning glance. Message understood. Fayth tiptoed around the paperwork, trying not to get muddy footprints on the crisp white paper. She looked like a spy, navigating around a security system as she tried to get to the diamond on the other side of the room.

She picked up her friend then carried her back down to the car. Hollie didn't wake up on the journey home, or when Fayth carried her into her room. After taking off her shoes and pulling the covers over her, Fayth and Astin left Hollie to sleep.

'She's going to go mad in the morning,' said Fayth.

'Yeah,' agreed Astin.

'We did do the right thing, didn't we?'

'Doesn't matter. It's too late now.'

*

The ground underneath Hollie's back was squishy. Her head felt like it was against a pillow. But she'd definitely fallen asleep in the studio. The studio floor was *not* that squishy. She opened her eyes. She was in her room. Fully clothed, thank god. But her shoes had been taken off and placed neatly by the door. Fayth. She hated shoes on furniture.

She jumped out of bed. The room spun and her vision disappeared. She fell back onto the bed. What the hell? Why couldn't she see? What—oh, that was better. The room came back into focus and everything stopped spinning. She stood up again and went to Fayth's door, then banged on it.

'All right, all right,' said Fayth. She emerged, pulling a green dressing gown over her pyjamas.

'What did you do!' snapped Hollie.

Fayth pulled the door closed behind her. 'I didn't want you sleeping there. It won't do you any good.'

'It's not your decision to make! How did you even get me up here?'

'You're not that heavy,' said Fayth.

'I helped,' said Astin, coming out of his room. Of course he had.

'Well isn't that great? The two of you becoming BFFs. The traitor and the hypocrite.'

'That's not fair!' said Fayth. 'We're worried about you! We wanted to help!'

'I didn't ask for your fucking help!'

'You fell asleep on the floor of where you work. That's not healthy,' said Astin.

'You fucking hypocrite.' How dare he tell her how to live her life when he'd never listened to her? She stormed into the bathroom and slammed the door behind her. How fucking dare they?

*

Fayth fell back onto the sofa. 'That went well.'

'We knew she'd be pissed,' said Astin, sitting beside her.

'Why'd she keep calling you a hypocrite?'

Astin fidgeted in his seat. Fayth watched him with anticipation. He sighed. 'Almost every time she tried to help me after the accident, I brushed her off. I refused to accept her help or advice.'

'Ah,' said Fayth. 'I wish you'd told me that sooner.'

'Why?'

'Because I would've taken Liam with me instead.'

A look of hurt flashed across his face.

'I just don't want her to be any more pissed off with you than she already is,' she said. 'She'll forgive me, and she'd feel guilty for hating Liam right now. She has valid reasons to hate you.'

'Thanks.'

'Well she does. Even if you've been really good to her lately. I mean, she's warming to you—'

Astin scoffed.

'She is. The melting of the polar ice caps was slow at first. It takes time to get going. But once it does, it's pretty dramatic.'

'You're comparing Hollie to the polar ice caps?'

'It's early. It's the best analogy I've got.'

TWELVE

A Golden Goodbye

We thought we'd said goodbye to Trinity Gold, but it looks like there's more to the story. Sources that were once close to her have exclusively revealed that her ex-boyfriend Liam York is her sole heir. That means her estate – which is thought to be worth several billion dollars – will go to him, and only him. Not her half-siblings, or her father (whom she's been emancipated from since she was fifteen), nor her former staff or even a charity.

We don't know about you, but it feels like there's more to it, don't you think?

Liam thumped the desk. How did they find out? Had someone at the police station leaked it? Who else would've blabbed? Someone on Trinity's team? Possibly. Their loyalty was to her, after all.

Even though the post wasn't that old, comments had started to accumulate. Not a single one said anything in his defence. They all accused him of murder.

He threw his laptop onto the bed behind him. Why would he kill her for her money? He didn't *need* money. He wasn't motivated by it, either. Money caused more problems than it was worth.

He needed to get out and clear his head. He changed into his gym gear then went into the kitchen to fill up his water bottle.

Tate was sat on the sofa, typing on her phone, when he walked into the kitchen. She looked up. 'Mind if I come?' she asked. 'I'm so bored of yoga.'

He kind of wanted to be alone, but if anyone understood his situation, it was her, so he agreed.

*

Fayth flicked through the photos on her laptop screen for the hundredth time. Francisco and Ramira had convinced her to exhibit before leaving at the end of March, but she had no idea what she wanted to exhibit. What kind of photos would appeal to their audience? What kind of photos even appealed to her? The more she flicked through her photos, the more she hated them. She slammed her laptop shut.

'Laptop upset you?' asked Ramira, walking into the small break room. She placed a takeaway flask on Fayth's desk. 'Tea, just the way you like it,' she said with a smile. 'Oh, and I got you a sandwich, too. Noticed you didn't have anything with you earlier and since you couldn't leave until I was back, thought I'd save you the lunchtime queues.'

'You didn't have to do that,' said Fayth. 'But thank you. What time is Francisco back from the doctors?'

Ramira looked up at the clock on the wall and shrugged. 'Depends if they're running on time.' She pulled out a chair from underneath the table and sat opposite Fayth. 'You know, you didn't have to help us with our website that day. And don't tell me you were just doing that because you wanted a job. I've seen you talking to people. You're not the kind of person to help someone just to get something in return.'

Fayth unwrapped the sandwich. The small of bacon, lettuce, and tomato wafted through the room. Yum. 'It seemed wrong not to help when I knew what the issue was.'

'Perhaps I can return the favour?' said Ramira, gesturing to Fayth's laptop.

'Is it that obvious I'm having issues deciding on photos to exhibit?'

Ramira nodded. 'You've spent every lunchtime in here staring at that thing, and your expression gets more frustrated every time.'

Fayth snorted. 'Sounds about right.' She picked up her sandwich and took a bite. 'I don't know what I want to say. I don't know what the common thread is.' She opened her laptop and turned the display to Ramira. 'And the more I stare at my photos, the more I hate them.'

'Could that be because you've stared at them too much?'

'Yeah, I'd say so,' agreed Fayth. 'But now I just can't tell the difference between what's worth exhibiting and what isn't. I hate them all.'

'Don't hate your photos. You're a wonderful photographer.'

Fayth blushed. 'Thanks.'

'Now, let's take a look at these photos.'

*

Fayth returned home from work feeling like she'd actually made some progress on her exhibition. Ramira had helped her pick a few, then Franscico had chimed in too when he'd got back from his doctor's appointment.

Liam was angrily typing away on his laptop when she got back. She kissed his cheek, catching sight of what he was typing in the corner of her eye. A letter to his PR team. Shit.

'Everything all right?'

'No,' he said.

Double shit.

'More stories about Trinity and me. They think that I snuck off to hers behind your back for a secret booty call in broad fucking daylight, and things went wrong and that's how she died.' He banged the desk. He hit send on the email then stood up. 'Ugh.' He flumped onto the bed. He stood up. 'I need to get out. Wanna go for a coffee?'

'No thanks. I've been running around all afternoon. My legs are killing me.' She lay back on the bed, her legs stretched out. 'Make sure you take Wade or someone else with you,' she added. She hated sounding like a nag, but he was terrible for going on long walkabouts and being impossible to find. The last she needed was even more reason to worry about him.

'Wade is already on his way, don't worry.'

'I do worry,' said Fayth. And sometimes she worried just a little too much…

*

Astin walked through the door, his body burning from the hours he'd spent at the gym. He probably shouldn't have spent that long there, but he'd needed to burn off some of the nervous energy after the argument with Hollie. And damn that gym session had felt good. It was the closest he'd felt to his old self since the accident. The old him would never come back, but a part of him still wished to be that carefree again. Life was so much easier when you weren't as attached.

'Heeeey Astin!' said Fayth. She sat on the sofa, some show playing on the TV. She had a bottle in her hand.

'Is that vodka?'

'Yep!' said Fayth. 'Wan' some?' she offered, holding the bottle out to him.

'How much have you had?'

'Jus' a wee bi',' she said with a giggle.

He'd never seen Fayth drunk before. Her accent was thicker than ever, and he almost couldn't understand it. She'd been a bartender so she was used to being around alcohol, but this seemed different. She didn't strike him as the type to drink alone. Then again, he hadn't done a great job of reading people lately.

'Where is everyone?'

'Liam and Tate are oot somewhere, an' Hollie is…' She shrugged. Great. Hollie was working late again. How much further could she push herself before she crashed?

Astin sighed. 'Is that why you're drinking?'

'I like vodka,' said Fayth. She tried to stand, but she lost her balance and fell back down again. She giggled. Astin walked over to her and helped her up. 'Yer differen',' she said.

'Am I?'

'Yeah,' she said, flicking his hand away and making her way to the kitchen. He followed her, leaning against the fridge/freezer just in case there was any more vodka hidden in there. Drinking away her sorrows wouldn't help anything. He knew that all too well.

'Yer used tae be a lo' less…*helpful.*'

How was he supposed to react to that?

'Naw, ah mean.' She tapped her foot a few times. 'Yer use' tae stay oot of other people's business; yer'd be reluctant tae help even if they asked. Buh now…yer differen'.'

He'd never heard her speak in such a thick Scottish accent before. It threw him off, and it took him a minute to work out what she was saying. Was he really that different to how he used to be? No, she was right. He was.

'What?' she said.

'Sorry, your accent is throwing me off. It takes me a minute to work out what you're saying,' he said.

Fayth snorted. '*My* accent is funny? Have yer listened tae yourself?'

He chuckled. 'I don't have an accent.'

She snorted. 'If tha's wha' yer wan' tae believe.'

The front door swung open. Hollie slammed it, then ran into her room and slammed that door, too.

'Ah'll go,' said Fayth, stumbling as she stepped forwards.

'No, I'll go,' said Astin. 'You smell like a brewery.'

'Nothin' new theyah,' said Fayth, waving the vodka bottle. 'Go play Prince Charmin'. We both know yer want tae.'

'Um…'

She waved the vodka bottle in the direction of Hollie's door. 'Go! Ah'm givin' yer me blessin'!'

'Are you safe on your own?'

Fayth snorted. 'Please. Ah'm Scawttish. This isn' drunk. This is jus' a wee bi' tipsy.'

'If you say so.' Astin grabbed a chocolate bar from the cupboard and knocked on Hollie's door. She didn't answer. He pushed it open and found her curled up on the floor, sobbing. He sat beside her and handed her the chocolate bar.

'Thanks,' she whispered, unwrapping it and snapping off a section. She offered it to him. He took it, even though he didn't really want it. Her offering him a square of chocolate meant a lot. Hollie wasn't one to share chocolate. They sat silently for a few moments as she devoured the chocolate bar. When she'd finished, she twisted the wrapper between her fingers.

'Do you want to talk about it?' Astin said, unable to handle not knowing what was wrong any longer.

'One of my models quit. Her grandmother is ill so she needs to look after her – which I totally get – but that's more work I've got to do! As if I don't have enough to do already! It took us ages to find all those models! How am I supposed to get everything done?' She started sobbing again. Astin put his arm around her shoulder and pulled her into him. She continued to cry, putting her hands on his arms. His skin tingled at her touch. He put his hand on top of hers. 'What am I supposed to do?'

'We'll sort it,' said Astin.

Hollie turned her head. '"We"?'

'I did used to be a model, you know.'

'I know, but that was years ago. You hate it when people remind you of that.'

'I'll help you find someone. If the two of us are searching, we'll find someone faster.'

'Don't you have something else to do?'

'I don't mind helping,' he said.

'OK,' said Hollie. She patted at her eyes with the back of her hand.

He stroked her hair. She hadn't let him so close to her since they'd broken up. A part of him felt like he was taking advantage of her, but the other part of him knew that she needed someone, and he was the best person to help with her nan in another country and Fayth drunk (whether she admitted it or not).

'Come on,' said Astin, helping her up. 'You should get some sleep.'

She kicked her shoes off. He helped her into bed then began to walk away.

'Astin?' she whispered.

'Yeah?'

'Will you stay with me?'

His stomach tied itself in knots. They hadn't shared a bed together in almost a year. He'd dreamed of it, wishing he could fall asleep with her in his arms, but he'd never thought it would happen ever again. Not after what he'd done. She pulled back the covers. He gulped. He hadn't been so nervous around a girl since he'd first met her.

He took off his shoes and climbed into bed beside her. She pulled the covers over them and wrapped his arm around her. They fell asleep, his breath on her neck and his arm around her waist.

Thirteen

Hollie and Astin spent the following day ringing agencies and organising go-sees. It was tedious, but they managed to line up several potential models. Hollie returned home feeling mildly optimistic. As a reward, she made herself a hot chocolate then curled up on the sofa beside Tate, who was watching *Ru Paul's Drag Race.*

Astin had gone to the gym when they'd finished ringing agencies. It'd been a couple of hours, so she assumed he'd had a shower there or gone for a massage or something. He came in, they exchanged pleasantries, then he walked around the sofa and came into view. He was limping. Why was he limping? He'd been fine earlier.

'Astin?' said Tate.

He stopped, his hand hovering over his bedroom door handle.

'Why are you limping?'

'No reason,' he said.

Tate hardened her features.

'I pulled a muscle at the gym. It's no big deal.'

'Astin!' said Tate, turning the TV down. Hmph. Hollie had been watching that. 'You still need to take it easy.'

'I know, Mom.'

'Do you? Is that why you go to the gym every day when you're supposed to be recovering?'

'I'm not going to recover if I don't build my strength back up, am I?' said Astin.

'I believe you told me that the doctor said you can build your strength back up but that you need to take it easy. That doesn't look like taking it easy,' said Tate. 'What do you think, Hollie?'

Hollie picked up her hot chocolate from the coffee table and stood up. 'If Astin wants to self-destruct, that's his problem, not ours.'

She went into her room without another word. Inside, she wanted to lecture him just as much as Tate was, if not more. But lecturing him didn't make a difference. He wouldn't listen. So why waste her breath?

*

'Look what you did!' said Tate.

'Tate, I really just want to sit down right now,' said Astin, resting his weight on his closed bedroom door.

'Then you should've thought of that before you did too much at the gym!'

'Did you ever think about why I do too much at the gym sometimes?'

Tate glanced at Hollie's bedroom door and sighed. 'She's not a Hydra.'

'No, but you never know which mood you're going to get. I can't keep up and who knows what the go-sees will be like tomorrow? She wouldn't even look at me while we were making the phone calls.'

'What, you've never been nervous around someone?' said Tate.

'Why is she nervous around me?'

'You are not that dumb,' said Tate.

He sighed. 'Don't start this again Tate, please.'

'I didn't start anything. You asked a question, I gave you the answer. Just because you don't like my response that doesn't mean it isn't true. Now, do you need any painkillers or have you got some in your room?'

'I don't need any; I'll be fine.'

Tate ground her teeth together. 'You'd better be there tomorrow.'

'I will be.'

*

'This is a bad idea. This is a really really bad idea,' said Hollie, pacing the studio. Having Astin present for the go-sees just added more pressure. Not only did she have to pick a model last-minute, but she'd also have Astin just a few feet away from her. That had happened far too often recently and it had to stop.

'Chillax, would you?' said Tate. She sat at Hollie's desk, painting her nails crimson. Thankfully she was resting her hands on a tissue. Red nail varnish on a white desk was not a good idea.

'Maybe he won't even show up,' said Hollie. 'He wasn't walking very well last night.'

'Have you ever known Astin not show up when he says he will?' said Tate.

'No,' said Hollie with a sigh. Why had he even offered to help? OK so he knew about modelling, but he'd admitted himself that he didn't know much about catwalk – he'd been a print model.

There was a knock at the door. Hollie ran to it, hoping it would be a potential model. Nope. It was Astin. He looked so casual in his ripped jeans and loose-fitting black t-shirt that she wanted to slap him. How could someone make jeans and a t-shirt look that good? And why was he not freezing in jeans and a t-shirt? It wasn't *that* warm out.

Astin held out a coffee cup for her. He had a cardboard holder in his other hand. 'Vanilla latte,' he said with a smile.

'Thanks,' she said, smiling back. Butterflies formed in her stomach. She wanted to vomit. Dammit. She sipped her coffee, hoping that the warm liquid would soothe her nausea. 'How's your leg?'

'Fine,' he said, walking inside with only a slight limp. Would that be bad for his back? Why didn't he use a walking stick?

He took another coffee from the holder and put it in front of Tate. 'One half caf extra hot hazelnut latte with coconut milk.'

'You still remember,' she said, shooting him a saccharine smile.

'Once that order is drilled into your head, it's hard to forget,' he said.

Tate cocked an eyebrow at him. She turned to Hollie. 'You can always tell how much attention someone pays to you by how well they remember your coffee order.'

What did it mean that he remembered her obnoxious coffee order? They'd slept together in the past. Did it mean that he still had feelings for her, if he was prepared to memorise something that bloody long?

'And how long you've known someone,' added Astin.

Or there was that.

'So what time's the first go-see?' he asked.

Tate checked the clock on the screen in front of her. 'Fifteen minutes. Maddy should be here shortly with all my notes.' She blew on her nails. She knew that would create air bubbles, right?

'We've got three coming over this morning, then another three after lunch,' said Hollie.

'Good. We only need one, so that should give us plenty of options,' said Tate. She splayed out her fingers, grasped the cup, and sipped her coffee. 'Hollie, I adore you, but you're making me dizzy with all your pacing.'

Hollie flinched. She hadn't even realised she'd started pacing again.

'There's nothing to worry about,' said Tate. 'We've got this covered.'

'Yeah, I hope so,' said Hollie.

*

Hollie had a new least favourite job: finding models. All the ones she'd found originally were perfect, and yet she had to replace one of them. It was sod's law at its finest. The first few models they saw were OK, but something didn't feel right.

And then the door flung open. A woman wearing a black trench coat and patent black stilettos walked in. The trench coat created curves in all the right places. Her sharp haircut and crimson lips gave her an intimidating fierceness. She opened her arms. 'I. Am. Lorena.' Without further prompt, she ripped open her trench coat to reveal silk lace underwear. Hollie widened her eyes and shrunk down into her chair. She wanted to look over at Astin to see his reaction, but she was too mortified. What on earth was this woman doing?

Unfazed, she took off her coat and threw it across the room. And then her gaze landed on Astin.

Oh no.

'And who are you?' she said with a smirk, sashaying over to him.

'Not the decision maker,' he said. His voice was level. He sounded perfectly normal. Of course he did. He'd been a fucking underwear model. He was used to seeing strangers in next to nothing. Hollie was not.

'Oh I'm sure you have some sway,' said Lorena.

'Actually,' said Hollie, 'he doesn't.' She had to reclaim some sort of control over the situation. Fast.

'Oh? So who does?' said Lorena, her gaze still fixed on Astin.

'I do,' said Hollie. She sat up and forced her shoulders back.

Lorena looked her up and down. 'What clothes do you have for me?'

Hollie glanced to Maddy. 'Can you get the wrap dress please?'

Maddy got the wrap dress and passed it to Lorena. She got dressed in front of them, not caring that Astin was right there. Astin remained unfazed. Did he have a killer poker face or was he really fine with the whole thing?

Lorena demonstrated her strut along the room. It was more of a stomp. Like she was taking up all her pent-up anger out on the floor.

'Could you do that a bit less aggressively please?' said Hollie.

'What's wrong with my walk?' said Lorena.

'It's aggressive,' said Hollie. 'That's not what we're going for.'

Lorena stopped and folded her arms. 'How would you know? You're a new designer.'

'So?' said Hollie.

'So you should be begging me to work with you,' said Lorena. 'I can promote your designs to all my followers on social.'

Hollie suppressed a snort. 'We looked you up before you arrived. My Golden Retriever has more Instagram followers than you. Please take that dress off and leave.'

'How dare you speak to me like that!'

'No,' said Hollie, folding her arms. 'How dare *you* speak to anyone like that? You're not superior because you look good in your underwear. Leave. Now.'

'Fine.' Lorena stomped her foot. Like, actually stomped. She made a show of removing the dress, threw it on the floor, wrapped herself back up in her coat, and left.

'Well,' said Tate. 'That was interesting.'

'That's one word for it,' said Hollie. 'Why were you so quiet?'

'I wanted to see how you handled it. And you handled it perfectly. Now I don't know about you, but I need some food. There's a vegan place around the corner. Who's in?'

*

Tate and Maddy went to get food, conveniently leaving Hollie and Astin alone. Hollie had tried to go with them, but Tate and Maddy had insisted that it was only a two-person job.

Hollie sunk into a beanbag. Astin stared out of the window at the busy street several stories below.

'I'm sorry about that woman,' said Hollie.

'It's fine,' said Astin.

'It's not. She was out of order.'

Astin shrugged. 'It wasn't what I expected when I offered to help out, but I was a model. I know what it's like.'

'You mean it's standard to show people your underwear in go-sees?'

'Well people ask – especially if you're going to be modelling half-naked for them – but most people don't walk in like that. Maybe she was trying to leave an impression.'

'Oh, she did that all right.'

Astin ran his hand over his heavily gelled hair. He really suited that style. It brought out his sharp jawline. Which looked super sexy with its five o'clock shadow.

Dammit.

Hollie sighed. 'What if we don't find someone?'

He turned to face her. His gaze was strong, self-assured. And just as intense and penetrating as ever. It was like he could see through her facade and right to her deepest, darkest secrets. Like how she was still—never mind.

'We will,' he reassured her. 'If we don't find someone today, there'll be plenty of others.'

'But we're running out of time. There are only three weeks to go until the show.'

'All of the clothes are ready, aren't they?'

'Almost,' mumbled Hollie.

'Exactly.'

'But I've got orders to do as well. I don't have time for this.'

He walked over and perched on the beanbag beside hers. 'We'll sort it. We've all got your back.'

Deep breath. Don't cry. Jeez, why was she so emotional? She wasn't even on her period. 'Thank you,' she said, reaching out and touching his hand. He put his other hand on top of hers. Realising what she'd done, she pulled her hand away and stood up. 'We should clear up some space so that we can eat.'

Fourteen

Hollie paced the length of the studio, her eyes glued to one of the mannequins. The other three sat beside it, looking just right. But that one…there was something about the dress that wasn't right. She'd thought she was done, but no. That dress just wasn't working. But what was wrong with it? The puff sleeves? The sweetheart neckline? What could she possibly change that would make it better? And really, this late, would any of it matter? What was she even doing?

She slumped onto the studio chair and let it spin her around. It had gone dark outside and she hadn't even noticed. Where had the day gone? It had been morning the last time she'd looked out of the window. She sighed, spinning the chair back around to face the mannequin. That was it! It needed to be shorter. Of course! Why had she ever thought making a calf-length dress was a good idea? Especially with puff sleeves like that! The shape needed to be balanced out.

She grabbed her scissors from the table beside her and approached the dress. A car horn honked outside and she flinched, the scissors jerking in her hand. They went straight across the front of the dress.

'No!'

The damage was done. The scissors had cut a hole right through the middle of the garment. There was no way of repairing that. She threw the scissors at the wall. They planted themselves into it as if they were mocking her. She stood up and yanked them from it. They'd made quite the hole. Who knew she was so strong? How was she going to explain *that* to the landlord? Blame the Incredible Hulk?

She wanted to scream. Nothing was working. She grabbed her coat from the coat stand and stormed out of the studio. She'd had enough. She needed to get away from it all. Her hands clenched into fists, she stomped down the street. As usual, it was teeming with people. Fucking tourists enjoying themselves. Why did they have to hover like that, taking pixelated photos on their crappy phones? It was too dark to see anything anyway. If it was that busy in February, what would it be like in peak tourist season? Ugh, imagine the crowds. The claustrophobia. She couldn't think of anything worse. But by the time Barcelona was that busy, she'd be long gone. She'd be back home, living with her mum and nan, deciding on her next move. Whatever that was.

When she reentered the apartment, she was still seething. She slammed the door shut and rested against it.

Astin walked out from his room in his gym gear. He studied her, his eyebrows raised.

'Don't ask,' she said.

'All right then,' he said. He closed the door to his room then went over to the kitchen to fill his water bottle.

'Yoga time?' she asked.

'Not tonight. I'm going for a jog. You're welcome to join.'

Hollie scoffed.

'I'm serious. It might do you good.'

'Sure it will.'

'Why'd you think Liam jogs?'

'I never thought about it before,' she admitted.

'I recommended it to him a few years ago to help with his anxiety. He's done it ever since,' said Astin, turning off the tap.

'Get you, a regular Mr Motivator.'

Astin shrugged.

'Even if I did want to go, I don't have anything to wear.' And anyway, what was she thinking, going for a jog? Let alone going for a jog *with Astin*?

'Tate probably has some stuff you could borrow. I'm sure she wouldn't mind,' said Astin.

*

Five minutes later, Hollie was dressed in a pair of Tate's purple Lululemons and a baggy t-shirt she'd found in her drawer. Tate's gym tops left too little to the imagination for Hollie's liking.

She'd half-hoped to run into Fayth or Liam or Tate or anyone really that could talk her out of it while she got ready, but the others had all gone to a theatre show. He hadn't gone because he wasn't interested in whatever it was they'd gone to see. He couldn't remember its name, just that the premise had sounded boring. Why hadn't they invited her? Was she really that boring that they didn't even bother asking her any more? She hadn't even known about it until Astin had told her. What kind of friend did that make her?

'I'm really not very good at jogging,' said Hollie as they descended the stairs.

'You're more of a yoga kind of girl, I remember.'

How did he remember that she'd said that? She'd said that back when they were in New York and she and Fayth had crashed his kickboxing class. That had been embarrassing. She was so not fit enough for kickboxing. And yet he'd still been interested in her. Would her terrible jogging efforts put him off? Was he even still interested? He'd said he wanted to move on. There was no point getting her hopes up about anything happening between them, not when she wasn't even sure if she could ever trust him again.

'Don't worry; I'll go easy on you,' he said with a wink.

'Where's the fun in that?' she teased back. Oh how she missed flirting with him.

'In that case,' he said as he pushed open the door of the apartment building, 'try to keep up.' He started jogging, and almost immediately she fell behind. Damn him. How could she flirt with him if he was way ahead of her?

No. She must not flirt.

She needed to focus on her breathing. Breathing meant that she could survive said jog.

Astin was a few feet ahead. He was clearly holding himself back so that she could keep up. It was both cute and annoying of him. 'Ready to speed things up?' he said.

'That was slow?' she said, panting. They hadn't stopped moving, but they had slowed a little so that they could talk.

He chuckled. 'Think about everything that's making you angry or anxious right now. Let that energy build up inside you. Then… run.'

'That's it?'

'That's it,' he said.

'All right.'

What was making her angry or anxious? So, so many things. The very person she was hanging out with, for starters. Did they still have a relationship? Was she even ready for another one? Was Astin, for that matter?

And then there was the reason they were there in the first place: the fashion show. She'd worked so hard on it for the last few months, but what if it didn't turn out how she wanted it to? What if everything wasn't ready in time? What if nobody liked her work? What if Tate changed her mind and pulled her funding?

Before she knew it, she was running. Running away from the thoughts and the fears and the anxiety and everything that was holding her back. Her chest tightened as the cold air bit at her lungs, but she kept going. And then she tripped.

She hadn't seen the damn drain cover. She fell, face-first, onto the pavement. Astin was beside her in an instant.

'Ow,' she yelped.

He helped her up, his eyes studying her as he did so. 'How do you feel?'

'Ow.'

'Where hurts?'

She pointed to her face. Where else was she going to injure when she had an important meeting in the morning?

Astin reached out and brushed her face with his fingers. Being touched by him sent shivers through her, but it also felt like hundreds of tiny needles were scratching against her skin as the dirt was wiped away. How bad did she look?

'Come on, let's get you cleaned up,' said Astin, putting his arm around her and guiding her back in the direction of the apartment.

'You carry on, I can find my way back,' insisted Hollie. She tried to shake his arm off, but he wouldn't let go.

'I want to make sure you're all right. It *is* my fault you face planted the sidewalk.'

'Was it really that bad?'

'Could've been worse,' he said.

'Well that's reassuring.'

*

Astin patted at Hollie's cheek with a flannel. She flinched. 'Sorry,' he said.

'It's all right. Do what you have to do.' It was better to get the muck out of her wounds before they healed, rather than letting them heal with the dirt still inside. Ew. She cringed.

'That grossed out by me cleaning your wounds?' said Astin, the tone in his voice suggesting he was only half-joking.

'I'd rather you clean them out than I end up like my mum,' said Hollie. 'She fell off a bike when she was younger and still has a stone embedded in her hand.'

'That's gross, but kind of cool.'

Hollie kicked him with her foot, almost losing her balance on the side of the bath. Astin reached out and grabbed her. 'So clumsy,' he said. 'Do I need to wrap you in bubble wrap?'

'I'm starting to wonder,' she said, 'although that may make threading needles difficult.'

'We'll think of something,' said Astin.

We. He kept using that word…

Oh god.

Hollie closed her eyes. Astin was being so nice to her. Was he just trying to get into her knickers, or had he actually grown up during their time apart? Was this who he really was, not the grumpy sod she'd lived with in London?

'I can't figure you out,' said Hollie.

'Oh?' said Astin, returning to bathing her wounds.

'You're being so nice to me, but when we lived in London…'

'I was a dick,' said Astin.

'You said it, not me.'

'I'm pretty sure you said it a lot when we were in London, too, but I wouldn't listen. I was angry at myself, at Roskowski, at the world. The only thing I wasn't angry at was you. But I was also worried that I'd hold you back, so I pushed you away.'

'You could never hold me back, Astin. I wouldn't be in the position I'm in now if it wasn't for you.'

'I'm sure there are a lot of positions you wouldn't have been in if it hadn't been for me,' he said with a sly grin.

She giggled. 'I mean it, though. Jokes aside. I never thanked you for helping me.'

He shrugged. 'I just put a good word in with Tate, that's all. She didn't have to take my advice.'

'But she did.'

'Trust me, she doesn't always.'

'Can I ask you something?' It was something that had been bothering her for a long time. She had to know.

'Sure. I can't guarantee I'll answer.'

'What really happened with you and Tate? You said you two had sex but that was it. I find that hard to believe. You two are so good together.'

He sighed. 'I don't want to bad mouth her, but she did some things I didn't agree with. I love her like a sister, but the way she lives her life…I couldn't be in a relationship with someone like that.'

'Oh,' said Hollie. She hadn't expected that. Was Tate really that immature?

'We were just kids when we met. Neither of us really knew what we wanted. Even then, though, Tate knew she wanted Jack by her side. She just didn't want to admit it because he was kind of a dick.'

'Who was worse?'

'They were both just as bad as each other,' said Astin. 'That's part of why they worked, and part of why they didn't.'

'Do you think they have a future like that?'

'Who knows? That's for them to decide.'

*

'Oh my god, I'm so late!' squealed Hollie, diving out of bed. She'd somehow managed to sleep past her alarm. Stupid Astin taking her jogging then having to clean up her wounds. Shit, how bad did her skin look with all those cuts?

The room spun as she got up. She leaned against the wall to steady herself. Whoa. Head rush. What was wrong with her? The lightheadedness was getting more and more frequent. Was something wrong? Even if it was, she'd lost enough time to getting her feet sorted after burning them and slicing them open. She couldn't afford to lose any more time to getting her body fixed.

The room stopped spinning and she frantically shoved things into her bag. She'd have to shower later if she wanted to get to the meeting in time. It was over the other side of the city. She barely had time as it was. How had she overslept? What the hell had happened to her alarm? And why had she left her laptop at the studio and not taken it home like she usually did? Stupid productivity advice telling her to separate her work and personal time.

She pulled on the outfit she'd planned for the day (ripped skinny jeans with a loose-fitting t-shirt and a blazer) and skidded into the living room. The smell of freshly-cooked omelettes came from the kitchen.

'Morning,' said Astin.

'This is your fault!'

'What is?'

'I have a meeting in twenty minutes with the organisers of the fashion show! There's no way I'll get there in time!'

'Can't you reschedule?' he asked, leaning against the counter, all casual.

'No! Everyone involved in the showcase is going to be there!'

'Why don't you take the car?' he said, pushing himself away from the counter.

'I don't know how to get there driving!' Plus they drove backwards in Barcelona and that would make her even more on edge.

She pulled on a coat and scarf then skidded out of the door. Who did he think he was, anyway? Telling her what to do? Telling her how to handle her anxiety when he couldn't keep a lid on his cantankerousness?

She ran down the stairs and stomped off down the street. It was a dark and rainy day; it reminded her of being back home in England. Most winter days were dark and rainy. And autumn. And spring. And summer, actually. Rain was better than snow, though. They hadn't had much snow lately. Not that she minded. She hated snow. It had been because of a snowstorm in New York that she and Astin had made up the first time…

Fuck.

She stopped walking for a moment. Where was she? Somehow she'd veered away from her usual path and ended up on a busy street that she didn't recognise. So much for autopilot.

She grabbed her phone from her bag. A battery symbol flashed on the screen. Oh no. She *always* charged it while she was asleep. Had she forgotten to turn the charger on? She couldn't have. Could she?

That would explain why her alarm hadn't gone off…

None of the buildings around her were familiar. She couldn't make out the top of the Sagrada Familia above anything, either, which meant she had no idea which direction she'd walked in. How was she supposed to find her way if she didn't know where she was?

Her stomach grumbled. It needed to shut up. She didn't have time to eat. If she'd had time for food, she wouldn't have been running so late in the first place.

She turned back the way she came, hoping to retrace her steps. Without her phone, she had no idea what time it was, but there was no chance she'd be on time. What would she tell them? That she slept through her alarm because her ex-boyfriend made her go for an evening jog, and she was up all night thinking about him?

As she walked in the direction she thought she'd come from, she noticed a sign for the metro. Of course! She could use the map to help her get to the nearest metro station to the venue. The stations were always close to the big tourist attractions. She studied the map outside. Getting the metro would involve changing a few times. But she could do it. Not that she had a choice.

Hollie found her way onto the first train. It was moderately busy but not claustrophobic. Not any more claustrophobic than being underground, anyway. She rubbed her hands together, desperate to get to the venue. Without a phone wire, she couldn't charge her phone even if she found a plug. She wasn't usually so disorganised. What had gone wrong?

Several changes and lots of power walking later, Hollie found herself at the Fira Barcelona. She was fifteen minutes late, which wasn't as bad as she'd thought. She ran to where she thought the meeting was, then paused outside the door. Voice echoed. She heard the word 'fashion'. Yep, that was where she belonged.

*

'How did the meeting go?' Fayth asked as Hollie walked in. She was surrounded by photos she'd taken since getting her new camera back in May. Her eyes were so tired from looking at photos that Hollie was blurry when she looked up. She wasn't blurry enough for Fayth to miss the redness in her eyes, though. Her skin was covered in tiny cuts, too. What had she done? Why hadn't she applied any make-up to cover them up? She always wore make-up.

Hollie rubbed at her eyes. 'OK. I was late. They were picking the slots. I got a crummy one in the middle because, for obvious reasons, I got to choose last.'

'Yeah, but you're forgetting something,' said Fayth.

'What?' said Hollie.

'That you've got this far. That's still a hell of an achievement,' said Fayth.

'Yeah,' said Hollie. 'I guess.'

FIFTEEN

As the fashion show grew nearer, Hollie's blood pressure rose. She went from barely sleeping to not sleeping at all. Whenever she tried, she tossed and turned like a pancake. Her eyes were so puffy and the bags underneath them so big she could take them for the weekly grocery shop. In an effort to make herself feel better, she decided to make an old school favourite: jam tarts. They were simple but effective. Soft, crumbly, chewy.

Rubbing the butter and flour between her fingers as she made the pastry soothed her. Breathe in, pick crumbs up. Breathe out, drop crumbs back down. It became a meditative state. For a while, she felt better.

Her jam tarts in the oven, she went for a quick shower. Fifteen minutes later, the smell of burning filled the apartment.

Hollie pulled the jam tarts from the oven. They were black. The jam had boiled over, sticking to the tray. As she tried to unstick the tarts from the metal tray, she noticed that the bases were still raw. The jam had boiled over but the fucking pastry hadn't cooked. Could she do nothing right? She threw the jam tarts across the room. They clattered against the units, landing in a heap on the edge of the kitchenette. Hollie sunk down against the cupboard and sobbed. The washing machine vibrated beside her, as if it was laughing at her. Who was she kidding? She couldn't even bake jam tarts. How the hell was she supposed to stage a fashion show, let alone run a business? She was a fraud. A failure. A—

A key rattled in the lock. Shit.

She couldn't see who it was from her spot on the floor. She half-hoped whoever it was would go into their room and not notice the crumpled heap on the floor, or the smell of burned jam tarts hanging in the air.

'Hello?' came Astin's voice as the door closed.

Shit.

'What's that smell?'

'Soggy bottoms,' mumbled Hollie.

'Hollie?'

She raised her hand. Her face was no doubt red and blotchy with mascara streaming down her face. She was past caring.

'Why are you on the floor? And what's that smell?'

She pointed to the jam tarts across the room.

'Why are you crying over tarts?'

'I fucked them up.'

He offered her his hand. She took it, allowing herself to fall into him as she stood up. She needed to feel close to someone. It being someone who'd broken her heart didn't matter. She'd broken her own heart enough times lately but hadn't stopped speaking to herself. He wrapped her in his arms and guided her to the sofa. 'Come on,' he said. She sobbed harder. Why had she let him go? He was a good person, really. Sure, he'd made a few mistakes, but hadn't they all? She'd abandoned him when he'd needed her the most. What kind of monster was she?

'Hey, come on,' he said as she sobbed into his Superdry t-shirt. He tucked her hair behind her ear and rubbed her back, just like he had when they were together. A voice at the back of her head reminded her that letting him touch her was a bad idea. She ignored it. Her anxiety had ruined enough already.

'What happened?'

She sniffled a few times. 'I can't do this. I can't run a business, or stage a fashion show, or any of this. I'm a fraud. I can't take it.'

He tilted her head up so that she looked at him. 'Don't you ever say that.'

'But—'

'No. You've worked your butt off. You're not a fraud. You can do this.'

'How can you have so much faith in me?'

He stroked the side of her face, tucking the other side of her hair behind her ear. 'Because you're strong. Stronger than any of us.'

She scoffed. 'No I'm not.'

'Yes, you are.' His tone was confident, assuring. Even more so than usual. 'Do you want to go for a coffee?'

She nodded. Coffee was a *brilliant* idea. Hollie looked down at her outfit. Her tulip skirt and black t-shirt were covered in jam and flour. Why did she have to be such a messy cook? Why couldn't she be a nice, clean cook like Fayth?

'Hollie?' said Astin.

'Give me a couple of minutes to get changed?'

'Sure.'

Inside the safety of her room, she took a few deep breaths. She had so much work to do, but she just couldn't concentrate. At least when she and Astin had lived together she'd had Jamal to help. Jamal had been their personal butler, and he'd dropped parcels off at the Post Office for her. Since leaving the hotel, she was back to doing it all on her own. As business increased, she had more and more to do. Everyone chipped in when they could, but she couldn't keep asking them to do this or that. It was her job, her career.

She changed into skintight leatherette trousers, a purple boat neck jumper, and her favourite chunky boots. Her make-up topped up to hide how much she'd been crying, she returned to the living room.

'There she is,' said Astin with a smile. 'New trousers?' he added, his eyes lingering on her legs.

'Yeah,' she said, both embarrassed and exhilarated at him checking her out. 'I made them just before Christmas.' The fabric had been a right pain in the arse, but it had been worth it.

'They suit you,' he said, cocking an eyebrow flirtatiously.

Hollie smirked, walking in front so that he could see her arse as she walked away.

*

After going for a Starbucks – a vanilla latte for Hollie and a macchiato for Astin, of course – they wandered through the scenic Park Güell and the bustling streets of Barcelona. It was a bright but chilly day, so Hollie pulled her scarf up high to protect her neck from the cold. The curves and character of the Gothic architecture filled her brain with all sorts of ideas, but she forced them to the back of her mind so that she could focus on Astin. Not in that way, but in a she-didn't-want-to-be-rude way. Mostly.

'Have you had much of a chance to explore since you got here?' said Astin.

'Not really,' admitted Hollie, wrapping her arms around herself. 'I haven't had much chance to do anything in months.'

'No wonder you're so burned out.'

Hollie stopped walking. 'I am *not* burned out!'

'You jump at everything! And if you're not jumping, you're snapping.'

A man barged into her. Hollie turned around and gave him her most powerful death stare. He hadn't even apologised. It was a busy street but it wasn't busy enough that he couldn't have walked around her. Arsehole. 'I am not!' She crossed her arms.

'You're doing it now.'

Hollie tightened her jaw. No she wasn't. 'You don't get to tell me what to do or how to do it.'

'I'm not trying to,' said Astin. 'I'm just worried, that's all.'

'Well don't be,' she said, storming off down the street. Astin barely had to speed up to catch up with her. Stupid tall people.

'I just want you to be careful. We all do.'

Hollie glared at him. 'No one else has said anything.'

'I've heard Fayth tell you how worried she is. You just don't listen.'

'I do too!'

Astin sighed. He tried to reach for Hollie's hand, but she jerked it out of his grasp. 'Please just be careful?' His tone went from lecturing to concerned. There was tangible pain in his voice. Why did he care so much anyway? 'It's easier to burn yourself out than you think.'

His change of tone caught her off guard. She found herself softening too. She sighed. 'All right.' Not that there was anything she could do differently. There was just over a fortnight left until the fashion show. So long as she reached that goal, she could figure the rest out afterwards. If she lasted that long.

'You know where this is, don't you?' said Astin, abruptly stopping in the middle of the street.

Hollie stopped too. 'Should I?'

He looked up. 'This is where Trinity fell.'

'How do you know?' said Hollie. He hadn't even been in Spain when she'd fallen.

He pointed to a few feet away, where hundreds of bunches of flowers had been laid out on the ground. Hollie walked over, admiring the sea of white lilies (Trinity's favourite, and, eerily, the flower of death). She crouched down to read some of the notes. People wished her peace in heaven, hoping she was finally free of her addiction; fans told her of how much she'd be missed. Astin had fallen too. If he hadn't had a crash mat to fall onto, there was no way he would've survived. The damage to his body was temporary. The damage to Trinity's…

Hollie stood up and wiped a tear from her eye. Even though she hated Trinity, nobody deserved to die like that. Nobody deserved to be used like she had been. Her life hadn't been as perfect as she'd pretended it to be, yet most of the outside world had no idea how terrible it really was. It was only through hearing the stories that Liam and Tate shared that Hollie realised just how crappy Trinity had really had it. It was no wonder she was a bitch that didn't trust anyone – she *hadn't* been able to trust anyone. Even Liam and Tate had hurt her. Hollie swallowed down the lump in her throat.

'You OK?' said Astin, putting his hand on Hollie's back.

She leaned into his shoulder, resting her hand on his chest. 'Do you ever think about how…how that could've been you?'

He sighed. 'All the time.' He moved his hand to around her waist and pulled her closer to him. 'When it first happened, a part of me wished I *had* died. I couldn't handle the thought of being bed or wheelchair bound for months. It terrified me.'

'Death didn't?'

'No. Death doesn't scare me. That's why I always used to live life to the fullest.'

'Used to?'

'I don't want to be that person ever again,' he said, his jaw set.

Hollie turned to face him, her hand still on his chest. 'But you're not that person any more. I know it wasn't really you.'

His face lit up. 'You do?'

She nodded. 'Nobody knows how they'll react in a situation like that until they're in it. I'm not exactly Little Miss Sunshine when I'm stressed.'

'You're not that much of a dick, either.'

Hollie shoved him. He barely moved, but the message seemed to have been received. 'Do *not* say that about yourself! You were hurting.'

'That doesn't justify my actions.'

'Doesn't it? We take our anger out on the people we love, thinking that we can push them harder because they're less likely to leave us.'

'But everyone has their breaking point,' said Astin. He looked up at the sky. Hollie was pretty sure his eyes were filling with tears, but she couldn't see for sure.

Hollie leaned forwards and pulled him into the tightest hug she could manage. No, he wasn't perfect, but neither was she.

*

In Barcelona, almost all roads led to the beach, so naturally, that's where Hollie and Astin ended up. The sound of the waves lapping at the sand added an ambience to their walk. It was – dare Hollie think it? – romantic. And really relaxing. While she liked to keep her feet firmly on the ground – that was part of why she hated flying – she loved watching the water. She loved seeing people's faces as they climbed off a jet ski or from one of those crazy water rides. She stopped walking and looked out across the ocean. It was one of those nights where the sun cast an orange glow over everything as it set. God, it was beautiful. The water shimmered in its amber light.

'It's so pretty,' said Hollie.

'Yeah,' said Astin, although she felt his gaze on her, not on the sunset.

A jet ski buzzed past the horizon.

'Now that looks fun,' said Astin.

'No, no it does not,' said Hollie.

'Why doesn't it?'

'I don't do boats. I like to keep my feet on the ground.'

'How did you get here, then? Portkey? Orbing?'

'Haha. I fly when I have to,' she said, forcing herself to ignore that he'd just referenced *Harry Potter* and *Charmed* in one breath. Him liking the same things as her was not a sign of compatibility. Compatibility ran deeper than that.

'Perhaps if you associated it with something fun then you wouldn't hate it so much.' He gave her his trademark cheeky smile. Oh no. That butter-wouldn't-melt smile wreaked hell with her lady parts.

'We don't have our swimsuits or anything with us.' There. That would do it.

'I'm sure we could find somewhere around here that could sell us something,' he said, jerking his head in the direction of a shop selling swimwear. Oh no.

SIXTEEN

Tate stopped jogging along the promenade and stared out across the ocean. The sun was setting and its reflection was sparkling in the water. She took her phone from the band on her arm and snapped a few photos.

Liam and Wade caught up with her.

Tate lowered her phone, a quizzical look on her face. 'Hey, isn't that Hollie and Astin?'

'Where?' said Liam. 'How can you tell from this far away?'

'Hollie's hair is pretty distinct,' said Tate. She huffed. 'And she really shouldn't be getting it so wet when the dye isn't that old.'

Typical Tate, thinking about hair dye over, you know, having fun. 'I still don't see them.'

'Over there,' said Wade, pointing to a jet ski skidding across the water a few hundred yards away.

Liam squinted. He couldn't really see; he'd forgot to put his contacts in. He didn't usually need them for jogging. 'Could be.' He walked to the edge of the promenade and leaned on the wall, narrowing his eyes further.

'You and your glasses,' said Tate with an eye roll.

'It's them,' said Wade.

'Are you sure? Hollie hates boats,' said Liam.

'It's definitely them,' said Tate. She smirked. 'They look *very* cosy.'

Liam rolled his eyes. 'You've interfered enough.'

'*Moi?*' said Tate, feigning innocence.

'You know you were wrong to move Astin in with us.'

'I did it for you,' she said, still trying to sound innocent.

'You did it so that you could play Cupid again,' said Liam.

'What's wrong with that? Do they not look happy?'

'They're too far away to tell,' said Liam.

'You mean you're too blind to see,' said Tate.

Liam turned and glared at her. 'Can you see their facial expressions from here?'

'No,' said Tate, 'but you don't rent a jet ski with someone you can't stand.'

'They would've found their way back to each other eventually,' said Liam.

'So then what's the harm in giving them a little nudge?' said Tate.

'It wasn't your place to interfere,' said Liam.

'But if things turn out for the better, then maybe it was.'

Liam wasn't in the mood to argue with her. She was impossible in an argument.

'Hey look, it's Tate Gardener and Liam York!'

Fuck.

'Bus stop,' said Wade, jerking his head behind them.

There was a group of people staring at them and pointing, their phones out and inevitably recording. Why hadn't they brought Tate's bodyguard, too? Why had they thought they'd be fine out for an evening jog? Ugh.

Before anyone had even spoken – or shouted – at him, he started to hear them in his head: *Did you kill Trinity Gold? Why did you push her? How does Fayth feel knowing that you're still in love with your dead ex-girlfriend?* He wasn't, not in the romantic sense, but the press and former fans were convinced that he'd gone to her apartment for a secret rendezvous. He flexed his fingers, resisting the urge to curl his hands into fists.

Wade shielded Liam and Tate as best he could, forcing his way through the crowd so that they could get to a taxi. He helped them into the nearest one, then told the driver where to take them.

*

Hollie hated to admit it, but she *loved* jet skiing. She'd even driven at one point, meaning that Astin had had to cling on to her. Not a bad feeling. She loved the simultaneous feelings of control and freedom. It was unlike anything else she'd ever experienced. And she'd bought a super cute tartan bikini to go underneath her wetsuit, which she'd spotted Astin checking her out in.

'Was it as bad as you thought it would be?' said Astin as they walked back towards the apartment. The water had removed almost all of the gel from his hair. It flopped into his eyes in a totally sexy way that made her want him. Stat.

'No,' she said. She grabbed his hand, pulled him to her, and kissed his cheek. 'Thank you.' It had been just what she'd needed to channel her anxiety and calm her racing mind.

He smiled back at her. It was one of those sad, hopeful smiles that until his arrival in Barcelona she'd never seen him do before. Was that his way of saying *'You're welcome, I miss you'* all in one facial expression? No. He'd said he wanted to move on, for god's sake.

But then…

The more she thought about it, the more she missed him. He brought out her adventurous side. Her fun side. Her daring side. He encouraged her to be ambitious while still looking after herself, and really, was there anyone better to have by your side? He'd fallen into a dark hole after his accident, but could she really blame him? He'd lost everything. He hadn't even been able to wipe his arse after going to the loo. Wouldn't that make anyone angry and depressed? He'd gone for therapy, and as far as she knew, was still doing it. It seemed to be helping. Living with him in a different place in a different situation made her see him in a new light. He wasn't angry any more, he was sad. Sad and lonely. Which is how she'd felt for months. But then, that was her own doing. She'd pushed people away so that she could spend time on her fashion line. But at the expense of what? Her sanity? Sure, her friends would stay by her side when she was being a bitch, but they shouldn't have to. She shouldn't treat them like that in the first place.

'I'm sorry for being a total bitch lately,' she said as they continued walking, hand-in-hand.

He kissed the top of her head. 'It's OK.'

And with those two words, she realised it was.

*

Shouting echoed down the corridor as Hollie and Astin made their way back to the apartment. Was it related to the crowds outside their building? They didn't recognise Hollie and Astin so they'd got through unscathed, but could they have been there for Liam and Tate? God, she hoped not. That would *really* help things. Help things turn more sour, that was.

Hollie and Astin exchanged worried glances, then headed inside.

Tate paced around the living area, shaking her head. Fayth and Liam sat on the sofa, while Wade stood by the door. Nobody looked up when they entered.

'Relax, would you?' said Liam.

'Relax!' cried Tate, waving her arms in the air. 'There are dozens of them out there!'

'You're exaggerating,' said Wade. 'There's a handful, at most.'

'I know what I saw,' said Tate.

'Why do you even care?' said Liam. 'You've been hounded by your fans hundreds of times.'

Hollie and Astin hovered by the door. They'd definitely walked into the middle of something.

'Do you have any idea what effect this could have on me?' said Tate.

'What, so you can be seen with drug addicts but not suspected murderers?' Liam stood up and folded his arms.

Fayth stood up too, putting her hand on his chest.

'Is it so wrong to want to protect my reputation? I've worked hard to get to where I am!' said Tate.

'So have I!' said Liam.

'Should we say anything?' mumbled Hollie.

'There's not much we can say,' said Astin.

'Yeah, and you did a great job of maintaining it, didn't you?' snarled Tate.

'That's enough!' shouted Fayth. Fayth never shouted. It *was* bad. 'Pack it in, both of you!'

Liam stormed into his and Fayth's room and slammed the door.

'Well, at least he's not going walkabout,' said Wade.

Tate huffed, disappearing into her room and slamming her door just as loudly.

Fayth shook her head.

'I'll be at my hotel if you need me,' said Wade. Even Liam's bodyguard couldn't protect him from his friends…

Fayth nodded.

Nobody spoke again until Wade left.

'What was that about?' said Hollie.

'The fans descended on them while they were out for a jog. Tate's worried being seen with Liam will be bad for her rep,' said Fayth.

Hollie raised an eyebrow. 'Seriously?'

'Seriously,' said Fayth, shaking her head.

'Tate likes being in control,' said Astin. 'With photos like that – especially ones taken by fans – she can't control the narrative.'

'But she can't with paparazzi shots anyway,' said Hollie. She lowered her gaze. 'Can she?'

'Sometimes,' said Astin. 'She occasionally arranges photo ops so that they can get the photos they need then leave her in peace the rest of the time. It usually works.'

'Wow. I never realised they were so orchestrated,' said Fayth.

'That's fame for you,' said Astin.

'I'd better go check on Liam,' said Fayth. 'Talk to you in a bit.'

Hollie nodded. A few hours ago, she'd desperately needed her best friend. But her best friend was needed more by her boyfriend. Hollie, meanwhile, would have to continue to find comfort in her ex. Which really wasn't as bad as she'd thought it would be...

'Coffee?' offered Astin.

'Please.' She sunk onto the recently vacated sofa. 'I don't get why Tate was so upset.'

'The higher up you are, the harder you fall,' said Astin as he made the drinks. 'And for women in Hollywood, it's a lot harder to be respected, let alone forgiven.'

'But she hasn't done anything wrong,' said Hollie.

'Doesn't matter,' said Astin.

Hollie huffed. 'It's so stupid.'

'Yeah,' agreed Astin. He sat beside her and put their drinks on the coffee table. Hollie leaned forwards and picked up her drink. Astin knocked her as he reached for his drink, too. Her drink splashed, landing on her jumper.

'Shit!' She put her coffee on the table and pulled her jumper over her head as she shoved it into the washer. The longer the stain had to settle in to a fabric like that, the harder it'd be to get it out of the fabric.

The washer sprung to life, the fate of her purple jumper in its hands.

She turned around. Astin stood behind her, leaning against the fridge/freezer. She blushed, suddenly self-conscious. She was stood in front of him with no top on. She'd taken it off without even thinking.

'Calvin Klein. It suits you,' he said, admiring her bra. 'I remember when we first met, you were scared to even take your shirt off around me.'

Her cheeks burned. She'd been more concerned about the fate of her jumper than getting semi-naked in front of her ex.

'I...'

'I think that was a rouse. I don't really think there are any marks on that sweater. You just wanted to seduce me.'

'You wish,' said Hollie, stepping closer.

'What if I do?' he said. Those blue, blue eyes stared right through her. They knew everything about her, the good and the bad. And, despite everything, he was still there. His arms were tight around her, his legs open so that when she stood between them, she could feel the erection forming underneath his jeans. Their chests moved rapidly and in sync. Neither broke eye contact. Until he leaned forwards and kissed her. Fire shot through her. It was like a defibrillator bringing her back to life. His lips pressed against hers with an urgency she'd never felt from him before. She kissed him back just as passionately. How had they been apart for so long? Why had she denied herself something she wanted so badly?

He picked her up, their lips still pressed together. She wrapped her legs around him as he carried her into his room and threw her onto the bed. Standing over her, he stared at her and smiled. She nudged him with her foot. He grinned, pulling his t-shirt off and leaning over her. She fiddled with his belt buckle as he kissed her neck, his hand sliding down her body and inside her knickers. There was something so wrong, yet so right, about being close to him again. She needed him, and he needed her. She'd known it all along.

Seventeen

Hollie opened her eyes. She wasn't in her room. She was in Astin's.

Shit.

He lay beside her, his breathing steady. And she had his t-shirt on.

None of what had happened the night before was supposed to have happened. They weren't supposed to enjoy each other's company, and they most definitely weren't supposed to end up getting naked. Things were about to get very, *very* complicated.

It was still early. If she crept out she'd be back in her own room before anyone else woke up. But then what? Would they act like nothing had happened? Would the others figure out that something had?

She pulled the covers from her. A hand reached out and grabbed her arm. 'Going somewhere?' said Astin, a teasing note in his voice.

She turned back to him. He was smirking. 'Embarrassed, are we?'

No, she wasn't embarrassed. She was mortified.

He chuckled. Even when he mocked her, his laugh was still endearing. She turned back towards him. 'It's complicated.'

'I think we passed complicated last night,' he replied.

She crossed her legs, then, remembering she didn't have any knickers on, tucked her legs underneath her and pulled Astin's t-shirt over her knees. He was right. They totally had. What had they done?

'You regret it, don't you?' he said, studying her bowed head and slumped shoulders.

'It's not regret, exactly,' she said, 'it's more…confusion. What have we done?'

'I can recap if you want me to,' he said, sitting up beside her.

'This isn't funny!'

'It kinda is. You're making a big deal out of nothing. So we had sex.' He shrugged.

'Is that all it was to you?'

'What was it to *you*?'

What was it indeed? Was it just sex, or was it the first step towards rekindling their relationship? She didn't know which prospect was scarier, and that's what made it worse. She'd tried to avoid his company for a reason. With him living in the same apartment as her, avoiding him hadn't been so easy. And, by some miracle, he was almost like the guy she'd fallen in love with back in New York. Would he have been like that if he hadn't been in an accident? Would they still have broken up if it hadn't happened?

She gulped. She didn't know. 'I have to go.'

Before he could stop her, she ran out of his room and back into her own. She'd left her clothes in his room, but they could stay there until he was out. She needed some time to think.

*

When Hollie returned to her room, she rang Cameron for advice. He was on an early shift so would be getting up any minute and therefore wouldn't mind her ringing right before his alarm was due to go off. Or at least, she hoped not.

'Hollie?' he said. 'Shouldn't you be asleep?'

'If only,' she said. 'Can I ask you something?'

'Shoot.'

'How did you forgive Luke?'

If anyone knew about getting back together with someone that had burned them, it was Cameron. He and Luke had broken up twice and had somehow turned into a happy couple. There had to be some secret, right?

Cameron sighed. 'I knew it wasn't really him. He was letting other people control him, and I hated the thought of him just being someone else's puppet.'

Hollie wrapped the duvet tighter around herself. Did she know the person responsible for all those terrible things Astin had said and done wasn't him? She'd seen the pain in his eyes. She knew he was depressed and that depression could manifest as anger. Did that make her a bad person for not staying by his side when he'd been at his lowest? No, it made him a bad person for saying he'd lost everything when he'd lost his stunt career when she'd still been there. If she mattered to him so little, she was better off without him.

And then Cameron asked the most important question of all: 'Do you want to give him another chance?'

*

Banging noises erupted from elsewhere in the apartment as Hollie finished talking to Cameron.

'Catfight?' said Cameron.

'Very funny,' said Hollie. 'I'd better go see what's going on.'

'Keep me posted!'

'You and your gossip,' said Hollie.

'You know you love me.'

Hollie pulled on her own pyjamas, flattened her hair, and went to investigate. Tate and Maddy were tugging gigantic suitcases towards the door.

'What's going on?' said Hollie.

'I'm leaving,' said Tate.

Hollie ran over to her. 'What?'

'I can't stay here any more,' said Tate.

Rage burned inside Hollie. 'You invited my ex-boyfriend to stay here, made me feel guilty when I wanted to leave, then you get into one argument with Liam and you bail? What the fuck?'

'It's more than that, Hollie. This is my reputation on the line.'

'And my mental health doesn't matter to you?'

'Nobody made you stay, Hollie. You may put the blame on me, but I'm not guilty.'

Was that true? Had Hollie crumbled so easily because she'd subconsciously wanted him there?

While Hollie ruminated, Tate took her chance and left. Coward.

'Did you really think me moving in here was bad for your mental health?' said Astin.

Hollie jumped. Why did he always appear out of nowhere? He was stood in his bedroom doorway, his head lowered.

'I...' She didn't know how to answer that. It was a loaded question. Especially after the night before.

'It was confusing,' she said.

He looked genuinely hurt. Like she'd stabbed him through the chest and was twisting the knife. She walked over to him, wrought with guilt. 'Are you honestly telling me you weren't nervous, too?'

'I was terrified,' he informed her lime green toenails. 'But I had to know.'

'Know what?' she said.

'How you felt.'

'Was that the only reason you came all this way?'

'No,' he said, 'but it was a big part.'

'What was the other part?'

He scrunched his face up, like it pained him to discuss it. 'Being back in Texas helped me to put things into perspective. I don't fit in there any more. But I was so lonely in New York. None of my friends were there. And...and I needed a friend.' He wiped at his eyes. Holy shit, he was crying. She pulled him into a hug, not sure how else to react. She'd never seen him so openly vulnerable. 'I lost myself, and there was only so many martial arts classes I could teach to make myself feel better.'

'I'm sorry,' said Hollie.

Astin lifted his head from her shoulder. 'For what?'

'I had no idea you were still hurting.'

'I've been hurting ever since I let you go.'

EIGHTEEN

Fayth and Liam hadn't heard Tate move out – they'd been fast asleep. When Liam found out, he went back into their room and closed the door. He immersed himself in games for the day, only emerging to get food and drinks. Fayth went to work and left him to it. He seemed like he needed the alone time.

When she got back, he was rifling through his wardrobe and tossing shirts onto the bed. 'I need to go out for a bit, clear my head. Want to come?'

'Are you sure you're all right?' said Fayth. She leaned back on the bed, calm as anything. How was she so calm after everything Tate had said?

He stopped looking for a shirt and turned to face her. 'Not really, but what can I do? I've known what Tate's like for a long time. She's not changed as much as she thinks she has.'

'Is that the only thing that's bothering you?'

'You know it isn't,' said Liam, returning to his wardrobe.

Fayth walked up to him and put her arms around him. She kissed his cheek. 'Come on, let's get you some fresh air.'

*

Fayth and Liam found a quiet bar nearby to hang out in. The music was good, the atmosphere was relaxing, and it wasn't noisy enough that they couldn't talk. It was just what he needed. Until one of his old friends from the *Highwater* films found them. He'd pulled away from a lot of that circle because he was embarrassed about his behaviour back then. It had been after his sister's death and at the height of his addiction. He'd said and done too many things he would've preferred to forget.

He couldn't avoid them all the time – it was hard with such a big convention circuit – but the less he saw them, the less embarrassed he was. At least the fans hadn't found out how bad he'd been when he was an addict. Not that it mattered when they all thought he was a murderer.

But, as sod's law would have it, he and Fayth had chosen to go to the very same bar as some of his old Spanish friends that night. Of all the bars in Barcelona…

'Hey Liam, long time. You didn't say you were back in Barcelona,' said Antoni.

'Good to see you,' Liam lied, giving his old colleague a half-hug. 'This is my girlfriend, Fayth. Fayth, this is Antoni. He was one of the cinematographers on *Highwater*.'

Fayth shook his hand. Antoni sat down at their table. Great.

'So how come you're still in Barcelona? I thought you would've left after what happened.'

Liam ran his hands over his hair. He'd seriously considered staying in New York after Trinity's funeral, but his friends were in Barcelona, and he needed them more than ever after recent events.

'We're here to support a friend at her fashion show,' said Fayth. She reached over and touched Liam's knee. Some of the tension in his body released.

'Oh, that's cool. Listen, a bunch of us are having some drinks. Why don't you come join us?'

Fayth looked to Liam. He wanted to say no, but he couldn't really say that, could he? He put on his best fake smile. 'Sure.'

*

Fayth leaned in to Liam. 'Do you mind if I go home? I'm exhausted and I have work in the morning.'

Liam put his hand on her shoulder. 'Do you want me to come with you?' He hadn't wanted to join his old friends, but it'd ended up being more fun than he'd thought. It wasn't awkward or embarrassing, it was just what he needed.

'No, you stay. I don't want to spoil your fun.'

'All right. I love you,' he said, kissing her cheek.

'I love you too. Enjoy your catch up.' She kissed him, said goodbye to the group, then headed off.

'I never expected you to end up with someone so low maintenance,' chuckled Núria. She tossed her auburn hair over her shoulder.

'Yeah, I thought for sure if you didn't end up with Trinity you'd be with someone equally high maintenance,' said Antoni. At the mention of Trinity, the other five people around the table fell silent, exchanging awkward glances.

Liam tensed at the mention of her name. Everyone *had* expected them to be together. The fans. The media. Even their friends. It had been in the making for a long time. Until Fayth had come along…

Núria slapped Antoni's arm. He flinched. 'Why would you do that? Why would you bring her up?'

'Sorry,' said Antoni, lowering his head. 'That was bad of me.'

'It's fine,' said Liam. 'You don't have to filter what you say.'

'Speaking of filter…' He went into his pocket and, hidden in a roll-up packet, was some weed. 'Want some?'

Liam widened his eyes. He hadn't touched anything other than alcohol and caffeine since leaving rehab. He wouldn't even touch painkillers. Would they think less of him if he said no? Would it leak to the media? Well, it wasn't like his reputation wasn't damaged enough already.

Saying yes *was* tempting. He could do with something to relax him after the last few weeks. But the temptation was almost too strong. It was a slippery path that he knew all too well. He was burying his troubles in alcohol and he knew it. But he could pull himself out of that if he wanted to. Or at least, that's what he told himself. He wasn't an alcoholic. He could stop any time. He just had a lot going on and didn't want to think about it. Which would make weed the perfect remedy.

He reached out to take it, then pulled his hand away. 'I can't. I'm sorry. I have to go.' He stood up, leaving his barely touched pint of Guinness on the table.

*

Liam crept into the apartment. He'd wanted to say yes. He'd wanted to say yes so badly. Anything to numb the guilt that plagued him about Trinity's death. But he wouldn't hide from the pain like he did last time. Numbing the pain just caused more problems.

But leaving so abruptly had left him feeling like a coward. But there was nothing wrong with saying no. So why was he so embarrassed? Did saying no make him a stick in the mud?

So that he didn't smell like a bar when he went to bed, he went for a quick shower. When he emerged a few minutes later, he caught sight of his reflection in the bathroom mirror. He still wasn't used to his shorter hair. His hair constantly being in his face had been part of his identity. His hair flicks didn't have the same effect when there was nothing to flick. But losing his hair had also been cathartic. It had reminded him that anything could change, including him. He could do whatever he wanted. The only thing stopping him was himself. And if he fucked up – like got a really stupid haircut – he could fix it. There was almost always a way to fix things.

While Tate's rants about her reputation had infuriated him, he knew she was right. Even though people still blamed him for Trinity's death, there was a high chance Hollywood would move on and forgive him. It wasn't so forgiving for female stars, especially as they grew closer to 30.

But even if he could repair his reputation, he wasn't sure if he wanted to. Hollywood had turned its back on him. He'd contemplated quitting several times in the past few years. Then a great role had appeared and changed his mind. But this time, those great roles had turned their backs on him. And there were plenty of other actors to fill those roles if he wasn't around. His looks wouldn't last forever, even if he got better at acting as time went on. Did he really want to end up like Ed Harris or Anthony Hopkins? Did he want to dedicate the rest of his life to acting? Was that his future? He loved entertaining people, and he knew that to some cinemagoers, movies were as much a form of therapy as they were art. But was it enough?

No, not any more.

Liam leaned over the sink so that he could see into the mirror to take out his contact lenses. He hated wearing them, but laser eye surgery scared him more. He didn't have a face for glasses, either, which meant his only option was contact lenses. He pulled one out and reached over to put it into the case, but he slipped on a patch of water on the bathroom floor. The contact lens fell out of his hand and into the toilet. No. Fuck no.

One eye with blurred vision and one eye with perfect vision, he ran into the kitchen, got some rubber gloves, then returned to the bathroom. Was he really going to fish it out? Well he couldn't let it go down the toilet. But would he really wear it after? No, he wouldn't. But he didn't want to pollute the waterways, either. His face scrunched up, he reached into the toilet, pulled out his contact lens, and shoved it onto the edge of the sink. Now what? He couldn't wear it. He didn't have any glasses, either. And it was his last pair. He had them on repeat, but he wasn't in New York. That pair were meant to have lasted him for months. His parents had warned him to always have a back up. Why did they have to be right?

He took out his phone to text Ola then realised she'd be asleep. He couldn't disturb her. She always kept her notifications on over night just in case he needed her, but it wasn't important enough to wake her up. She needed sleep too. He'd have her deal with it in the morning.

*

Liam woke up the next morning and texted Ola to ask her to sort something. Her response was several shocked emojis, followed by *I'll sort it.* Thank god for a reliable assistant. He would've been lost without her.

Fayth slept beside him, her mouth hanging open as she made soft snoring noises. He lay back down and closed his eyes. What state would he be in now if he had accepted that weed? What would he have told Fayth? *Would* he have told her, or would he have tried to hide it? If he hid it, it was a sign that there was something to worry about. If he didn't hide anything from her, it meant he didn't have a problem. Right?

*

Fayth's alarm buzzed. Time to get up for work. Liam rolled over in bed and propped his head up with his hand. He looked like he hadn't slept all night. What time had he got home? 'I'm thinking of quitting acting.'

Fayth did a double take. 'What? Why?' Was she still asleep, or had he really just said that? He was such a great actor. It would be a shame for his talent to go to waste. But after the way his fans had reacted to him after Trinity's death, his pity audition, and his and Fayth's stalker, was it really that surprising he felt that way? The fans had been brutal to him. Especially the die-hard *Highwater* fans that had once been so loyal. Even though he'd been cleared of anything to do with Trinity's death, they refused to believe he was faultless. The simple fact that he'd been there and hadn't been fast enough to stop her was enough for them to blame him. Hell, it was enough for him to blame himself.

'I've been thinking about it for a while, but after everything that's happened the last few months…' He sighed. 'I'm just not sure I want to live in a fishbowl any more.'

Fayth reached over and touched his arm. 'Whatever you choose, I'll be here.'

'That's the problem, though – I don't know what to choose.'

'You'll figure it out.'

'When?'

'When you stop putting pressure on yourself,' she said. 'I figured out I wanted to be a photographer while I was talking to you about something completely unrelated. Sometimes that's all you need.'

'I guess,' he said.

'You have the money to take a break for a while, so why don't you? You don't have any upcoming projects or anything, and after everything, you've kinda earned it.'

He sat up. 'You're right. I have. I've been working almost nonstop since I was 10. I *deserve* a break.'

'A wee bit,' said Fayth. 'You work harder than most people I know but seem to realise it less.'

He gave a small laugh. 'Do I?'

She nodded. 'Yeah. Just because you're on a film set and you're not writing or directing or producing, that doesn't mean you're not still working hard. You spend all day pretending to be someone else. That must be exhausting.'

He paused for a moment. 'I've never really thought about it like that before. It's what I've always done, you know?'

'That doesn't mean you can't change it.'

MARCH

ONE

The ninth of March. Hollie's birthday. And for the first time ever, she didn't want to celebrate it. What did she have to celebrate? That she was another year older and everything was going wrong? That this time last year she'd had the most amazing birthday where everything was going right and less than three weeks later everything had gone tits up?

The year before, she and Astin had stayed at the Savoy in London. They'd gone to a modern-day speakeasy. They'd had the most amazing, fun-filled, romantic day. A year later, she didn't even know if she could trust him anymore. She wanted to, but that wasn't enough. He'd betrayed her. He'd said that he'd lost everything after the accident even though she'd stayed by his side. Surely that meant that she didn't matter to him? She scrunched her eyes up, as if that would help her to shake the visions of her and Astin's break-up from her mind. Whenever she wanted to give him another chance, those images came back. The feeling of her heart breaking as he'd said those horrible things. Was he still that person? Was she?

They worked so well together. When things went well, they went *really* well. When they went badly, well…to call it a car crash would be an understatement. Were they just going through the storming phase of their relationship? Would they soon be at the norming stage, where they could find their happily ever after?

Who was she kidding? There was no such thing as happily ever after.

Hollie sighed.

Fayth had planned something for her birthday. There was no doubt about that. It was an unspoken rule between the two of them that whenever they spent birthdays together, the other person would plan something. The unspoken rule had never bothered Hollie before, but this time, it did.

While she wanted to hide under her duvet all day, she knew she couldn't. After checking her emails and responding to the important ones, she got up and went into the living area. Fayth and Liam were already in there, making breakfast.

'There's the birthday girl!' said Fayth, running over to Hollie and hugging her. 'We've just put breakfast on.'

Hollie eyed Liam standing over the cooker. 'Is that safe?' He had a reputation for being a notoriously bad cook, and his previous cooking experiments in Barcelona didn't instil much faith.

'I'm watching him closely,' said Fayth with a cheeky grin. 'You can't go wrong with a fry up. Can you?'

'I mean I've written off a pan with baked beans before so don't look at me,' said Hollie.

Fayth widened her eyes. 'What? How?'

'Don't ask,' said Hollie. Moral of the story: don't use hobs when tired.

'Happy birthday,' said Liam, hugging her as she entered the kitchen area. He had on a black apron with white frills. Interesting choice.

'Thanks,' said Hollie.

'Coffee thingy's done its thing if you want a drink,' said Fayth.

'Thanks. That was very descriptive of you,' said Hollie as she fished a mug from the cupboard.

'Wasn't it? I should write poetry.'

'You mean you should keep writing poetry so that I can read it?' said Hollie. Fayth wrote great poetry, but she had no idea how good it was. Hollie had encouraged her to read it aloud while they were in New York, and it had gone down amazingly. It seemed to have boosted Fayth's self-confidence, too, which was a plus.

'It's not *that* good,' said Fayth.

'Is too. I studied English Literature at A Level, therefore I know good poetry.'

'You know that's not how it works, right?'

'You know that's how it works in Hollie's head and that's what matters, right?' said Liam.

Fayth glared at him. But he was totally right.

'Food is almost ready,' said Liam.

'Where's Astin?' asked Hollie.

Fayth cocked an eyebrow.

'What? I just assumed he'd want to join us, that's all.' And yeah, OK, she wanted to see him. She'd struggled to get him out of her head before they'd slept together again. Since then, it was almost impossible. The things he could do with those hands of his...

'Gym. He said he'd be back for breakfast,' said Fayth.

'He probably got carried away,' said Liam. 'You know what he's like with exercise.'

Just as he said that, the door opened and in walked Astin. 'Hey.' He joined them in the kitchen and kissed Hollie's cheek.

'Someone had a good workout,' said Hollie. He was *dripping* with sweat. That made her want to jump him even more. There was something she found very attractive about Astin after a workout. She'd never figured out what it was.

'Mmm yeah. I'm just gonna go shower. I'll be with y'all in five.' He kissed Hollie's cheek again, then disappeared into the bathroom.

'Are you two…?' began Liam.

Fayth picked up a towel from the side and spanked him with it.

'Ow!'

'Don't be so bloody nosy then!' said Fayth.

'He's just looking out for his friend, same as you would,' said Hollie.

Liam waved the spatula at her. 'What she said. Except I'm looking out for *both* my friends.'

'Doesn't that put you in an awkward position?' said Hollie.

'No. What's been awkward is knowing how much the two of you want to jump each other the last few weeks,' said Fayth.

'It hasn't been *that* bad,' said Hollie. Had it?

'Yeah, kind of has,' said Liam.

'So you knew when…?' Oh god. Mortified, much?

Fayth put her arms around Hollie's shoulder and patted it. 'Oh yeah. We knew. We also knew not to say anything.' She kicked Liam. 'Then this idiot goes and opens his mouth today. Of all days.'

Liam flashed her an innocent grin.

Fayth rolled her eyes.

'It's OK. I get why he asked. I don't know what the deal is yet. I don't want to rush anything, you know?' said Hollie.

Fayth squeezed her shoulders. 'Yeah. Don't worry about the rest of us. Just focus on what you want.'

'Thanks. I will.' Just as soon as she figured out what it was.

*

It was a quiet birthday, but a better one than Hollie had anticipated. After breakfast the four of them had gone to Barcelona Cathedral, which Fayth had insisted on taking Hollie to even though she'd already done it with Liam. Fayth was right – Hollie *did* love it. Getting neck cramp from staring up at the ornate stained glass windows was a long-overdue break from how hard she'd been working lately. It was never going to last, but it was nice while it did.

When they got home, Hollie excused herself to lie down. After changing into her pyjamas, she cocooned herself in her duvet. There was just over a week to go until her fashion show. It would all be over soon, and she couldn't wait. She'd had so little sleep over the past few weeks that she could barely keep her eyes open. But then, when she did try to sleep, suddenly her mind was a hamster running frantically on a wheel. If one more person told her to try aromatherapy or sleep hygiene she'd be forced to commit violence. They meant well, sure, but most of them didn't know what burn out felt like. They'd never pushed themselves *that* far. Hollie, on the other hand, knew that she was on the brink of burning out. But, like a car racing towards the edge of a cliff at 100mph, she couldn't stop herself.

Two

One week to go. And there was still so, *so* much to do. Hollie pulled the quilt over her head. Nope. She couldn't deal with the world any longer. She'd had enough. The fashion show would just have to go on without her. The organisers wouldn't miss her if she didn't turn up. None of the people attending would even notice if she didn't go.

But if she didn't go, she'd be letting herself down. She'd be letting Tate down. And Fayth. And her mum. And her nan. Ugh. She hoisted herself out of bed and began to get ready. Wet-look trousers. Sequinned blazer. Straight hair. Lots of make-up.

She could do this.

*

'Breakfast will be ready in a minute,' said Fayth, gesturing to the oven. Hollie suppressed a gag. She *really* didn't want food, but Fayth had gone to the effort of making pancakes for everyone so that they had plenty of energy for the upcoming day.

They were relocating to Francisco and Ramira's gallery for the day where they'd have more room to put together a makeshift runway, and room for people to get changed and do hair and make-up. Once they'd decided on the outfits for each model, Fayth would take photos of them so that they knew the styling of each outfit. It was going to be a long day, and while a part of Hollie was excited for it, she also knew that the physical reactions to excitement were the same as those for anxiety. No, she had to stay calm and keep a clear head. She had to suppress all emotions so that she didn't get controlled by them.

'You ready for today?' Fayth asked, handing her a cup of coffee. 'Still don't trust you to make it yourself,' Fayth added with a cheeky grin.

'Thanks,' said Hollie, giving her best friend a hug and resting her head on her shoulder. 'I just want to get today over with. Is that bad?'

'No, but you should at least try to enjoy it. This is the first time you've ever done something like this, and we're all working together on it.' Fayth squeezed Hollie's arm. 'We won't let you down.'

*

'The first model arrives at ten, then we get half an hour with each to try on different outfits with them. They'll then be off to hair and make-up for styling,' Maddy informed them. All of Hollie's friends and their assistants were stood in the main area of the gallery. All the furniture had been moved to create a makeshift runway, and they'd set up a white backdrop at the far end of the room to take photos of each of the outfits. Ready or not, the second most important day of Hollie's life was about to begin.

'What time are hair and make-up arriving?' asked Ola.

'Quarter past ten, so they've got time to set up before the models need them,' said Maddy.

'Thanks,' said Hollie, her heart thudding in her chest. 'So if Tate and Liam, you could help me with styling the models, then Astin and Jack you help Fayth with the photos. We'll want photos of the outfits to go with each outfit on the day and for social media.'

'Why am I on photo duty? Something wrong with my fashion sense?' said Jack, gesturing to his t-shirt, which featured a neon print of the Sagrada Familia.

Hollie stared at him blankly. 'You know the answer to that. And it's because you're more photogenic and have done a lot of modelling.'

He framed his face in a *Vogue* pose. 'You think I'm photogenic?'

'You're very photogenic, dear,' said Tate, patting his shoulder.

'Are you being sarcastic?' He turned to Hollie: 'Do you think she's being sarcastic?'

'I'd never be sarcastic,' said Tate, a wry smirk creeping over her face.

'Sure sure,' said Jack.

'Right, are we ready to get started?' said Hollie.

'Let's do this!' said Tate. If only Hollie could muster up her enthusiasm.

*

'Your first model has arrived,' said Francisco, walking in with her in tow. 'Can I get you a drink?'

'No, thank you,' she said with a bright smile.

Francisco bowed out, leaving them ready to set up.

'I love your hair,' said Hollie. She had thick, dark hair that was tightly curled.

'Thanks. I'm happy to straighten it if you want me to.'

'No no, that won't be necessary,' said Hollie. She studied the clothing rack, running her fingers along the outfits. Her hand fell on a PVC minidress and matching black trench coat. 'Try this,' she said, handing it to the model.

Tate led her into the changing room, where Maddy and Ola would help with the fittings.

When the model had disappeared into another room, Hollie exhaled. Fayth came from the kitchen and passed her a coffee. When had she even left the room? Was she really paying so little attention? 'Thanks,' said Hollie.

'Don't worry, it'll be fine,' said Fayth.

'Uh-huh,' said Hollie, taking a few sips of the coffee. She couldn't handle much more; swallowing was difficult. Her body seemed to want to keep out any form of sustenance.

The model emerged, strutting the length of the studio. Hollie shook her head. 'It doesn't work,' she said.

'Why not?' said Fayth.

'It's too…I don't know. Something is off.' Hollie pursed her lips. She returned to the clothes rack and took out a dress with a corset top and tutu bottom. It was white with orange and pink polka dots on it. 'Try this,' she said, passing it to the model.

A blonde model with poker-straight hair and incredible cheekbones joined them shortly after. She would look *perfect* in the PVC dress and coat. Hollie asked Ola and Maddy to change her into that as the first model emerged wearing the tutu dress. She looked amazing.

'I love it,' said Tate. 'Her hair goes so well with the outfit. It balances out. And the waist on that dress! Gorgeous!'

'I want your hair,' said Jack as she walked past him.

'Focus, sweetie!' said Tate.

'I *am* focusing. I'm deciding which angles will work best for her when we photograph her outfit, while also being jealous that my hair will never look that good.'

Hollie ignored him and addressed the model. 'Your hair is gorgeous as it is, so we'll keep it like this. As for make-up, keep it minimal. Pink lip, white eyes.'

'Will that work with the other outfits she wears?' said Tate. 'We need to stick with one hair and make-up look for each model, remember.'

'Good point,' said Hollie. 'We'll make a note of that idea, then decide on the rest of the outfits first.' She took a white suit from the collection and handed it to her. 'Try this on.'

*

By the end of the day, they had ten models in four outfits each. The hair and make-up was done, and the photos were taken. Hollie was emotionally and physically drained, and she wanted nothing more than to curl up into a ball and sleep. But she couldn't – there were adjustments to be made. She stayed up all night, bringing this in, taking that out, moving things a centimetre this way or that. By the time she was done, she could barely see straight. She'd get an earful from everyone for staying at the studio all night, but the door was locked and she didn't have her earphones in. She would've heard if a lunatic had tried to break-in. Her crazy eyes would likely be enough to scare them off anyway. When she went into the bathroom, her mascara – that had been applied almost 24 hours earlier – was halfway down her face. All her other make-up had moved, too. Her face was contoured in all the wrong places, and her sparkly eyeshadow gave her a sparkly chin. She took a make-up wipe from the cupboard in the bathroom and removed it all. She looked even worse after having taken it off. Her skin was red and blotchy; her eyes were swollen and puffy; the purple bags underneath her eyes were bigger than ever.

She looked better than she felt, though. Her body ached in weird places like her arse and the bottom of her foot. Her jaw was so tight she was pretty sure she'd have no teeth left if she kept grinding them like she was.

Just a few more days. She could make it. She had to.

THREE

The models were in place. Tate was ready to go. Hollie couldn't breathe.

Fayth rubbed her back. 'You've got this. You can do this.'

Hollie's throat was too tight for her to respond. She'd spent her whole life working towards this moment. If it didn't go according to plan, what would she do? Would that be the end of her fashion career before it had ever really begun?

Fayth guided Hollie to a chair behind the curtain. That was the only thing blocking them from the audience's view. They could hear the crowd murmuring in the background. Were they reading the PR materials she'd spent weeks writing, or had they discarded them already?

There was a 10-minute break between each show, giving them time to set up and the models time to get changed. That break was almost over.

Hollie sat down, burying her head in her hands. The musky smell of the models' perfumes mixing together made her want to throw up. Why were they spraying it so fucking liberally? They wouldn't even be in those outfits for very long.

The black linoleum stared back at her. Blackness. Nothingness. Oh, how amazing it would be if she could go back to feeling nothing. Feeling nothing was better than feeling everything. Being afraid of everything. You can't be afraid if you can't feel. Fear cripples. But as much as she wanted to curl up into a ball until it was all over, she couldn't. It was her show. It needed her to run.

Someone tapped her on the shoulder. She looked up. Maddy was holding out a glass of water for her.

'Thanks,' said Hollie with a meek smile. Was she really pathetic enough that people needed to bring her water?

'I need to go set up for the photos. Will you be all right?' said Fayth.

'Yep. I'll be fine,' said Hollie. She looked down at the glass of water. She'd drunk the whole thing in the time it had taken Fayth to speak two sentences.

Fayth gave Hollie a quick hug. 'Remember: you can do this.' She gave Hollie's arm one last squeeze. 'Keep an eye on her,' she mumbled to Maddy before disappearing.

Maddy checked her watch. 'ONE MINUTE!' she shouted. Oh god. Hollie needed to throw up. She shouldn't have chugged that water. 'Ready to go?' she asked Hollie.

It wasn't like she had a choice. Everything depended on her. The event wouldn't even be happening if it wasn't for her. Maybe that would've been for the best. Why hadn't she thought of that before? Was it really too late to cancel?

The ten models queued beside her in their first outfits. They each had four quick changes that had to be timed perfectly. Forty outfits that needed to be ready to go. Forty outfits that if they weren't perfect now, never would be.

She wiped her sweaty palms on her leather skirt. It did nothing to help.

Tate appeared at the front of the queue wearing the silver playsuit Hollie had created for her *Comet* music video. The design that had launched Hollie's career. Hollie looked at it almost a year later and wanted to change the hem by a couple of inches, adjust the shoulder so that it sat slightly differently on Tate's slender frame. But, as with everything else, it was too late.

'Ready?' said Tate.

Hollie forced a nod. If she spoke, there was every chance she'd throw up. Tate would perform for the duration of the show, but in some sections she'd be blacked out so that people focused on the outfits and not on her. She'd start off by singing *Comet*, move on to one of her more upbeat songs, then finish with a cover of Taylor Swift's *Style*. If all went well, the transition between the songs would be seamless. Was it really a good idea to have her out there the whole time? Would they be more interested in her than the outfits?

Tate kissed Hollie's cheek. 'Break a leg!' She ran onto the darkened stage. Showtime.

*

Fayth stood in front of the stage. After everything Hollie had been through, she was about to do her first real fashion show. She was so proud! Fayth had expected her to hire a professional photographer, but Hollie had insisted on Fayth taking the photos. Fayth couldn't have been more honoured.

She positioned herself at the end of the catwalk, just to the left. The room wasn't full, but it wasn't empty, either. For a fashion showcase of unknown designers, it was a decent turnout. Some of that turnout was likely to be Tate's influence, but what was the point in her investing if she wasn't willing to get people to turn up to events?

More people trickled in through the doors as the start time grew closer. The show would start any minute. Was Hollie OK? She'd looked bad. Really bad. The last few months had really taken their toll on her. If Hollie could make it through the fashion show, maybe then she'd finally rest. Maybe they'd have to force her to rest. Fayth would happily find a way to do that if it stopped Hollie from burning out any more than she already had.

Another photographer pushed into her, forcing her chest into the sharp edge of the catwalk. Fuck. She turned to glare at the person responsible, but he'd already walked off. Arsehole. She massaged her winded chest. It would not stop her from taking the best photos she'd ever taken for Hollie's defining moment.

The room plunged into darkness. It was filled with silence. Then, the opening chords of *Comet* started. A spotlight focused in on Tate. She clicked to the music, her head bowed. She looked up, her eyes sparkling as she began to sing.

*

'Kiss me slow, kiss me fast, kiss me harder. Every time I see you, my heart flutters,' sung Tate.

Ugh. Yes. Astin did make her heart flutter. Fashion shows, on the other hand, made her nauseous. Thank fuck she hadn't had breakfast.

The models came offstage, high-fiving her as they went past. All seemed to be going well. Just ten more minutes to survive. She could do that.

Maddy tapped her on the shoulder. 'One of the straps has broken on Alicia's dress.'

'You're joking?' As if there wasn't enough to worry about already. She and Maddy ran over to Alicia. The strap on her dress was indeed broken. It was a flimsy thing, but that shouldn't have mattered.

'I'm sorry!' said Alicia in her thick Spanish accent.

'It's not your fault,' said Hollie. It was her stupid fault for using such flimsy fabric. She'd thought it would hold for a couple of minutes on a catwalk. Apparently not. 'Have we got scissors?'

Maddy held out a pair.

'Perfect.' With no time to mess about, Hollie cut the strap off. 'Think you can hold it?'

'Sure thing,' she said.

The top of the dress was structured, but the flimsy straps offered extra security. They didn't add anything to the outfit itself.

'I'll have to cut the other one off to make it even,' said Hollie.

'Go for it.'

'Thirty seconds before she needs to go out,' said Maddy.

Hollie cut the other strap off. 'Change your poses at the end if you have to.'

Alicia nodded, then ran towards the door.

'Feeling OK?' asked Maddy.

'Nope,' said Hollie. Her mouth was drier than the Sahara. Had she really chugged a whole glass of water just a few minutes ago? She needed to keep going. In ten minutes it would all be over. Weeks, months, *years* of work, and it would all be over. Then what? What would she do then? Was this really what she wanted to do for the rest of her life?

*

Tate finished singing. The spotlight on her went off. The models stepped out, clapping as they walked around the catwalk. Tate joined the end of the queue. The models lined up at the back of the stage. Tate remained on the catwalk, a huge grin on her face. 'Ladies and gentlemen, the woman behind it all, Hollie Baxter!'

The crowd cheered. Everyone looked in the direction of where the models had emerged, but nobody came out. Where was she? It was her big moment. She wouldn't miss it. Not unless…

Astin looked over at Fayth, who was stood at the front, posed ready to take Hollie's photo. Fayth turned to look at him as if to say, *do you know where she is?* He shrugged in response. Where *was* she? Liam, Jack, and Wade, who were sat with him on the second row, were just as confused. Shit.

The applause began to slow as people exchanged murmurs.

Then, she appeared. And she looked pale. Paler than he'd ever seen her. Ghostly pale. *Worryingly* pale. Her shoulders were hunched, and even in flats she could barely walk.

Astin shifted forwards in his seat. There was something off about her.

'I…' She began. It looked like forming just that one syllable caused her pain. 'Thank…you…'

Something definitely wasn't right.

Hollie clutched on to Tate, who put her arm around her and beamed. Hollie's legs gave way. Tate caught her before she hit the floor. People gasped; cameras flashed.

Astin catapulted out of his seat, leaping over the barrier to get to her. Tate lowered her onto the stage with the help of Fayth, who'd climbed onto the stage too.

The door opened and the audience were ushered out. Some tried to stay in their seats, but Wade, Maddy, and the venue's staff were quick to start escorting people out. The models hovered awkwardly on the catwalk.

'Careful,' said Tate as Astin went to pick her up.

'Well then what do we do?' he snapped.

'Has anyone called for an ambulance?'

'They're on their way,' said Liam. He stood by the front row, his face knitted with concern. Jack and Wade stood beside him looking just as worried.

'Thanks,' said Fayth.

Cameras continued to flash.

'Don't y'all have any decency?' growled Astin into the crowd.

'Actually,' said Tate, crouching down to whisper into his ear. 'In terms of marketing...'

He glared at her. 'Are you fucking serious?'

'We both know she'd agree.'

She would. But that didn't mean he liked it. Hollie was unconscious in a room full of people who seemed to revel in her pain. It wasn't the time to be thinking about how best to market her fashion line. Her fashion line was the reason she was unconscious.

He turned around and noticed one of the models pointing her camera right at them. 'You'd better not be recording right now.'

She took a few steps back. She was. She so fucking was. Rage boiled inside him. He ran over to her and snatched the phone from her hands. Sure enough, it was recording. It took all his strength not to break it. His jaw tight, he deleted the video and shoved it back at her. 'Get the fuck out of here.' She scurried away, clearly terrified of him. Good. 'Anyone else want to film?' he snapped to the rest of the models. Maddy began to guide them backstage.

He ran back over to Hollie and crouched by her side. 'Please wake up,' he begged, neatening her hair with his hand. 'Please.'

Four

Fayth paced the small space in front of Hollie's hospital room. 'I failed her. I fucking failed her.'

Liam sat up in the cheap, plastic chair. 'How did you?'

'I promised her mum and nan I'd look after her! Letting her end up in hospital twice in one trip is not looking after her!'

'It's also not your fault,' said Liam, leaning back in the chair. He stretched his feet out. Fayth had to jump over them so that she didn't trip up as she paced. Was sticking his feet out his way of telling her to stop pacing? If so, it wouldn't work. She had to do *something* to get rid of all her nervous energy. Hollie was unconscious and in hospital and they had no idea why. The doctors suspected it was exhaustion, but they were doing tests just in case.

'What am I supposed to tell her mum and nan? I can't put it off much longer or they'll see it on the news!'

'I doubt Hollie's technophobic family will find out what happened to her online, and it's not like this will be all over the news channels.'

'It might be on the news, you never know! It involved Tate. It's not a small deal.'

Liam stood in front of Fayth and pulled her to him. 'No, but as much as we all love Hollie, it's not that big of a deal in the grand scheme of things.' He kissed the top of her head.

'But it is to her! She's spent her whole life working towards this! What if she never recovers?'

'Then it wasn't meant to be. Why don't you go and sit with her for a bit, give Astin a break?'

'I can't,' she said. 'I can't see her like that.'

He pulled her closer. Being in his arms offered her some comfort, but it didn't make her feel any less guilty. It had been her job to look after Hollie. She'd made a promise.

'Why don't you talk to her when she wakes up, then?' he suggested.

'About what?'

'Ask her what was going through her head; why she didn't talk to you.'

'I guess I could.'

'I think you should,' he said. 'It'll at least make you realise none of what happened is your fault.'

Would it? Or would it make her feel worse for not having noticed how bad Hollie really was?

'I never should've got a job while I was here. If I hadn't, I would've been able to keep a closer eye on her and—'

'If I recall, *she* told *you* to go and get a job so that you didn't hover.'

Goddamn him. He was right. Fayth glared. Liam beamed.

'I hate you,' grumbled Fayth.

'No you don't,' he said. 'Are you sure you don't want to go sit with her for a bit?'

'I can't.'

Liam cocked his head. Then he widened his eyes as he remembered why she was terrified of hospitals. Nothing good ever came out of her being in a hospital. The last time she'd been in hospital someone had just tried to kill them both. The time before that, her mum and sister had died in a car accident. Was it any wonder she was restless? 'It won't be like that this time,' he reassured her.

'You don't know that,' said Fayth. 'We don't know what's wrong with her. The doctors are just guessing. And besides, we both know the damage long-term stress can do. What's she done to herself? Why did we let it get this bad?'

*

Beep. Beep. Beep.

Oh no.

Was that…hospital beeping?

'How long until she wakes up?' asked Astin.

Hollie tried to open her eyes, but her eyelids wouldn't budge. Her mouth wouldn't open and let her speak, either. She was there! She was right there!

'She'll wake up when she's ready,' said another voice. He had a Catalan accent. Was he a doctor?

'What does that mean? You don't know?' said Astin. She couldn't hear the sounds of other people's monitors or talking, which meant she must have her own room. Good. The last thing she wanted was other people around her. She hated people around her at the best of times, let alone when her body didn't even want to let her open her eyes so that she could see what was going on.

'She's exhausted. Her body needs time to repair itself,' said the unfamiliar voice.

Astin sighed. A door closed. Footsteps echoed. Silence.

Someone – Astin? – touched her hand. 'I don't know if you can hear me, but…I just…I'm sorry. For everything. Please don't leave me. I need you. I was wrong when I said I'd lost everything after the accident. I didn't lose everything until I lost you.' He paused. It sounded like he was crying. 'Even if you hate me, even if you never forgive me, please don't give up. Please wake up. Please.' He let go of her hand. There was no doubt he was crying.

'I don't hate you,' Hollie croaked. By some miracle, her body had chosen just the right moment to start functioning again, even if every word she spoke felt like her vocal chords were being forced against a cheese grater.

'Hollie!' Astin jumped up from the chair beside the bed and hugged her. She reached up and put her arms around him. His familiar scent of patchouli and citrus pulled her right back to that night in New York when they'd gone on their first date. He'd given her his leather jacket because she was cold. It had been a simple yet magical night. It still boggled her mind how much had changed since then. She tried to speak, but it turned into a cough because her throat was so dry. Astin pulled away and poured her a glass of water.

'Thanks,' she said after she'd taken a sip. 'What happened?'

She rubbed her eyes. That's when she saw it. A cannula was in the back of her hand, attached to a drip. Her eyes widened. Needle. Sort of.

'You passed out.'

'What?' she asked. Needle. Why was there a needle? No, wait. It wasn't a needle, technically. It put a hole in the back of her hand instead. Wait. That was just as bad. And wasn't that technically what a needle was?

'At the end of the fashion show,' said Astin.

'Oh god. I don't remember any of it. How long was I out?'

Neeeeeedle.

'A while.'

'Ugh,' she said, leaning back into the lumpy pillow and closing her eyes. What had she done?

Needle!

Astin reached over and rubbed her hand. The one without the needle in. She laced her fingers with his. Having him there was one of the few things that made the whole experience more bearable. Until she moved and felt the cannula in her hand move.

'Needle. Needle!'

'It's fine, it's fine!' insisted Astin.

'It's not,' she said, her heart rate increasing. 'Please get a nurse and get them to get me some sedatives. Or some sleeping tablets. Or take the needle out. I don't care, just do something about the needle!'

'OK, OK,' he said. He kissed her forehead then ran out into the corridor.

She closed her eyes. She had a cannula in her hand, which, to her mind, was even worse than a needle. The wound could get infected if it wasn't taken out properly. And it was sharp and pointy and she could feel it when she moved. There was no escaping it because she needed it but—

'Hollie?' said a nurse.

Hollie opened one eye. She held out her hands to demonstrate how much she was shaking.

'We'll get you some food and some mild sedatives,' said the nurse.

'Thank you,' said Hollie. The nurse left to get the food and sedatives. Astin returned to the chair beside her. 'Where is everyone?'

'Floating around somewhere.'

'What time is it?'

'Doesn't matter. You just focus on resting.'

Hollie scoffed. 'Resting? What's that?'

'Something it's about time you learned.'

FIVE

Fayth took a deep breath. She didn't want to see Hollie so weak, but she knew that Hollie would want to see her. Maybe seeing her would be reassuring. She might see that Hollie was perfectly fine and there was nothing to worry about. Ha. Not likely.

She walked into the room. Hollie was attached to a drip with a dopey look on her face.

'They gave me drugs,' said Hollie with a giggle.

'Sedatives,' corrected Astin as he stood up from the chair by the bed. 'I'll leave you two alone.' He put his hand on Fayth's arm as he walked past.

She was still pale and fragile-looking, but then that was Hollie's general look anyway. Most people wouldn't know the difference. It was only the people who truly knew her that could tell when something was wrong.

Fayth turned away and wiped a tear from her eye.

'Hey, don't cry,' said Hollie. 'I didn't want to make you cry.' She pouted.

'It's not…it's not you,' said Fayth. Although it kind of was. 'I just wish you'd come to me.'

Hollie hugged herself. 'I wish I hadn't dug myself into a trench so dirty and horrible I came out with trench foot.'

Only Hollie could make a self-deprecating joke about World War I while on sedatives. Fayth gave a small laugh. 'How are you feeling?'

'Meh,' said Hollie with a shrug. 'You should go home. You hate hospitals.'

'I know, but I love you more than I hate hospitals.' She bent over and hugged her friend. Hollie was awake. She was alive. She'd be OK. She had to be OK. Hollie hit Fayth's shoulder. 'Stop crying on me!'

'Sorry,' said Fayth, wiping her eyes. 'You really worried me.'

'I worried me, too. But when you're a high-speed train it's awfully hard to stop.'

'Then we need to turn you into a slow, rickety steam train.'

'Where's the fun in that?'

'You get to enjoy more of the scenery,' said Fayth. 'You should try it some time.'

Hollie frowned.

'Have you spoken to your nan?' said Fayth, changing the subject.

'Not yet. Thanks for telling them. I wasn't ready to speak to them.'

'No problem. I didn't want them to find out from someone else. I thought it was best coming from me.'

'Yeah.' Hollie sighed. 'I just wish they hadn't had to find out at all. Not that I didn't want you to tell them. Just that I hadn't ended up here.'

Fayth nudged her shoulder. 'Maybe next time you'll listen when someone tells you to rest.'

Hollie scoffed. 'Have we met?'

'Yeah, and it's about time your desire for success was balanced by a desire for rest or you're not going to make it to thirty.'

Hollie lowered her head.

Had she been too harsh? 'Sorry.'

'No, you're right,' said Hollie. 'I didn't think about what I was doing. I just needed to finish it. I needed to prove to myself that I could do it. Not to anyone else. Just me. I needed to prove to myself I wasn't the failure I was always told I was going to be.'

'Who told you you'd be a failure?'

'Society, because I came from a single-parent household. My so-called school friends, because I don't know. And my dad…'

'What?' Fayth sat on the edge of the bed.

'I heard him argue with my mum once. He said I'd never amount to anything. That I'd only ever do just enough to get by.' She wiped at her eyes with the hand that didn't have the cannula in the back of it. 'Do you think that's why he left? Because he had a failure of a daughter?'

'No! He left because he was a wanker.'

Hollie laughed. It was the biggest laugh Fayth had seen from her in months. It was a magical sound. If only it hadn't come from such a horrible conversation.

'Anyone who thinks you'll never amount to anything doesn't know you as well as they think they do. You're the most ambitious, driven person I know. Don't ever lose that.'

Hollie gave a meek smile. 'I won't.'

'But maybe just learn when to put the brakes on,' added Fayth with a chuckle.

'Yeah, that might help.'

'"Might"?' echoed Fayth.

'Well, you know. Hopefully next time I won't work quite so hard. I'll just drive a bit slower.'

'That's my girl.'

*

After food and drugs, Hollie felt mildly better. Her anxiety had calmed somewhat, and she no longer focused on the sharp, pointy object in the back of her hand. It being there still made her uncomfortable, but she was too drugged up to care. And distracted by the fact that Astin was still there. Didn't he have something more interesting to do? He didn't even have a book with him. He always had a book with him! She kept trying to raise it with him, but he ignored her. Then, just as she was drifting off to sleep, he handed her the phone. She hadn't even heard it ring.

'Who is it?' she asked.

'Your nan.'

Oh god.

Hollie took the phone from him. 'Hi Nan.'

'What did I tell you about looking after yourself?' said her nan.

'I did. Sort of.'

'Ending up in hospital in a foreign country twice in a month isn't looking after yourself.'

'It was longer than a month!'

'Barely,' growled her nan. 'And that doesn't change my point.'

'I'm sorry,' she said, hanging her head.

'You worried us.'

'I'm all right.' She leaned back in bed, her head throbbing. Stupid body. Stupid brain. Why had she put herself through all that?

'What did the doctor say?'

'I haven't seen him yet. I'm on a drip and sedated because of the stupid thing in the back of my hand.'

'And how do you feel?'

'Meh.' She sat up. Why couldn't she get comfortable? Oh, because hospital beds were like sleeping on rocks. Apparently that didn't change regardless of what country you were in.

'Are they looking after you?'

Hollie glanced over at Astin, who was clearly eavesdropping. She smiled. He winked. Her heart fluttered. Goddamn he was cute. 'Uh-huh.'

'Good. I'll kick your arse when you get home then.'

'Do you have to?'

'You should listen to me then. You should know by now – Nan knows best.'

'Not always.'

'I beg your pardon! When does your nan not know best?'

Fashion. Technology. Music. Film… 'Never mind.'

'Exactly. Now go get some rest and I'll talk to you soon.'

'Yes Nan. Bye Nan.'

'Bye sweetheart.'

Hollie hung up and passed the phone back to Astin. 'Your Nan's cute,' he said.

'Yeah, she is,' said Hollie with a smile. Her nan had always had good people instincts, and she'd always liked Astin. She hadn't judged his actions after the break up, just listened while Hollie talked. Was that intentional? Was she leaving it for Hollie to judge the situation herself? Knowing her, that was exactly what she was doing.

'You should go get some sleep,' said Hollie. 'The nurses will kick you out soon.'

'No they won't,' said Astin with a smirk.

'Sleeping here won't do you any good. You're still healing too.'

'I let you go twice. I won't make that mistake again,' said Astin.

She reached out and touched his hand. 'I let you go too. But what you went through is a hell of a lot more serious than this. I'm not the only one who's been too hard on themselves.'

He'd been at the gym almost every day, giving his body little time to rest in between. Would that cause further damage to his back, or was it helping to rebuild its strength?

'I needed an outlet for my stress,' he confessed.

'I'm sorry for causing some of it.'

He gave her a meek smile.

'Go home and get some sleep. We've got the rest of our lives to sleep together.'

Astin's face lit up. 'You mean that?'

Hollie smiled. 'Only if you bugger off and get some sleep now.'

He hopped up from his chair and kissed her. 'See you in the morning.'

*

Hollie clung to the back of Fayth's jumper. Why had she insisted on taking the sodding stairs back to their apartment? Exercise was so overrated.

The doctors had kept her in for a couple of days so that they could run some tests, rehydrate her, and make sure everything was working OK. After running numerous tests they concluded she was suffering from exhaustion and dehydration. Through the drip – *shudder* – they'd rehydrated her with some fancy electrolyte thingies. They'd then sent her home on the condition that she rested. Pfft. Rest. Rest was for the elderly.

Astin put his hand on Hollie's back, half pushing her up the stairs. Hollie turned back to look at him and glared. She wasn't walking *that* slowly.

'Just making sure you don't fall,' said Astin, moving his hand only slightly away from her.

Fayth unlocked the door. Liam, Tate, and Jack ran over to her and hugged her.

'We're so glad you're OK!' said Tate. Hollie was surprised she was at the apartment. Things must've been bad if she was willing to return. Did that mean she was living there again?

'Welcome home,' said Liam.

Jack flashed her a sombre smile.

'Thanks,' said Hollie. 'Do you mind if I go lie down?'

'Course not,' said Fayth. She gave Hollie a hug then let her go.

Astin guided her into her room then helped her onto the bed. He sat beside her.

'Why'd you do it?' she asked, hugging her knees.

'Do what?' he said, sitting on the end of the bed.

'Stay at the hospital until I woke up.'

'You know why.'

'But…after everything?'

'You're the one that shouldn't love me, not the other way around.'

She hugged her knees tighter. 'Love fades.'

'No it doesn't. Not real love. Not the kind of love that you'd do anything for. The kind of love that makes you fall asleep smiling, and wake up happy because you know you'll never be alone. Not the kind of love that we have.'

She turned to look at him. His blue, blue eyes were filled with love. 'Astin—'

He pressed his lips to hers. It lit a fuse within her, running through her body until she burned with desire. He'd been there for her when she'd been clinging to the edge, just like she'd tried to be there for him. The difference was, she didn't want to push him away. She wanted to pull him closer; to hide under the duvet with him and only emerge when it was safe and everything had calmed down.

He pulled away, cupping her face with his hands. 'I'm sorry. I know saying it doesn't fix anything, but I need you to hear me say it. I'm sorry for how I treated you before. I took you for granted. I expected too much of you as a girlfriend, but pushed you too hard as a businessperson. I don't deserve you.'

She put her finger to his lips. 'We don't get what we deserve. We get what we earn.' She removed her finger from his lips and placed her hand on his lap. 'I left because I couldn't trust you any more. I didn't know you any more. And you know what? Maybe we moved too fast. But we were young. Naive.'

'No we weren't. I was just a dick.' He stroked the side of her face. She leaned in to him, his touch gentle against her skin. 'When your nan had her stroke, you dropped everything. You always drop everything when someone you love needs you. But when you did that for me, instead of being grateful, I slammed the door in your face. So when Tate invited me to be there for Liam, I wanted to follow your example even if seeing you again would be hard.'

'And was it?'

'It was like being stabbed repeatedly in the gut.'

'You should help Luke write boy band lyrics with lines like that,' she teased.

He chuckled. She'd missed that laugh. Oh, how she'd missed it. His lips still curled into a smile, she leaned forwards and kissed him.

Six

'So, how's my favourite fashion designer?' Jack asked, hopping onto the bed and lying beside Hollie.

'Meh,' said Hollie with a shrug. She picked up the coffee Liam had made her from the bedside table and took a few gulps. It was decaf, but it was better than nothing.

Jack stole the mug from her hands and took a few sips. 'Ew. This isn't coffee. This is warm milk.'

'It's a decaf latte,' she corrected him.

'Like I said: warm milk.'

'I didn't ask you to drink it,' said Hollie, taking the mug back from him and hugging it to her.

'You know, you and Astin are more alike than you think,' said Jack.

Hollie scoffed. 'Sure we are.'

'You're both too hard on yourselves,' he said.

Hollie frowned.

'Don't frown at me just 'cause you know I'm right,' he said with a cheeky smirk on his face.

'Pot, kettle.'

'Yeah, well. How do you think I'm so good at identifying these things in other people?'

Hollie put her coffee down and reached for her phone.

'What you checking that for? You haven't missed anything,' said Jack, taking her phone from her hands and putting it on the other side of the bed, out of her reach, before she'd even had a chance to unlock it.

'I do have friends and family outside of Barcelona, you know.'

'Fayth's keeping them updated, don't you worry about that,' said Jack.

'How do you know?'

'I heard her on the phone to your mom earlier. And she mentioned texting some guy called Cameron, whom I vaguely remember you mentioning before. So you see? Nothing to worry about. Just let it aaaaaaall wash over you.'

Hollie sighed. 'Wish I could. Even now my mind is still racing and refuses to switch off.'

'Have you tried compartmentalising?'

'What do you mean?'

'Tell yourself that you won't worry about this on this day, and you won't worry about that on that day. Allot times to worry about different things, then when you're done, move on to resting or getting shit done.'

'Is that what worked for you?'

'No. More drugs worked for me. But yeah, therapy helped too.'

*

Hollie spent the next few days resting. She'd never spent so little time away from her phone, but she kind of liked it. Eventually, though, she had to return to reality. Her stiff joints protested as she stretched across the sofa. With a yawn, she grabbed her neglected phone. Fayth slid onto the sofa beside her, as silent as a ninja. 'Whatcha doing?'

Hollie eyed her warily. Fayth didn't talk like that. 'What do you want?'

'Nothing!'

'You sound very suspicious.'

'Me? Never.'

'Right now you do. What's up?'

'Just wondered if you wanted to go for a coffee.'

'You don't drink coffee. And I need to check social and emails. I'm behind enough as it is.'

'Maddy's monitoring them. Take some actual time off for once.'

'What's that supposed to mean?'

'It means you just got out of hospital and the doctors told you to rest,' said Fayth.

'I have been resting! I can't afford for things to fall any further behind.'

'But why didn't you ask for more help? Why did you let things get so bad?'

Hollie returned her phone to the coffee table. Why hadn't she asked for more help? She'd known she was overworked. She could still feel it physically and mentally. She wasn't sure if she ever wanted to look at a sewing machine ever again. 'I guess I had no idea how much work it would actually be until I got in too deep.

Then I was in so deep that I couldn't see a way out – I just had to keep going.'

'That doesn't explain why you didn't ask for more help though. Why didn't you hire more people? Or ask us?'

'When did this become a therapy session?'

'Sorry. I'll stop.'

'It's a valid question I guess. I didn't want to bother the rest of you. You and Liam were having fun exploring Barcelona, Tate and Maddy were already doing so much, and things with Astin were…complicated. I never really thought about hiring more people to take the load off. I'm not business-minded like you are.'

Fayth snorted. 'I'm not business-minded, I just paid attention to what Mum and Dad did when they ran the pub. If things got too busy – like during the summer – they'd hire extra help. All the students that were back from uni and were desperate for cash were the perfect temps.'

'See now that makes sense. But I just…' She sunk farther down the sofa and rested her feet on Fayth's lap. 'Maybe I'm not cut out for this.'

'Cut out for what?'

'Running my own business. Maybe I should work as a Creative Director somewhere instead.'

'You're forgetting something,' said Fayth.

'What?'

'To work for someone else you have to like being told what to do.'

Hollie glared at her.

'You know I'm right.'

She was. She so was. Hollie *hated* being told what to do by other people. She liked to be in control. She preferred to call it tenacity over stubbornness. But still. She wouldn't last five minutes in a traditional nine-to-five. But could she cut it being self-employed for the rest of her life?

'Maybe I need to rethink my business plan. And, you know, pay more attention to it.'

'Paying attention to it always helps.'

Hollie picked up her phone.

'What are you doing?'

'Checking Twitter.'

'Why? It's not healthy to be on social media all the time.'

'All right, what am I missing? You're clearly trying to keep me away from my phone.'

'No I'm not.'

'You suck at lying. Every time I've reached for my phone lately someone seems to be on me. You, Astin, Liam, Tate, Maddy. Even Jack. What's going on? Why are you keeping me away from my phone?'

'I'm not!'

Hollie narrowed her eyes. She picked up her phone and opened Twitter. Her personal profile had so many notifications it was stuck at 20+. How many would the company account have? She opened the notifications. It was full of people commenting on her passing out onstage. Some were sympathetic. Most weren't.

Fayth put her arms around Hollie. 'We wanted to protect you for as long as possible.'

'Well at least your weird behaviour makes sense now.' It had been like there was a conspiracy to keep her away from her phone and laptop for as long as possible. Initially she'd assumed it was because she needed to rest. Turned out there was more to it. 'Thanks.' Sighing, Hollie got up and went into her room. She needed to be alone.

*

Masochist that she was, Hollie spent the next couple of hours reading reviews of her fashion show. Almost all of them were negative or indifferent. Even the more positive ones seemed to end on a negative note. She'd burned herself out for nothing. They hated her designs. They hated *her*.

Hollie Baxter: from breakthrough to boring

Hollie Baxter's first fashion show reeks of desperation. Her show doesn't hold a candle to the trend-setting outfit she designed for Tate Gardener's Comet *music video. Is she a one-trick pony? Has she been buoyed up by the false hope of her celebrity friends? It's pretty clear to us she should stick to designing clothes for the people in the small town where she grew up and save the trendsetting for her celebrity friends.*

The range lacked any real cohesion. Unless the angle she was going for was confused. If that's the case, she nailed it.

Unable to read any more, Hollie threw her phone across the bed. It landed just on the edge, then slipped and thudded onto the floor. Hollie burst into tears. Metaphor, much? She'd teetered on the edge for months. Then she'd slipped and crashed. HARD. And the whole fucking world had seen. She was a meme. A goddamn meme. And not even a complimentary one. How was she supposed to deal with that? What was she supposed to do next? They'd called her boring. Boring! She'd never been called boring in her life! Not to her face, anyway. Was that really how the outside world saw her?

Tears streamed down her face. Everything she'd spent her life working towards was ruined. Fucking ruined by her fucking stupidity. By her desire to do everything. By her desperate need to prove to herself that she wasn't a failure. That she could do what she wanted to, despite what people used to say about her. They'd always said when she was at school that she was all ideas but no execution. Well, she'd proved that she *could* do something: run full-force into a tornado.

'Bear? Are you OK?' called Astin's voice from the other side of the door. At the sound of him using the pet name he'd given her, Hollie cried even harder. Her body convulsed as she sobbed. She was crying too much to respond. Astin entered, saw her crying, and ran over. He didn't ask her what was wrong. Fayth had probably told him that she'd seen the comments. He joined her on the bed and pulled her into him without a word. And, in that moment, that was exactly what she needed.

*

Hollie fell asleep curled up beside Astin. When she woke up, his head was resting against hers. His warm breath tickled her neck. She needed to move as her neck was stiff, but she didn't want to wake him up. Slowly, she shifted downwards. He opened his eyes.

'Sorry. Didn't mean to wake you up.'

'I wasn't asleep,' he said.

An awkward silence fell. It was clear he wanted to talk about why she'd been so upset, but she wasn't sure that she was ready. But would getting it out of her system help? Was that why Fayth had encouraged her to talk?

She turned around and hugged her knees. 'They called me boring,' she mumbled.

'How much did you read?'

'Enough to make me wonder why I'm even bothering. Especially after what happened. Is this really what I want to do for the rest of my life?'

'Only you know that.'

But did she? She was so confused. It was all she'd ever wanted. All she'd spent the last fifteen years of her life wanting more than anything else. But when she'd finally done it, it hadn't been what she'd expected. She'd spent years living in a fantasy. And now that the illusion was shattered, she wasn't sure she could live with what was left. What was she supposed to do? Everyone kept looking to her for answers as if she knew how to fix things. She most definitely didn't.

'I don't, though. That's the problem,' said Hollie.

'You will.'

'When? Where? How? I don't have time to sit and stew. I have too much relying on me.'

'Like what?'

'My customers expect stuff from me. I have orders to fulfil.'

'Why don't you outsource then?'

Hollie scoffed.

'I'm serious. You need a break. That's why outsourcing exists. You can't do everything forever. Hell, you can't even do it now.' He stroked her hair. 'Please, Bear, at least consider it.'

'But I don't want to outsource stuff,' she said.

'So, what? You're going to push yourself to exhaustion every day? You know that's not practical.'

'So what am I supposed to do?'

He shrugged. 'Cancel your orders. Quit while you're ahead.'

'You think I should give up? That I shouldn't have even bothered with that stupid fucking fashion show?'

'No!' He crossed his arms. 'Why can't you accept that you made a mistake and learn from it for once?'

Hollie huffed. She hadn't made a mistake. She'd just gone about things the wrong way.

'You think I'm a failure, is that it?'

'You know me better than that.'

'Do I? Do I really know you at all?'

Astin stood up. 'Of course you do.'

'Maybe I don't. Maybe you just want me to think that I know you.'

He shook his head. 'Can you hear yourself right now?' He walked out, leaving her to ruminate in her self-pity.

*

Fayth was sat on the sofa playing *MarioKart* when Astin emerged from Hollie's bedroom. 'What happened?'

'I don't know what to do any more.' He sat beside her. 'Just as I start to feel like she might give me another chance, she picks a fight with me again.'

Fayth turned off her 3DS and spun around to face him. 'I wish I could say something to help, but I don't know what to say. I don't know where her head is.'

Astin sighed. 'Am I being naive? Should I give up?'

'She loves you. I know that much.'

Astin wiped at his eyes with his fist. He would not start to cry because Hollie was being unfair again.

'But,' started Fayth. She stopped herself.

'But what?' probed Astin.

'Well, you did kinda do the same thing to her.'

'So, what, this is revenge?'

'No! Hollie isn't that petty. But you understand what she's going through. She's beating herself up for something that didn't go how it was supposed to. Doesn't that sound familiar?'

'She's not in a wheelchair,' grumbled Astin.

'Not physically, but emotionally she's a wee bit drained right now. What did you want when you felt like that?'

He clutched the edge of the sofa. What had he wanted? Sometimes he'd wanted alone time, but he'd mostly just wanted to punch something. And...and what? He'd been so shut off from everything and everyone, but that was his own doing. Was there anything he could do to stop Hollie from doing the same thing to herself?

He marched back into Hollie's room. She was curled up in the foetal position, sobbing. He curled up behind her. At first, she didn't move. After a few seconds, she snuggled into him, pulling his arms around her and hugging them to her chest.

SEVEN

With just a few days left in Barcelona, Liam was keen to explore as much as possible on his jogs. There was always somewhere left to go, something new to see. As it got closer to tourist season, the weather warmed up and there were more people around every day. Liam and Wade were jogging back to the apartment when they heard someone shouting.

'You killed her! You killed her!'

Liam upped his jogging pace. Were they talking to him? Wade kept up with him, his eyes and ears on the lookout. They weren't that far from the apartment. They just needed to make it past the Sagrada Familia, through Park Güell, then down their street. They could be rid of the shouting person by then, right?

'Hey! I'm talking to you, Liam York!'

Shit.

He upped his jog to a sprint. It wasn't enough.

A small, round woman blocked their path. Liam and Wade skidded to a halt. 'Are you deaf?' she said. 'I was calling you.'

'I…'

'What? Am sorry for killing Trinity?'

'I didn't kill her. She fell because she was standing on the terrace wall and lost her balance,' he said.

'So you didn't push her?' The woman snorted. 'Right.'

'If you don't mind, we have somewhere else to be,' said Wade, taking Liam's arm and starting to guide him away.

'Actually, I *do* mind,' said the woman, keeping up pace with them. How was someone so small and round so fast? 'He needs to be held accountable for his actions.'

'What actions!' said Liam. 'I didn't *do* anything!' What was this, trial by social media? It had been two months! How much longer did people need before they let it go?

Wade shoved Liam into a tourist bus and followed him inside. He blocked the door so that the woman couldn't get on while Liam paid. The bus pulled away a few seconds later, but it felt like an age. The woman glared as the bus drove away, her middle finger stuck up at them. How many people felt like her but weren't willing to be so public about it? Did his former fans really hate him that much?

Liam exhaled. They were inside the tourist bus but that didn't mean everything was fine. Any one of the people on the – admittedly quiet – bus could start blaming him for Trinity's death. It wasn't enough for them that he blamed himself. Oh no – they had to remind him that it really was his fault. They blamed the fact that he'd dumped her. They blamed the fact that he couldn't help her. They blamed the fact that his reflexes weren't fast enough to grab her before she fell.

He took out his phone and opened Twitter. There it was already – a video of the woman shouting at him and blaming him for Trinity's death. That hadn't taken long. That hadn't taken long at all.

*

Liam held a bottle of 2011 Dominio de Pingus in front of him. He'd stopped off on his way home and bought the most expensive wine he could find. He couldn't get that woman's face out of his head. Or the horrible way she'd spoken to him. It wasn't the first time he'd been spoken to like that, but it was the first time someone had accused him of murdering Trinity to his face after he'd been cleared by the police.

It would be so easy to numb the pain and confusion with alcohol or drugs. But how would that be any different to what he'd done after his sister's death? He knew all too well that that was a dangerous path. He didn't want to end up like Jack. Or Trinity.

Astin walked out from the bathroom. When he saw his friend, he narrowed his eyes. 'You all right?'

Was it really that obvious that something was wrong? 'Where is everyone?'

'Packing up the studio. Why?'

Liam put the bottle on the side. 'You know when you were on that morphine drip in the hospital?'

Astin cringed. Bringing that up was probably a bad idea. Oops. 'Barely, I was too drugged up,' said Astin.

'When you were on morphine, it didn't bother me. But now… every so often, I catch myself craving it again. I just don't know how to deal right now.' He ran his hand over his hair.

'Would anyone?'

Liam shrugged. 'I don't know.'

'It's a pretty unique situation. Most people aren't there when their ex dies.'

'Depends if they killed them or not.'

'You didn't kill Trinity.'

'No, but I couldn't save her. Isn't that just as bad?'

'You know it wasn't your job to save her, right?'

'Wasn't it?'

'No! She didn't want help. You can't help someone who doesn't want your help. She cried for help, but what she really wanted was attention. Whenever someone tried to be there for her she just threw it back in their faces. You not being able to save her isn't your fault. It never was, and it never will be.'

Liam wiped at his eyes as they filled with tears. 'She trusted me. I was the only one she trusted. That should've meant something.'

'And it did mean something. You know how many songs she wrote about you. Some of them are so romantic they make *me* cry. But that still doesn't mean it was your job to save her. Nobody can save anyone but themselves.'

Liam tilted his head. 'Yeah, I guess you're right. It was seeing my parents that made me want to go to rehab, but that wasn't what motivated me to get better.'

'What was it?'

'Getting arrested. I didn't want to end up in prison! I'd never survive!'

'That's true,' said Astin. 'Even now you still spend longer getting ready than I do.'

'I'm always worried I'll run into someone and they'll judge me if I don't look perfect.' He sighed. 'It's all I've ever known, but the last couple months have made me realise how much of a bubble I've been living in. I want to break out of that bubble.'

'Then do it,' said Astin.

'How? It's not that simple,' said Liam, putting the bottle of wine on the side.

'Sure it is. If I can break out of my comfort zone and admit I have enough of a problem to need counselling, you can break out of the Hollywood bubble,' said Astin.

'You went to therapy? You never said.'

'What can I say? I'm a Southerner.' He gave a sheepish laugh. 'I've been talking to someone online for the last few weeks. It made me realise that I would've healed faster if I hadn't been holding myself back. I was so busy feeling sorry for myself and wallowing in how my life was over I didn't think about the opportunities it could create.'

'What opportunities?'

He shrugged. 'Anything. Everything. One doctor told me I'd never be able to do stunt work again. Another said I could. Nobody's word is gospel.'

'So you're going to go back to stunt work?' asked Liam, resting his foot against the cabinet. Fayth would go mad if she found out he'd done that with shoes on, but she wasn't there.

'One day, maybe, but not right now. I have other things I want to do first. This has given me the chance to re-evaluate what I want in life.'

Liam smiled. 'You've been through more than you sometimes realise, you know.'

'Have I?' He shrugged. 'I don't know any better. To me it's just how things have always been. But I'm OK with that. I've said my peace with my parents. My grandparents and brother have forgiven me. And I hope Hollie will, too.'

'Now you just need to forgive yourself.'

'So do you,' said Astin, raising an eyebrow.

'When you figure out how, will you let me know?'

'I can try, but forgiving yourself for a stunt gone wrong is a different to forgiving yourself for not saving your ex-girlfriend,' said Astin.

'Is it? Or is forgiveness one of those things where, once you know how to do it, you can adapt it to any situation?' said Liam.

'I dunno. I've never been the forgiving type.'

'Are you saying you haven't forgiven your parents?'

Astin sighed. 'I'm not sure. If it wasn't for them I wouldn't be where I am now, but do I wish I had a normal childhood? Every day. It's all part of the journey though, right?'

Liam laughed. 'Man, you have had a lot of therapy.'

Astin picked a tea bag up from the box on the side and threw it at him. It hit his cheek and fell to the floor. 'Imagine how *you* sounded when you came out of rehab.'

'At least now you know where I was coming from.'

'Yeah, but it sounds better coming from me.'

Liam scoffed. 'You wish.'

*

Hollie stared around the studio. It was the last day of the lease. Time to pack everything up and get ready to head back to the UK.

In a week's time, she'd be living with her mum and nan again.

She'd taken Astin's advice and outsourced as much as she could. Her plan was to pull back, assess, and come back stronger. Everything had happened so fast in the last fourteen months that she hadn't had time to plan. The cyclone had grown faster and faster, and even with a few items in her inventory she couldn't keep up with what people wanted alone. She'd also stopped thinking about what *she* wanted.

It was drilled into her from her schooldays that you had to have all the answers straight away. There was no room to learn or to grow. But if you stuck by the same decisions you made when you left school, that meant being stuck in the same position for days, weeks, months, years. Indecision bred inactivity and boredom. And that wasn't the life she wanted. She wanted to adapt, to change, to be flexible. And whether that meant continuing down her current path or starting a new one, she was open to her options.

It wasn't about the mistake itself, it was about how she responded to it. Tate had helped her to outsource what she needed, giving Maddy more responsibility in the company so that they could both have some downtime. Tate had other staff that she could trust to pick up the slack; Hollie didn't.

The truth was, Hollie wasn't sure if she ever wanted to go back to sewing. She couldn't even look at her sewing machine. Sewing was her great love. It had always been there for her. But she'd worked herself into the ground with it. She'd pushed herself too hard and too fast, and for what? To create a confused line that was slated by the fashion industry.

Even though it was her own fault, she wasn't ready to go back to sewing yet. Her obsession with it had been what had led her down the rabbit hole. Until she found a way out, she wouldn't be able to sew again.

Fayth pointed to where the hole left by Hollie's scissors had once been. She'd filled it in a couple of days earlier and had just finished painting over it. 'What do you think?'

Hollie walked over to it. 'You can't even tell.'

Fayth grinned. 'Right? I think I did a pretty good job.'

'You did,' said Hollie, giving her a hug.

'So did you,' said Fayth.

Hollie scoffed.

'You *did*,' said Fayth. 'Most of those people badmouthing you wouldn't have the gumption or skills to do something like that themselves. Especially not at our age. They'd be too afraid.'

'I was bloody terrified.'

'But you did it anyway.'

'What does that say about me?'

Fayth rested her head against Hollie's shoulder. 'That no matter what happens, you'll be all right.'

Eight

Francisco and Ramira insisted on letting Fayth host her photography exhibition for free. They'd been so kind to her in the short time that she'd known them. She was glad she's left Regina K Photography and found them instead. She'd learned so much. While the gallery didn't do photoshoots, Francisco and Ramira had shared stories about their time taking photos for film stars, politicians, and even astronauts. They'd let her sit in on client meetings and take notes, and taught her more than she could've hoped for. Regina never would've done that for her.

It wasn't Fayth's first photography exhibition, but it was her first solo one. That was the scary part. There was nothing and nobody to hide behind this time: all the pressure was on her. It was no wonder Hollie had worked herself into the ground for her fashion show. Hollie had always been the type to put pressure on herself. And it had backfired. Fayth had tried to learn from her friend's mistakes and not work so hard, but she'd taken so many photos of things lately and still hated them all that she'd almost asked everyone else to pick out the photos to exhibit. The less to think about, the better.

In the end, she chose them herself with a little bit of help from Francisco and Ramira, since they knew the market better. When exhibition day arrived, Fayth had lost her appetite and didn't want to get out of bed. But once she got to the gallery and saw all her chosen photos displayed, she couldn't have felt more chuffed. Everything she'd done had paid off. Even if nobody turned up, she'd done it. She'd proven to herself that she was capable of doing something on her own. Sure, her friends had been by her side – and a few of the photos were of them – but she'd developed a skill all on her own.

'You did good, kid,' said Francisco, patting her on the back.

*

Hollie walked up to her best friend and hugged her. To see Fayth sharing her work so far away from home was a massive achievement. Just a couple of years ago, Fayth had been a homebody. She'd always planned to follow the same path since they'd met: marry her childhood sweetheart, work in the family pub, have two point four kids. While it had taken the loss of her mum and sister to make Fayth realise that wasn't what she wanted, Hollie knew they'd be happy for Fayth and how much she'd changed. Hollie couldn't be prouder. Not just of how far Fayth had come as a photographer, but of how much she'd grown in confidence, too. Even with people trying to belittle her and tell her she was worthless. Fayth had proven them wrong. Fayth had proven herself wrong.

She put her hands on Hollie's arms. 'Hey Bea.'

'Hey person I'm super proud of.'

Fayth slapped Hollie's arm.

'Don't hit me for paying you a compliment! I mean it. You don't pat yourself on the back enough. Let me do it for you.'

'If you must,' said Fayth.

'I must.'

'We must, too,' said a familiar voice.

Fayth turned around to see her dad and sister stood behind them, grinning. Fayth ran over to them and hugged them. 'What are you doing here?'

'What? You thought we'd miss your first solo photography exhibition? No way,' said her dad.

'Liam flew us over to surprise you,' said her sister Brooke.

Fayth hadn't expected them to travel to Barcelona just for her exhibition, but she was happy to see them there. After everything that had happened, it was about time her family had something to celebrate.

'So, what'd you think?' asked Fayth.

'Oh, I dunno. Some are all right,' said Brooke.

Fayth nudged her sister. Brooke grinned.

'They're wonderful,' said her dad.

*

Liam wandered around Fayth's exhibition, a smile plastered on his face. Her photos were so good. She'd always said that with her photos she wanted to get deep into people's hearts and minds. And she had.

He stopped in front of a photo of Hollie, Fayth, Astin, and himself. Fayth had put her camera on a timer to get the perfect shot of them on the beach. But it wasn't just a shot of a bunch of friends on vacation. They weren't posed awkwardly with their hands on each other's backs. They were looking at each other and laughing, but there was pain in their eyes, too. It was a photo of people who'd been through hell. Who were still going through hell. But who were determined to get out of it. He hadn't told her yet, but he'd purchased a copy of it to go in his apartment back in New York. He knew she'd give him a copy if she asked, but he didn't want that. He wanted to pay for it. He wanted to show her how much her work meant to him. It seemed like the perfect way to do it.

As he was walking over to her to tell her all that, his phone rang.

*

Liam sunk into a nearby chair. Just moments before, he'd been filled with positivity. One phone call had ruined everything.

Fayth came over and put her hand on his shoulder. 'What's wrong? You look like you saw a ghost.'

Liam scoffed. 'Funny you should say that.'

'What am I missing?' said Fayth.

'Do you know where the others are? They need to hear this too.'

'Is it that bad?' said Fayth. 'You wouldn't want everyone together if it wasn't bad.'

He stood up and held her hands. 'I'm sorry. I want to tell everyone at once, and it can't wait. I don't want anyone to be blindsided.'

Her eyes filled with fear. He kissed her forehead. None of it was her fault. Why did she have to get wrapped up in it? Why did he have to spoil her big night with such horrible news? It wasn't fair. What he was about to tell them could be just as damaging to her as it was to him. Being at the start of her career, she had even more to lose. But what could he do other than warn her?

'All right, I'll go find Hollie if you go find Astin,' said Fayth.

'Tate and Jack too,' said Liam.

Fayth's eyes widened. She knew how much he hated Jack. For him to want Jack to hear something, it had to be bad. And it was.

She didn't say anything else, just nodded then walked off to find them.

Liam found Astin practising his Catalan with Francisco and Ramira. He tapped his shoulder. 'Have you got a minute?'

'Sure,' said Astin. He turned back to the gallery owners: 'Excuse me.'

Liam and Astin made their way over to Hollie, Fayth, Tate, and Jack. They'd found a quiet corner of the gallery to talk and were waiting for Astin and Liam. The spot was away from the hustle and bustle of the crowds, or where people might eavesdrop. And, given what he was about to tell them, people would want to know. To outsiders, it was juicy. To them, it was cataclysmic.

'Yo, what's up?' said Jack. The hairs on the back of Liam's neck stood up. He really hated Jack, but Jack needed to know just as much as the rest of them.

'Fayth made it sound urgent,' said Tate.

Liam lowered his head. Fayth put her hand on his shoulder.

'Any time today,' said Jack, tapping his foot.

Tate hit him. 'It's obviously bad. Let him prepare himself.'

He took a deep breath. 'I just spoke to Trinity's former manager. It turns out that before she died, Trinity went behind her back to…to…'

'Spit it out!' snapped Jack.

Liam glared at him. 'Trinity wrote a book.'

'So?' said Jack.

'Please tell me it's some children's book with cute and fluffy animals,' said Hollie.

Liam pursed his lips.

'It's about us, isn't it?' said Tate.

Liam nodded. 'I don't know what's in it, but I do know that it's a tell-all memoir. I wanted to warn everyone so that nobody gets blindsided.'

Tate gripped Jack's arm so tightly her nails looked like they'd leave indentations. Hollie looked over at Fayth. Fayth looked like a deer that a car was about to crash into. Liam didn't blame her. Trinity had hated Fayth, blaming her for much of what was wrong with the last year of her life. It hadn't been long, but it had been recent. And recent pain was always easier to write about.

'Does anyone know anything else about it?' said Astin. Not that he had much to worry about – he'd always kept Trinity as far away as possible. Turned out to be a smart decision.

'Only the publishers, but they're not giving anything away.'

'I can't believe she didn't even tell her manager,' said Tate. 'That's such a Trinity thing to do.'

'Can't they find the manuscript on her hard drive or something?' said Hollie.

'Nobody knows where it is,' said Liam.

'What?' said Fayth.

'Nobody has seen her laptop since she died. It's like it's vanished.'

'What about her phone?' said Jack.

'It was in her pocket when she fell. She landed on it and smashed it into pieces.'

'Do you think she did this on purpose?' said Hollie.

Liam shrugged. He still didn't know if it had been an accident or a suicide. Not knowing that was what really haunted him. But when he found out about the book, he began to wonder. She *had* always preferred the path of most destruction, and if she didn't see a way out of her own situation, that was one way to ensure everyone else went down with her…

'Is it definitely going to be published?' said Hollie. 'Sometimes these things can be stopped.'

'If we stop it before we know what's in it, it could cause even more issues,' said Liam. 'It would make it look like we have something to hide.' Which most of them did, but they didn't want the press or public to know that. As soon as they found that out, they'd start digging and whatever was – or wasn't – in the book would come out anyway.

'But we're in it, right? There's no way we won't be in it,' said Tate.

'A tell-all memoir without her exes and former friends? Of course we're in it,' said Jack, helpful and comforting as ever.

Fayth tightened her grip on Liam's shoulder. 'So what do we do now?'

Acknowledgements

The last 12 months have been crazier and more unpredictable than I ever could've imagined. Thank you to my friends, family, and readers that have stuck by me and supported me along the way. The biggest thank you goes to Nan, who was always my biggest fan. I'm sorry you didn't get to finish reading about Hollie and Fayth. Your advice and support always meant the world to me, and I wouldn't be where I am today if it wasn't for your never ending faith and constant reminder that good things don't come to those who wait, they come to those who work. I know that if there is any kind of after life, you're watching over me, nodding along as I'm finally listening to your advice, nearly two decades after you first said it to me. (Better late than never, right?)

Thanks to Sarah for being the first person to read *What Happens in Barcelona*, and your suggestions on how to torture my characters more. Also thank you for our weekly lunches, as they've helped to take the edge off the pain of this last year.

Thanks to Tori, Kate, and Mum for beta reading too, and your (always hilarious) reactions. Extra thank you for Mum for helping me figure out how to break (and heal) my characters, and also for always being there for me, no matter what.

Carl, you're my rock, and I couldn't keep functioning without you.

Thank you to Alexa, Gudrun, Chelle and everyone else that shared their work-related horror stories that helped to inspire Fayth's storyline.

And finally, a big thanks to you, dear reader. Thank you for sticking with Hollie, Fayth, and me, for so long. Writing and publishing books as a one-woman band was always going to be difficult, but doing it with increasingly damaging chronic health issues is even harder. Despite that, I'm determined to release two more books this year, both of which you can find out more about on my author website. In the meantime, I hope that you loved this book as much as I loved writing it, and please do leave a review if you've got just a couple of minutes to spare. Reviews really do mean everything, and can make or break an author's career.

ABOUT THE AUTHOR

Kristina Adams is an author, poet, and blogger. She has a BA in Creative Writing from the University of Derby, and an MA in Creative Writing from Nottingham Trent University. When she's not writing, she's baking, sewing, or finding another way to avoid the real world. She lives in the UK with her partner.

Printed in Great Britain
by Amazon

78132609R00130